Daisy hurried out the door and hurried past the pool and other meeting rooms to the outside door and her van. She opened the door of the vehicle and climbed inside. The thermometer in the refrigeration unit said the temperature was on point. Relieved, she removed the mini tarts in their pastry boxes, closed the door to the van, and carried the boxes inside. As March in Pennsylvania was wont to do, the day had begun with a cold chill and it hadn't dissipated. Wind blew across the portico leading to the inside of the building and Daisy shivered. She hadn't bothered with her jacket to run in and out.

However, as she reentered the building, she heard a piercing scream that sent a frisson of fear up her spine. The sound had come from the pool.

Daisy dropped the boxes of tarts and ran for the double doors leading into the pool area. The frosted glass revealed nothing.

Yanking the door wide, she rushed inside. Stella Cotton was hanging over the side of the pool as Daisy hurried closer. As she took in the scene, she froze and felt like screaming herself.

Althea Higgins floated in the pool with one of the pool partition ropes wrapped around her neck. . . .

Books by Karen Rose Smith

Published by Kensington Publishing Corp.

A Daisy's Tea Garden Mystery

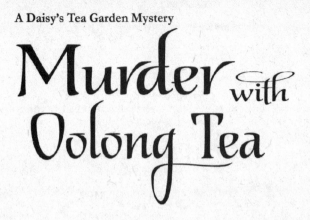

Murder with Oolong Tea

Karen Rose Smith

KENSINGTON
PUBLISHING CORP.
www.kensingtonbooks.com

KENSINGTON BOOKS are published by

Kensington Publishing Corp.
119 West 40th Street
New York, NY 10018

All Kensington titles, imprints, and distributed lines are available at special quantity discounts for bulk purchases for sales promotion, premiums, fundraising, educational, or institutional use.

Special book excerpts or customized printings can also be created to fit specific needs. For details, write or phone the office of the Kensington Sales Manager: Attn.: Sales Department. Kensington Publishing Corp., 119 West 40th Street, New York, NY 10018. Phone: 1-800-221-2647.

Kensington and the K logo Reg. U.S. Pat. & TM Off.

First Printing: January 2021
ISBN-13: 978-1-4967-2396-3
ISBN-10: 1-4967-2396-1

ISBN-13: 978-1-4967-2397-0 (eBook)
ISBN-10: 1-4967-2397-X (eBook)

10 9 8 7 6 5 4 3 2 1

Printed in the United States of America

*For all English teachers and readers
who appreciate Shakespeare.*

ACKNOWLEDGMENTS

I would like to thank Officer Greg Berry,
my law enforcement consultant, who so patiently
answers all my questions. His input is invaluable.

Chapter One

"Claudia never should have been hired," Althea Higgins proclaimed loudly enough for everyone in the teachers' lounge to hear.

Daisy Swanson, who was consulting with the principal of Willow Creek High School along with the guidance counselor, listened in spite of herself. Mrs. Higgins had been one of *her* English teachers when she'd been in high school. Daisy particularly remembered Mrs. Higgins's love of Shakespeare.

The older teacher, who Daisy gauged to be around sixty, wore her gray hair in a long ponytail that trailed down her back. With her high-necked white blouse and her midi-length tan skirt, she looked like a schoolmarm from olden days except . . . she more resembled an *unhappy* schoolmarm with her mouth pursed as if she'd tasted rhubarb and didn't like it.

Noticing Daisy glancing Althea's way, Megan Pratt, the principal, brushed her auburn shoulder-length hair back from her brow and murmured, "Althea campaigned for a woman she knows to fill the math department spot that became vacant when a teacher took early maternity leave.

But Claudia Moore presented herself with so much more energy and fresh ideas."

Now Stella Cotton, the guidance counselor who Daisy had dealt with on many occasions prior to this, shook her head with disapproval.

As in any workforce, there were tensions. Daisy knew that Stella, in her late fifties, kept up-to-date for herself and the students she counseled. Her hair was coal black and angled forward from her nape to her chin. Both her eyeliner and mascara were heavily layered. Daisy had consulted with her several times, usually about her teenage daughter, Jazzi. Each time Stella had been wearing bold bright colors. Today, maybe trying to encourage spring to make an early appearance even though the calendar read the beginning of March, Stella wore a two-piece dress in lemon yellow with lime-green flowers.

Stella studied Megan, who was at least fifteen years younger, and frowned as if Megan shouldn't have shared inside school information with Daisy.

Althea Higgins suddenly pushed back her orange vinyl–seated chrome chair and stood, gathering her bagged lunch. "I have lesson plans to work on in my classroom."

As Althea left the teachers' lounge, one of the other women at the round table where she'd been sitting said with a bit of sarcasm, "As if we don't *all* have lesson plans to develop."

Daisy checked her watch. She'd allotted an hour for this meeting with Megan and Stella to create the menu for their spring tea event later this week. Megan, a new principal this year, had decided serving tea to the faculty after the spring concert would show the district's appreciation for their service. Stella had agreed.

As co-owner of Daisy's Tea Garden with her aunt Iris, Daisy catered outside events as well as oversaw day-to-day operations at the tea garden. Her tea garden, housed in a restored Victorian downtown, was gearing up for spring and summer Amish country tourist trade in Lancaster County. She and her aunt welcomed the opportunity to share teas, soups, salads, and baked goods with their customers.

Daisy's shoulder-length blond hair swept along her cheek as she raised her head to discuss the reason for the meeting. "With spring arriving soon, I'm already creating fresh recipes as well as buying and blending teas."

"What do you suggest for *our* tea?" Megan asked.

"I created a new tea blend called Daisy's Spring Garden. It's an oolong tea with lemon and vanilla notes."

"What *is* oolong tea?" Megan asked. "I don't know black from green from Earl Grey."

"Oolong is a traditional Chinese tea," Daisy explained. "It's produced in a certain way. The leaves go through a process of being withered in the sun and oxidized."

"Can you provide more than one tea?" Stella inquired.

"Sure, I can," Daisy agreed with a smile.

"We'll rely on your judgment for the teas," Megan decided. "It's not as if we know anything about them."

"My servers will be glad to explain whatever we serve," Daisy assured the women. "As far as the food courses are concerned, I was considering an avocado-cucumber soup to start and tomato aspic for a different type of salad course. For the savory course—egg and olive sandwiches, beef on rye squares, and cucumber-watercress triangles. The tea garden also offers blueberry coffee cake that we can serve along with mini shoofly pies and lemon tarts."

Daisy handed each woman a printout of those menu possibilities along with alternatives.

"This looks wonderful," Stella decided. "I'll have to make a reservation for a full tea service once school is out for the summer."

"You're welcome anytime," Daisy said. "As far as this menu, just make sure you phone me with your selections by tomorrow night. Will we be serving in here . . . in the lounge?"

The teachers' lounge was a tight fit with a few round tables and many institutional chairs.

"Oh, no." Megan shook her head. "There's a room down the hall from the pool that we use for teacher functions when we want everyone at the same place at the same time. Teachers come and go here during lunch and free periods. We'd never fit everybody in this space at once. We'll show you the room before you leave."

They seemed to have discussed everything that needed to be discussed. Daisy checked her watch once more. She was about to push back her chair and excuse herself when Stella picked up the conversation again. Looking straight at Daisy, she asked, "Will you be attending the school board meeting mid-month?"

"Yes, I will. I want to hear the pros and cons about several items on the agenda."

"Has the gossip around town managed to announce the last item that's been added?" Megan asked.

Daisy gave the principal a questioning look. "The last I heard we were going to talk about after-school groups and how long they should stay at the school, whether service hours should be increased, especially on seniors, and what type of fundraising should be done for special trips and incorporating interactive whiteboards into classrooms. Did I miss anything?"

"Just the most important and probably the most controversial," Stella responded. "Megan and I are going to add to the agenda the idea of having a dress code in the high school."

That took Daisy aback. She hadn't had an inkling about that being added to the agenda. Controversial indeed. She imagined this discourse would be intense.

"We might even need security guards," Megan joked.

Stella jumped in. "This isn't any laughing matter."

Megan scrunched up her nose. "Someone has to have a good sense of humor about the subject or we'll end up in the swamp of Althea's complaints."

Daisy leaned forward and in a low voice asked, "Althea has a strong opinion?"

Daisy's question was met by the two women exchanging a knowing look. Finally, staring directly into Daisy's blue eyes, Stella answered, "I'm not talking out of school, so to speak, to tell you that Althea will be there with bells on. This is her bailiwick. She wants skirts, blouses, and vests ordered from the same company for girls as well as blazers, slacks, and ties for the boys."

"No room for options or alternatives?" Daisy wanted to know. She knew exactly how she felt about this idea.

"No, and it's not at all what I had in mind when I brought up a dress code," Stella explained. "I just wanted the school board, with the input of the parents, to make up general rules so the girls don't look provocative and the boys don't resemble gang members. I don't think that's too much to ask. Already we're seeing crop tops that are way too cropped, necklines with spaghetti straps that look like nightgowns, and even shorts that are as short as underwear! And the daytime temperature is still in the fifties."

Megan reached across and tapped Stella's hand. "Now don't exaggerate. Most of our kids have a sense of propriety."

Stella studied the principal. "Most?"

"All right," Megan acquiesced with a sigh. "Maybe half. It all depends on the latest fashions. I'd like to outlaw flip-flops too."

Daisy could suddenly see how complicated this discussion would be. "Who's leading the cause for *no* uniforms?" If Daisy's suspicions were correct, it would have to be someone with as much intensity and passion as Althea.

Megan answered this question. "To my surprise, Claudia Moore has stepped into that gap. Actually, there are several teachers who believe we shouldn't implement uniforms. I don't know if Claudia is specifically against it because of the way Althea has been spreading rumors saying her friend would be more competent teaching than Claudia. But I think Claudia really believes clothes are a matter of self-expression."

Daisy came down on that side of the debate too, though she did believe in propriety. She had to approve of what Jazzi wore to school, and she expected other parents to do the same. The tightrope between control and no control as a parent of a teenager was difficult to maneuver.

"I'm with you and the general rules, and I would think most parents would be. Or am I wrong about *that*?" Daisy looked from one professional to the other.

"We absolutely don't know," Megan responded. "If the

school board is too divided, we might have to take a vote. But the first step is an open meeting and that's what we're having. We're asking the students not to come to this session. We'll have an assembly about dress for school after the parents discuss it. Whatever we decide, we can't just spring it on everyone when school starts in the fall. Including feedback from most parents and making sure we listen to it is the school board's biggest challenge."

Daisy was sure Megan was right about that. Listening became hard when two competing sides were shouting at each other.

After her meeting with Stella and Megan, Daisy had gone back to work at the tea garden. Regular customers often came through the door in the late afternoon to take goodies home for their suppers. Tessa Miller, Daisy's kitchen manager and best friend, came out of the kitchen and sidled up to Daisy at the sales counter where she'd just sent a few customers on their way with goodies. "So does our menu for the teachers' tea look like the menu we discussed?"

Tessa and Daisy had gone to school and skipped a grade together. After high school, Daisy had enrolled in college, met her husband, married, and moved to Florida. Tessa had taken culinary courses here and there, apprenticed with a chef, but couldn't seem to find her way. When Daisy returned to Willow Creek with her two daughters, renovated an old barn into a home, and with her aunt set up the old Victorian as a tea garden with an apartment on the second floor, Tessa seemed to find her niche. She enjoyed working as Daisy's kitchen manager and living above the tea garden. Daisy and Tessa had never had any secrets from each other—not when they were kids and not since they'd been involved in murder investigations together.

Daisy stopped counting the baked goods left in the case and turned to Tessa. "Stella and Megan really seemed to like the preliminary menu I presented. They even selected teas to try on my recommendation. They were very easy to plan with."

"Do I hear a 'but' lurking in there somewhere?" Tessa asked.

"We'll have an all-occasion room to set up near the pool."

"That wing of the high school is the newest," Tessa remembered.

"It is. The state-of-the-art pool was a real bone of contention before it was built. But now they see how good it is for the kids. Do you remember Althea Higgins, the English teacher?"

"I do. I was scared to death of her. She made us memorize poetry and stand up and recite it. I was always afraid I'd get a D or an F if I didn't get every word right. She was as sharp as her pointed nose."

Daisy worked hard to suppress a smile. Althea did have a pointed nose. "She was exacting but her vocabulary drills for the SATs were right on the mark. I took an after-school class of hers on how to make the most of the study guide for the SATs. She was good. But I have to admit, she wasn't one of the teachers I'd enjoy sitting down and having a conversation with. I can't believe she's still there. Stella told me she's thinking about retiring. My guess is she's probably sixty-two. Violet had her for an English class but Jazzi has had other English teachers. You can learn from a drill sergeant or from a teacher who uses the Socratic method. I'd prefer the Socratic method."

The front door of the tea garden opened and the bell rang. Jazzi, Daisy's sixteen-year-old, breezed in to help serve and clean up before Daisy closed the shop for the day. Daisy studied her, so proud of her daughter that sometimes she could burst. Jazzi's black hair was sleek, straight, and swept below her shoulders. She had an oval face, high cheekbones, and a cute nose. Her eyes were as brown as the richest chocolate. She was lithe, long-limbed, and learning to have confidence in herself. When she'd gone on a search for her birth mother, she'd found her. Now Jazzi was learning how to fit in to Portia Smith Harding's family as well as her own. There had been potholes on that road but Jazzi had navigated them with the help of everyone who loved her.

Today Jazzi wore a denim skirt with a bib overall top and a yellow T-shirt underneath. Her denim jacket suited the weather. Her shoes had a chunky heel and laced up to the ankles. She took her backpack everywhere. It was loaded with enough books and paraphernalia to weigh at least what any camper's backpack would weigh when they were hiking.

Jazzi motioned to her mom and pointed to the office. She obviously wanted a few minutes alone with Daisy. That always rang warning bells in Daisy's head.

Daisy glanced around the tea garden's main serving room with its pale green walls, glass-topped tables, and mismatched antique chairs. The spillover tearoom past the sales counter was pale yellow with a diamond-cut glass bay window. The tea garden was quiet since they hadn't served afternoon tea today. When they scheduled those days, tea was served with reservations.

Tessa must have seen Daisy assessing what was going on at that exact moment because she said, "Go on with Jazzi. Iris and I can handle anyone new who comes in."

Daisy went through the doorway that led to a hall with the kitchen on the right and her office on the left. Her office had Plexiglass windows that she could see into and out of. Jazzi was unloading her backpack onto Daisy's desk chair.

Her daughter didn't waste any time getting to the point. "Do you remember me talking about Brielle?"

Jazzi was involved in a peer counseling group and had met Brielle Horn in that group. From what Daisy remembered, Brielle's parents were lawyers and traveled a lot. Although Jazzi mentioned her now and then, Daisy had never met her. "I remember you discussing Brielle."

"I have a favor to ask."

Leaning against her desk, Daisy smiled. "That look on your face tells me it's a big one."

"Not so big, really," Jazzi promised. "I'd like Brielle to spend two weeks with us, spring break and then a week after that."

Whoa! Daisy hadn't expected *that* request. "I don't know, Jazzi. I'm over at Vi's a lot to help her with Sammy. With my tea garden hours, I don't know if I want to take on anything else."

"I thought it all out," Jazzi said calmly, as if her explanation would help. "Vi and Foster are doing better, don't you think? Vi's over her postpartum depression from what I can tell. She's even going into Pirated Treasures some days to help Otis."

Daisy's oldest daughter, Violet, had gotten pregnant her first year of college, married, and had a baby in November. Postpartum depression had hit her hard but with early intervention she was now doing well. She and her husband, Foster, and their four-month-old son Sammy had found a routine that worked for them.

"They *are* doing better," Daisy agreed. "Why does Brielle need someone to stay with?"

"Her parents are going to some international lawyers conference in Geneva. If Brielle went along, she said she'd be alone in the hotel because her parents would be in meetings during the day and going to cocktail parties in the evenings. They also visit with their friends. After the conference, they intend to go stay with a couple in Norway. Brielle has been there before. It wasn't fun and she doesn't want to go again."

"Not take a trip to Geneva and Norway, Jazzi?" Daisy studied her teenager carefully. "What's really going on?"

"All right," her daughter conceded. "The truth is that Brielle doesn't want to hear her parents bicker about everything. She thinks they're going to get a divorce. If they're alone on this trip, maybe they can mend things and come back better. Her grammy lives in the area but she doesn't get around well. She'd like to stay with her but Brielle's parents think Brielle needs more control than her grammy can provide. Brielle feels all alone so much of the time. I think it would be good for her to be with us."

Thinking about Jazzi's request, Daisy considered what having a guest would mean. Two weeks *wasn't* an eternity. Daisy had been looking forward to spring break, thinking she would take a few days off and she and Jazzi could do things together. After all, next year was Jazzi's senior year and it wouldn't be long until her daughter went to college. But . . . maybe all three of them could spend some time together. This seemed to mean a lot to Jazzi.

"Please, Mom? Won't you think about it?"

Gazing at Jazzi, who had been such a gift when Daisy and Ryan were married and couldn't have more children, Daisy saw flashes of the life they'd all had in Florida. Since moving back to Willow Creek three years ago, Jazzi had grown from an unsure teen to a maturing young woman. Jazzi and Vi had been very close until Vi left for college. Married now with a baby, Vi had her own life. Daisy was sure Jazzi missed the bonds they'd once had. Was that why she wanted Brielle to come stay . . . for her own sake as well as Brielle's?

"I *will* think about it, honey. If I do decide to consider it, I have to meet Brielle and her parents before I say *yes*."

"Oh, thank you, Mom! Can you call them tonight?" Jazzi came around the desk and gave Daisy a big hug. Daisy knew her daughter believed having a houseguest was already a done deal.

Chapter Two

It was almost noon the following day when Jonas Groft entered the tea garden. A tourist bus crowd had just left, continuing on with their tour of Amish country. Daisy was arranging cookies in the sales case because their tray had been depleted.

Jonas's smile not only turned up the corners of his mouth but reached his green eyes as he approached the sales counter.

Daisy appreciated each and every one of those smiles. He'd been closed off more the past few months since a revelation by Detective Zeke Willet had rocked Jonas's life. Zeke had been emanating vibes of resentment toward Jonas ever since he'd come to Willow Creek to be a detective on the police force. Once a detective himself, Jonas now ran his own store—Woods—which carried handcrafted furniture that he and others in the area created.

Zeke's attitude had finally blown up in both of their faces. Back in Philadelphia, Jonas's partner, Brenda, had been killed in an ambush and Jonas had been injured. That night, before they'd gone out on their shift, Brenda had told him she was pregnant. She'd had her IUD removed without telling him because she'd wanted a family with him. When they'd gone to interview a murder suspect, the man's rifle had changed Jonas's world and taken Brenda's life. At the bonfire in Willow Creek before Christmas, Zeke—who had been drinking that night—revealed to Jonas that he also could have been the father of Brenda's child.

Daisy hurt for both men but mostly for Jonas. Zeke, who had been a friend, had betrayed Jonas. Brenda had also betrayed him. Now he was rethinking everything he thought he knew, *everyone* he thought he knew, maybe including Daisy.

Thank goodness today he must have had lighter thoughts on his mind. Maybe three months since the bonfire had given him perspective. She hoped so because she'd realized she loved him.

Jonas was one of those men who would stand out in any crowd, not only because of his handsome looks— black wavy hair that sometimes dipped over his brow, green, green eyes that could see into her heart, a physique any man would be proud of. But it was his calm demeanor, his confidence, his steady attention to every detail that assured her he was a man to be relied on.

"Those lemon tea cakes look good." He leaned closer to her and whispered, "As good as *you*."

She smiled back. "And what can I do for you today, kind sir? Taking a lunch break?"

"Do you have time for a cup of tea with me? How about some of that oolong that's a special this month."

Aunt Iris, who must have seen Jonas come in, crossed to the sales desk. "Go on," she said to Daisy with a sly wink. "Everything's ready for afternoon tea at two."

Daisy had seen the prosciutto and pear sandwiches in the kitchen's walk-in, as well as the tomato aspic and the mini chocolate tarts that Tessa had baked this morning. All last-minute preparations were ready. So was the spill-over tearoom with its pristinely clothed tables and white wood chairs topped with green, blue, and yellow pinstriped chair pads.

Daisy said to Jonas, "How about a table at the window? Or do we need more privacy?"

A shadowed expression passed over his face as if he was thinking about all the things they could talk about. Instead he motioned to the window. "We don't need privacy unless I want to steal a long kiss."

She felt a blush creep up her face. They hadn't taken a final step in solidifying their relationship—that very important physical one. They both wanted to be sure exactly what they were doing. But Jonas's kisses sped her into the future where they could really be together.

"The window table it is. I have cabbage sausage soup today. Would you like that with a chocolate biscuit?"

"Sounds good." With another smile just for her, he turned toward the table.

Five minutes later Daisy carried the tray to the table at the bay window. He helped her unload it, then put the large tray on the serving cart nearby. "It looks good, but then your food always makes my stomach grumble."

What she liked most about Jonas was that she could believe what he said.

"Do you have a full service for tea this afternoon?" He picked up his soup spoon and dipped it into the hearty soup filled with cabbage, sausage, potatoes, and carrots.

"We do. Tourist season has definitely started. I've kept

Tamlyn on full-time and I'm glad I did. She's an excellent worker."

Tamlyn Pittenger had been a housekeeper before Daisy hired her. Daisy had met her through her last murder investigation, which she didn't want to think about.

"You know how to pick reliable employees," Jonas said. "I'm thinking about letting my manager, Tony Fitch, take over some of the accounting chores. That would give me more time to work on furniture."

Daisy added a spoonful of honey to her tea. Jonas didn't add anything to his. As she stirred, he revealed with excitement in his eyes, "I've decided to plan an event for summer, highlighting our reclaimed wood furniture. Elijah has suggested the idea several times. He's willing to help me get ready. His oldest son is taking over more of the running of the farm. Jeremiah is getting married this summer and ready to move into the house that Elijah helped him build."

Elijah Beiler was a woodcrafter as well as a farmer. Jonas sold Elijah's pieces in his shop on consignment. Elijah was Amish and Jonas trusted him as he would a brother because of his humble personality, his values, and his appreciation for his family.

"Would just the two of you work on pieces for the event?" She had seen the reclaimed wood island with a quartz top that Jonas had built. It had been beautiful and he'd sold it as soon as he'd put it in his shop's window. In the summer with the tourist season in full force, he and Elijah shouldn't have any trouble selling their handcrafted wood pieces.

"I'm not sure yet. There are two other men who have woodshops on their properties who I might consider asking. But we might need more than the store space to sell everything. It's a lot to think about."

"Exciting too."

Jonas covered Daisy's hand with his. "Yes, it is. And it's good to think about—" Jonas just waved his hand in the air without finishing the sentence.

Daisy could finish it for him. Without thinking about his relationship with Zeke and what had happened with Brenda.

"I have news too."

He took a spoonful of soup and then studied her. "Good news?"

"I'm not sure yet. Jazzi wants to ask a classmate to stay with us over spring break and a week after that. She met her in peer counseling and Brielle must be sort of a lost soul. Her parents are lawyers and away a lot. They're going to a conference in Geneva and then lengthening the trip to visit friends in Norway. Brielle also thinks they're contemplating a divorce. Jazzi believes if Brielle stays with us, it will be a positive experience for her."

Taking his time to answer, Jonas took another spoonful of soup, then set down his spoon and gazed at her directly. "Do you want my honest opinion?"

"Always." She wasn't just saying that. She did. She always wanted Jonas's honesty.

"Vi is still on the road to good mental health. You were scared for her when she was so low. You said she was working more. Does that mean she'll depend on you to babysit Sammy?"

Daisy tucked in a blond strand of her hair that had escaped from her ponytail. "I already thought about that. Brielle's visit is only for two weeks. Vi seems to be stable now, even happy. I've been worrying more about Foster, that he's doing too much with working at the tea garden, going to school, taking on building websites so he can make more money. But whenever I'm over at their apartment, they seem good. This isn't a done deal yet. I have questions for Brielle and her parents, and I have to meet them. I asked them to dinner tonight but they can't come. Brielle is coming home from school with Jazzi."

"I guess the main question is . . ." Jonas paused. "Do you really want to take on the responsibility for a stranger's teenager?"

Daisy thought about it. "There's something in this girl that Jazzi likes. She doesn't just feel sorry for her. I have to trust Jazzi's judgment too. If she thinks Brielle needs us, then why not give it a try?"

Jonas returned his attention to enjoying his soup. "It sounds as if you've already made up your mind."

"Not completely. It all depends on what happens when I meet Brielle. Would you like to come to dinner too?"

Since Daisy had opened the tea garden, she'd had regular customers. Regular could mean once a day, once a week, or once a month. She made a point of learning their names and chatting with them. However, in all that time, she couldn't remember Althea Higgins coming in even once.

It was late afternoon when Althea walked in and took her time letting her gaze wander over the main tearoom. She seemed to be sizing everything up, from the dried lavender on each of the tables to the color of paint on the walls to each teacup lined up on a shelf for decoration or for sale. Daisy hoped Althea had come in to enjoy a cup of tea, a baked good, or a bowl of soup.

Would she indicate if she remembered Daisy from her high school days?

The woman seemed to have a mission as she spotted Daisy and headed for her.

Daisy smiled and asked pleasantly, "Mrs. Higgins. Can I show you to a table?"

"All right," Althea agreed. "I suppose we could sit while we talk."

Daisy had no idea what they were going to talk about.

She motioned the older woman to a table for two near a table of four women who would soon be finished.

As soon as Daisy and Althea were seated, Cora Sue, a full-time server, approached them. "Can I get you anything, Mrs. Higgins?" Cora Sue asked with a smile.

Althea looked Cora Sue over as if she might remember her as a student. "Not right now. I had my last period free and I came here to talk to Mrs. Swanson for a few minutes."

"Whatever you'd like is on the house," Daisy proposed, wondering if that was holding Althea back.

Cora Sue lifted her brows to Daisy, and Daisy just nodded that she should go back to what she was doing—cleaning out the case for the day.

"I heard about the menu you discussed with Mrs. Cotton and Miss Pratt."

"I see," Daisy said, sensing criticism in Althea's tone, the same criticism she'd heard from her in high school when she'd wrongly named Keats instead of Byron as the author of a poem.

"They didn't intend to discuss that menu with the faculty. Imagine that."

Since the gathering was to be an appreciation tea, Daisy guessed the two women thought of it as a gift to the teachers, not one that had to be analyzed by them all. Although Daisy didn't want to ask the question, she did. "Is there a problem with the menu?"

Althea glared. "There certainly is. I didn't see any accommodations made for gluten-free treats."

Thoughts of a gluten-free almond cookie hadn't come up in Daisy's conversation with the principal and the guidance counselor.

Before she could say that she'd gladly add a gluten-free cookie to the menu, Althea went on, "And will you be using organic produce? This tomato aspic you're going to prepare. Will those tomatoes be vine-ripened, no GMOs? If you serve a fruit cup, I hope it will be pesticide-free fruit."

"I can see this is important to you," Daisy said calmly. "Do you know how many teachers might require your specifications?"

"I don't know about anybody else. I just know about *me*. Besides, *my* health concerns would benefit everyone. At my age, I'm concerned about my constitution, and I go the extra mile whenever I can. Yes, it's a little more expensive, but it's worth it. I intend to live a long, happy life."

"Happy" wasn't a word that Daisy would associate with Althea Higgins. However, she didn't know her that well.

"I intend to retire next year," Althea added. "I've never had time to garden on the farm. I know that might seem odd, but we raise crops and tend to livestock."

Trying to put Althea at ease, Daisy said, "I have a small garden."

"Yes, well, running this shop isn't as demanding as teaching. Once I'm retired, I'll grow everything from seed to ensure I'm producing it as healthily as possible."

"That will be a fine hobby."

Althea frowned. "It will be more than a hobby. It will be a way of life. I intend to change a lot of things about how I'm living."

Knowing that topic would be too personal to probe, Daisy was about to change the course of their conversation when the women at the table next to them stood, ready to leave.

Althea looked up at the woman closest to her. "You're wearing an awful lot of perfume," she commented. "Don't you realize that could cause an asthma attack? Perfume nowadays is actually outlawed at many establishments." Althea targeted Daisy. "You should think about doing that."

The customer's face reddened. She turned to her companions as if to walk away, but then decided against it. Rounding on Althea, she advised, "And maybe you should keep your comments to yourself, or not go to public places with other women if your asthma is so bad."

Althea looked ready to stand and Daisy knew she had to nip this confrontation in the bud. She said to Althea, "Give me a sec." Then she hurriedly stood, slipped a coupon she always kept ready out of her apron pocket, and took her customer by the arm, leading her away from the table. She presented her with the coupon. "I'm so sorry if she embarrassed you."

"Is she right about my perfume? Is it terribly strong?"

Daisy caught a whiff of a light floral scent. "It's not strong at all, but I suppose in the future wearing perfume is something we should all be mindful of."

The woman looked down at the coupon. "Your cabbage sausage soup and carrot-grape salad were delicious. I'll certainly be back. But I hope she's not here then. There's a right way to say something and a wrong way. Do you know what I mean?"

"I certainly do. I hope you have a pleasant evening."

"You too," the woman said with a slight smile. She raised the coupon. "Thank you for this."

After Daisy returned to the table and sat with Althea once more, Althea looked down her long nose at Daisy. "You always were too conciliatory as a student. I thought you would have become more self-assured as an adult. Why did you do that?"

Constructive criticism was one thing. Personal attack was another. "I did that because I don't want to lose a customer," Daisy answered bluntly. "If something like that happens again, I suggest you move to a different table."

Althea gave a harrumph, put her hands on the table, and pushed herself to her feet. "Please think about what I said. All of it," she emphasized.

Before Daisy could wish Althea a good evening, the woman was gone.

Daisy let out a relieved breath. Apparently, the English teacher thought about herself more than anyone else. However, Daisy was thinking about her gluten-free cookies. As far as the organic produce was concerned, she'd talk to her supplier.

She couldn't help but wonder if Althea Higgins always got what she wanted.

Daisy wondered why Brielle's parents were too busy to come to dinner. Last night when Jazzi had pleaded with her mom not to make Brielle wait until they were free, she'd asked, "Couldn't Brielle come on her own?"

When Daisy had relented, she'd told Jazzi they would just have an ordinary night . . . ordinary for them. That meant she was babysitting Sammy while Vi and Foster had a chance to go out to dinner . . . and Jonas was joining them.

Daisy realized Jazzi wanted to help Brielle desperately when her daughter had agreed to all that.

Brielle would be coming home from school with Jazzi. Daisy made sure she was at the house early while her crew covered for her. She was lenient with them about emergencies and time off so they didn't mind filling in for her.

Daisy had changed into blue jeans and a swirled patterned sweater in shades of blue with an irregular hem. It dipped on one side and was higher on the other. She'd braided the sides of her hair at both of her temples and fastened it with a gold clip in back. Taking care of Sammy was easier when her hair wasn't in the way, though the little extra care she gave to her hairdo was for Jonas's benefit too, she had to admit.

Not knowing what Brielle might like to eat, she decided to keep the meal simple. She never knew when Sammy might have a fussy spell. After rubbing chicken pieces with olive oil, rosemary, and pineapple sage she'd dried last fall, she put the roasting pan in the oven along with baked potatoes. Since Sammy was still sleeping in his carrier, she decided roasted veggies would go well with the chicken. She'd cut up an assortment and have them ready to slip into the oven an hour after she put in the chicken. After adding sunflower oil to the cookie sheet and spreading it around, she chopped an assortment of veggies—zucchini in slices, carrot pieces, halved Brussels sprouts, half a fennel bulb cut into chunks, a sliced pepper, a few cauliflower florets, and half a sliced onion. She salted the vegetables, shook on garlic pepper powder, then laid a few pats of butter here and there on top of the vegetables. Afterward, she covered the tray with foil. It would take about an hour—the first half hour at 350 degrees covered, and then uncovered at 425 degrees. Jazzi knew the drill if Daisy got tied up with Sammy.

Jonas arrived before the girls did. He rang the bell and Daisy checked the camera app on her phone. It was Jonas. She wished he'd just walk in. She'd left the door open for him.

Picking up Sammy—she wasn't about to leave him alone in the kitchen—she found her felines Marjoram and Pepper already at the door ready to greet Jonas. They must have telepathy. They both liked him and followed him around.

After he came in, he leaned down to kiss Daisy, baby and all. The kiss filled Daisy's heart with so much emotion that she felt tears prick her eyes.

Jonas backed away a step and lifted her chin with his thumb. "Everything okay? With you and Sammy?"

"Everything's fine. I just got a little too happy there for a minute."

"We all deserve happiness, Daisy. Happy tears are a good thing. Don't try to hide them, especially from me."

"When was the last time *you* had happy tears?"

It didn't take Jonas long to answer. "When I found out you were safe after the last murder investigation."

Before they had a chance to discuss any of that further, four-month-old Sammy let out a cry.

"He needs a bottle." She was about to set Sammy in his carrier again when Jonas offered, "I can take him."

His care of Sammy always touched her deeply. "If you'd like."

As Jonas took Sammy into his arms, she wondered, not for the first time, exactly what Jonas was feeling. First, he'd had to go through the grief of losing a child along with his partner when Brenda had died. Then with Zeke's announcement at the bonfire, Jonas had experienced loss all over again, not knowing if the child even had been *his*. She didn't see sadness on his face now, though. In fact, he was smiling and tickling Sammy's tummy. He always seemed perfectly comfortable with the baby.

After she mixed the formula, he said, "I can feed him if you have something else to do in the kitchen."

"I brought home blueberry coffee cake from the tea garden. But I thought I might like to make drop biscuits to go with the chicken. I'll probably be finished by the time Sammy is done with his bottle."

Just then Jazzi burst through the front door, another teenager behind her. Daisy tried not to stare at Brielle as Jazzi introduced her.

Brielle's short spiked hair was black except for her pink bangs. She looked to be about ten to fifteen pounds overweight and had a nose ring, an eyebrow piercing, and Goth tattoos on her forearms.

Just what was Daisy getting herself into?

Chapter Three

Before Daisy could introduce herself to Jazzi's friend, Brielle looked around the downstairs. "This was a barn, wasn't it?"

"It was," Daisy responded.

Brielle lowered her eyes for a minute.

Daisy didn't want her to feel awkward. She went to Brielle and tapped her elbow. "Let me introduce everybody. This gentleman is Jonas Groft. He owns the shop downtown called Woods. It's right down the street from my tea garden."

"Is he your boyfriend?" Brielle asked. The question seemed brash but it wasn't asked in a brash tone. She was curious.

"He is," Daisy said, her eyes meeting Jonas's. There was a sparkle in his eyes that said he liked her answer. Daisy pointed to Sammy. "And this is my grandson. I have another daughter, Violet, and this is her baby."

"She's the one who had to get married," Brielle said as if she were putting Violet into a compartment of her own.

Deciding not to beat around the bush, Daisy added, "Vi and her husband Foster love each other very much. They were married in July and Sammy was born at the beginning of November."

"You're young to be a grandmother. My grammy's really old."

Maybe it would be better to move to a different topic. "Are you hungry? Everything should be ready. I just have to make gravy. Find a seat at the table and I'll put everything on serving dishes. Jazzi, can you help?"

"Sure, Mom," Jazzi said, giving a quick glance to Brielle to see if she was okay.

Her friend seemed to be as she continued to look around—at the stone floor-to-ceiling fireplace near the dining room table, at the table and chairs Daisy had refinished herself, at the table runner and the placemats.

"Should I put Sammy in his crib in the bedroom?" Jonas asked.

"Why don't you pull the crib into the living room, at least while we're having dinner," Daisy suggested. "He might lay there for a while and watch his mobile."

As Jonas handed Sammy to Daisy and went to get the crib, Brielle whispered to Jazzi, "Does your mom's boyfriend always handle the baby like that?"

Daisy smiled at Brielle so the girl would know she'd overheard. "Jonas is good with Sammy. It's the male to male bonding thing. Why do you seem surprised?" After all, if Brielle could ask questions, Daisy could too.

"My dad would never help like that. He'd never lift a dish unless it was to feed himself."

To Daisy's relief, Jazzi spoke up. "Everybody helps when they're here for dinner . . . or anytime really. If you stay with us, you'll have to help too. You're a guest tonight. That's why we're serving you."

Brielle seemed to absorb what Jazzi had said.

Jonas returned and Daisy laid Sammy in his crib. The baby batted his arms and legs. Marjoram and Pepper, who were both asleep on the sofa, stretched, watched the baby for a few minutes, and then went back to sleep. They were happy in their own little corner of the world.

Following up on what Jazzi had told Brielle, Daisy asked, "Do you have chores at home?"

"Nope."

"Your mom takes care of the meals and dishes?"

Brielle laughed. "Oh, no. She'd never do that. We have a housekeeper. She's supposed to be my babysitter too when they're away. But I'm too old for a babysitter. I do what I want and she doesn't even know it."

Daisy was almost afraid to ask what that was.

"She has her own set of rooms and everything," Brielle added.

Jonas brought the plate of chicken to the dinner table where the potatoes, gravy, and roasted vegetables were already positioned. As the platters were passed around, Brielle took a chicken breast and a few vegetables but nothing else.

Sitting beside her, Daisy asked in a low voice so not to embarrass her, "Aren't you hungry?"

"My mom says I need to be on a diet. She said I shouldn't fill my plate because you all would think I didn't know how to restrain myself."

That wasn't the advice Daisy would give *her* daughter if she was going to a friend's for dinner.

Jazzi picked up the bowl of potatoes and handed them across the table to Brielle. "Don't be silly. Mom makes all this so we eat it. When you come here for dinner, she wants you to eat whatever you want."

Brielle turned to look at Daisy, and in spite of the nose ring, the many piercings, the tattoos, Brielle's gaze looked almost innocent. "Is that true?"

"It is. I was a dietician before I bought the tea garden. If you ever want to talk about diets and what's good for you, just let me know. We could map out something. But tonight, just eat what you want . . . within reason," Daisy said with a sly smile.

Jonas spoke for the first time since they'd sat down. Daisy suspected he didn't want to add anything controversial since this wasn't his gig. Somehow she wanted to convince him he was part of their family and his opinion mattered.

"What Daisy's advising is save room for blueberry coffee cake. She made it at the tea garden this afternoon and it's really good." He tore the meat from his chicken leg and swirled it around in the gravy before he forked it into his mouth.

After that, conversation ran around the table about happenings at school, teachers, and outside activities. Brielle didn't seem hesitant to join in. "Mom says she wishes there was a stable in Willow Creek so that I could take riding lessons again. It's the one kind of exercise I *do* like."

"Where did you live before moving here?" Daisy asked.

"In Virginia. The private school I went to had horses. It was part of the curriculum. Pretty cool, huh?"

"I've never been on a horse," Jazzi said.

Suddenly, Brielle said in a low voice, "It was hard to leave my friends to come here."

Stepping in, Daisy agreed. "I bet it was. Jazzi and Vi left their friends in Florida when we moved here. It's never easy to leave behind people you love."

"My mom says I should just move on like they do. But I don't know if they have real friends."

"What do you mean *real* friends?" Jazzi asked without hesitation.

"You know," Brielle said, waving her fork. "Friends you can really tell things to. Their friends all talk about work and who bought the best car and where they're going on vacation. It's not anything *real*."

Smiling to herself, Daisy realized Brielle was actually endearing. Jazzi liked her. Daisy found herself liking her too. It would be an interesting two weeks if Brielle's parents let her stay with them.

The following morning, Daisy served the table of four women in the center of the tearoom. They were all retired from a company in Chambersburg and decided they'd visit Amish country for the day. Daisy enjoyed chatting with them as she served them tea. This was the fun part of the tea garden, learning all about her visitors. It was amazing how much they shared about their lives when they were drinking a calming brew.

Out of the corner of her eye, Daisy noticed Russ Windom, the man her aunt was dating. He was speaking with Iris at a table for two. As her aunt left him to return to the kitchen, she crossed to Daisy. "Russ would like to talk to you for a few minutes."

"No problem," Daisy said, wondering what he wanted to talk about. She finished pouring tea for the women, set down the blue-and-pink-flowered teapot on a cat-shaped trivet, and crossed to Russ's table. "Hi, Russ, Iris said you wanted to talk to me."

"I do. Do you have a couple of minutes?"

Daisy checked around the room and saw that everything seemed to be in order. All of her clients were served, sipping tea, eating baked goods or salads or soups, and chatting.

She pulled out the chair across from Russ and sank into it.

"I heard you're catering the appreciation tea at the high school on Friday."

"I am. I think it will be a fun service—a combination of a light lunch and tea after the morning concert."

"I attend the concert every year to show my support."

Russ was a retired teacher from Willow Creek High School. "I stopped over there on Tuesday," Daisy said, "to finalize the menu. I'm working with Stella Cotton and Megan Pratt. I like Stella a lot. She pointed me in the right direction more than once with Jazzi. Megan seems quite nice too."

"I know Stella," Russ said. "She's all about the students and what's best for them. Of course, I don't know Megan since she's new. But I hear she's doing a good job. Even though I'm retired, I'm still in the loop. I receive one of those teachers' e-loops from the district."

Daisy thought about her encounter with Althea Higgins in the tea garden yesterday. "Did you know Althea Higgins well?"

A look drifted over Russ's face somewhere between a frown and a disapproving expression. The lines around his eyes seemed to crease deeper. Did even the thought of Althea do that?

"Oh, I knew Althea," he said. "In fact, she's a historic figure at the high school. She has her finger in everybody's business."

"Really?" Daisy knew she shouldn't dive for more gossip but Althea was such a quirky woman she wanted to know more about her. "I have the feeling she can rile up a room pretty quickly."

Russ turned over the fork at his place setting. "That she can. I understand the next school board meeting is going to be a hot one. The subject of uniforms is on the table again. I can't tell you how many years that's come up, but nothing has ever been done about it because nobody can agree."

"Althea wants uniforms."

"That's no surprise. In some ways I suppose she's right about it."

Listening to Russ's viewpoint would give Daisy another perspective. "How do you mean?"

Leaning back in his chair, Russ explained, "Willow Creek High School still expects teachers to present a professional front, and I totally agree with that. Most of the men still wear ties, and the women for the most part dress conservatively. After all, we do have to set an example."

Daisy nodded for him to go on.

"Althea believes if students are dressed similar to their Sunday best, they'll learn better. They respect the teachers and the teachers respect them. If the girls are wearing crop tops cut above their belly buttons, and the boys wear jogging pants with holes, Althea feels they think they're at a slumber party or at a friend's house. That's not what school should be, in her mind."

"That *is* one way of thinking about it."

Russ took another sip of his tea and then set down his cup. "I wanted to talk to you about something else in case it comes up at the tea. Have you heard the gossip about Althea's self-published book?"

"I didn't know she'd published a book."

"She did, and it's all about teaching methods. But . . ." He paused as if he was figuring out exactly what he wanted to say to Daisy. He looked Daisy in the eye. "A teacher in Philadelphia is claiming Althea plagiarized some of her book. Althea denies it, of course. As proper as she is, I can't believe she'd *do* something like that."

"Has anything come of the accusation?"

"I've heard a lawsuit is in the offing, but nobody knows for sure. Althea can be very closed-lipped when she wants to be. Of course, other times she's not afraid to say exactly what she thinks."

"She does seem to have a lot of opinions to share."

"And you can bet at the next school board meeting, she will do exactly that."

It was early in the season to be checking her garden that evening, but Daisy couldn't wait to turn the earth over and plant something. Soon she could get onions in. She'd have to remember to go to her parents' garden center and pick up a set.

Jazzi, who had come outside and walked beside her, asked, "So what did you think of Brielle? Really, Mom."

"You realize, don't you, that having Brielle here is

not going to be the same as when you and Vi shared the upstairs."

Stopping to kick at a clump of soil with her sneaker, Jazzi asked, "What do you mean?"

"I mean—Vi respected her space *and* your space. You were used to her and her quirks. You've never had another roommate."

Jazzi squatted down and ran her hand through the soil. She looked up at Daisy, her dark brown eyes serious. "I know Brielle's not Vi. That's a good thing. I can talk to Brielle about things I couldn't talk to Vi about."

"Like what?"

Standing again, Jazzi said with exasperation, "Oh, Mom. Like boys! And Brielle's fashions and piercings and tattoos. About her life and where she's been and what she's seen. She's had an exciting life, Mom. She's been to Europe. I think she even went to China once with her parents. They've lived on the West Coast. Imagine all I could learn from her."

Daisy was imagining just that, but she still figured two weeks wasn't an eternity. They'd manage.

"Are you going to plant anything different this year?" Jazzi asked as if the subject had become too intense or she'd revealed too much.

Since Daisy didn't have much time to plan the garden, she usually planted herbs, zucchini and tomatoes, maybe a pepper or two. "What did you have in mind?"

"Maybe Brussels sprouts and spaghetti squash."

"We can try them. But even if we plant Brussels sprouts as soon as we can get them in, they won't be matured until fall."

"Wow. Really?"

"Remember, Joachim Adler has greenhouses. So do other farmers who raise vegetables throughout the year. We have to depend mostly on the weather. That's what Rachel does too."

"Do you think Rachel would give Brielle a ride in her buggy? That would be an experience she's never had."

Daisy had to smile. "If Rachel's too busy, one of her daughters might be able to do it. So you think Brielle would really enjoy bumping along the streets of Willow Creek?"

Jazzi grinned. "I think she enjoys anything different. That's why she tries anything she wants to."

Now Daisy gave Jazzi a probing look and stopped walking around the garden. "I hope you don't mean drugs."

"No, not drugs. Brielle cares about her body."

"That's why she gets piercings?"

"Mom, piercings accentuate parts of the body. You let me get my ears pierced."

Yes, she had. When Jazzi was fourteen, ear piercing was what she'd wanted for her birthday. The same with Vi. Did other piercings carry the same significance? That would be a conversation she could have with Brielle.

"Mom, you know Brielle is mostly nerdy."

Surprised, Daisy said, "I didn't get that impression at all."

"She seemed to get along with us. That's why. But she doesn't make friends easily so she spends a lot of time on her computer."

Daisy wasn't sure she liked the sound of *that* either. "I'd like to meet Brielle's grammy. Maybe we could visit her while Brielle's here."

"Brielle would like that," Jazzi agreed. "She wants to check on her grandmother more than her parents do. She can ride her bike there if she has enough time but her parents don't like her to do that." Jazzi laid her hand on her mom's arm. "I want to ask you something."

"Okay. Ask."

The late-day sun shone down on Jazzi's black hair, making it gleam. She wore it loose and it splayed around her shoulders like a magnificent black shawl. She was growing up and Daisy wished she could stop time.

"This tea you're giving for the teachers at the high school tomorrow."

"What about it?"

"You don't talk about me to anybody, do you? You met with Miss Pratt and Mrs. Cotton."

Daisy was glad Jazzi's name hadn't come up. "No one mentioned your name. If I had to talk to one of your teachers, I would tell you first. You know that."

"I hope. But if you're around my teachers in a casual way, I thought they might talk."

Teachers often did talk about their students. Daisy had heard that during the short time she'd been in the teachers' lounge. But mostly it was in consultation with another teacher about ways they could help students. "Not even any casual references. I promise."

Jazzi's cell phone played and she took it from her jacket pocket. She said to Daisy, "It's Portia."

"Go ahead and take it while I poke around in the garden. I can pull weeds."

Jazzi crossed to the patio and sat in one of the Adirondack chairs that Daisy kept outside all year round in case she wanted to sit and watch the sky or just think and look at the surrounding farmland.

At first Jazzi sounded animated but then she became

quiet. The phone conversation took about ten minutes, then she returned to Daisy at the garden.

Daisy laid a handful of weeds on the ground at the edge of the garden and straightened.

Jazzi was frowning. "Portia wants me to come to Allentown over spring break, but I told her about Brielle."

More than anything, Jazzi didn't want to disappoint her birth mother. "What did she say?"

"I think she was unhappy and disappointed."

"You made the commitment to Brielle first," Daisy reminded her.

"I know. But I'm not sure what to do."

Daisy considered the whole situation—Brielle staying with them, babysitting for Sammy, and dating Jonas. However, life was life and it would keep on turning no matter what she did. So why not do what felt right . . . for Jazzi.

"Why don't you consider asking Portia to visit, either while Brielle is with us or after? I know it's not the same thing, but maybe that would make her less disappointed."

Jazzi looked out over the farmland at the end of their property. No one had farmed it and the weeds were growing high along with the tall grass. Finally, she turned to Daisy. "If Brielle's here, that would be different, wouldn't it?"

"It would. I can't predict how it will work out. It's up to you."

After thinking about it longer, Jazzi decided, "I'll ask Portia to come."

* * *

The spring concert had been a success. As Daisy readied herself for the next few hours on Friday, she thought, *Sure, there had been some sour notes and missed cues.* The conductor's glasses had fallen down his nose at one point but he'd caught them. But overall, everyone had enjoyed the performance.

While the auditorium emptied and students packed up their instruments and filed out of the building to catch their buses, Daisy and her crew, which consisted of Tamlyn, Cora Sue, and Foster, set up their first courses for tea in the all-occasion room. Thirty-one teachers had accepted the invitations to tea that Stella had sent out. She'd insisted that sending them through the mail made them special. The envelopes had included RSVP cards. Stella had been pleased with the response.

There would be four tables with eight teachers at each table. Daisy, Cora Sue, Foster, and Tamlyn would each be servicing a table. With tourist season fast approaching, Daisy couldn't afford to have any more of her servers leave the tea garden and come along. If nothing unexpected happened, they should be able to serve four courses without a problem.

However, the refrigeration unit in her work van was giving her trouble. She'd had it repaired twice in the past few months, most recently last week. She'd tested it earlier in the week and it had seemed good to go. She checked it often to make sure the temperature would stay where it was supposed to.

A half hour later, Daisy had just served the avocado-cucumber soup and was refilling teacups with oolong tea when she heard a ruckus at the table across from her.

Tamlyn's table. Somehow Althea Higgins and Claudia Moore had been seated at the same table, across from each other no less.

Claudia had raised her voice. "If you didn't pass by my room so many times during the day, you wouldn't have anything to criticize."

Althea returned sharply, "The students in your room become so loud the whole school can hear them."

"You're exaggerating!" Claudia shot back.

Althea said calmly, "And you're too young to know decorum."

When Claudia pushed her chair back, a glass of water spilled on her dress. She tossed down her napkin and rushed from the all-purpose room. Daisy watched Stella stand also and go after Claudia, maybe to console her or calm her down.

Tamlyn crossed to Daisy. "What should I do?"

"Nothing," Daisy advised her. "We'll be serving the next course as planned. Teachers will come and go as we're serving and they can just settle in and catch up as they want to. Make sure when they do return that their tea is warmed up."

Tamlyn nodded that she understood and returned to her table.

The tomato aspic course proceeded as Daisy had predicted. Althea left as soon as they'd served the aspic. Maybe she didn't like it? Daisy noticed she had her cell phone in her hand as she headed for the hall.

One of the objectives of this tea, besides showing appreciation for the teachers, was to let them chat in a friendly atmosphere in between courses. Daisy and her staff also needed time to prepare them. The next course was the savory course.

During and after Daisy had served her table with mini sandwiches, she noticed Althea was still missing from her table and Claudia hadn't returned either. Several other teachers stood to stretch their legs and mill about as Daisy and her crew removed crumbs from the tablecloths, refilled teacups, and prepared for the dessert course.

Cora Sue met Daisy at a side table where the hot water urn sat. She said, "I brought in the blueberry coffee cake and the snickerdoodles, but the lemon tarts are still in the refrigerator in the van."

"I'll go get them," Daisy said, "while you and Tamlyn and Foster ready the dessert tiers. I want to make sure the refrigeration unit is as cold as it's supposed to be."

Daisy left the all-purpose room and hurried past the pool and other meeting rooms to the outside door and her van. She opened the door of the vehicle and climbed inside. The thermometer in the refrigeration unit said the temperature was on point. Relieved, she removed the mini tarts in their pastry boxes, closed the door to the van, and carried the boxes inside. As March in Pennsylvania was wont to do, the day had begun with a cold chill and it hadn't dissipated. Wind blew across the portico leading to the inside of the building and Daisy shivered. She hadn't bothered with her jacket to run in and out.

However, as she reentered the building, she heard a piercing scream that sent a frisson of fear up her spine. The sound had come from the pool.

Daisy dropped the boxes of tarts and ran for the double

doors leading into the pool area. The frosted glass revealed nothing.

Yanking the door wide, she rushed inside. Stella Cotton was hanging over the side of the pool as Daisy hurried closer. As she took in the scene, she froze and felt like screaming herself.

Althea Higgins floated in the pool with one of the pool partition ropes wrapped around her neck.

Chapter Four

Daisy had found a body once before, but she'd been able to close the door on it. This murder seemed very different.

Zeke Willet and Morris Rappaport and two patrol officers rushed into the pool area after the paramedics. Rappaport glanced at Daisy, whose arm was around Stella, then he helped herd everyone else out.

Daisy wasn't as wet as Stella. She'd helped pull Althea from the pool. But Stella had climbed down the pool's steps to reach the body. They couldn't just let her float in the water. Daisy, had wanted to make sure there wasn't a pulse.

There hadn't been.

The humidity inside the pool area almost made Daisy light-headed. She felt like she couldn't breathe in enough air. The crime scene technician the department had hired—Daisy had read about it in the *Willow Creek Messenger*—was equipped with a camera and was taking photos.

Daisy had to turn away.

Stella's skin was so pale against her dark hair. Daisy

wondered if she too looked like the ghost she felt like. Her hands were clammy but maybe that was from the humidity.

Stella kept saying to Daisy over and over again, "I didn't like her. Most of the teachers didn't. But I didn't want to see her *dead*."

Trying to clear her head, Daisy knew she had to tell Stella one thing. "Don't tell the police any more than what you did and what you saw. Nothing else. If they start asking questions that you don't want to answer, tell them you're going to call a lawyer. Got it?"

Stella blinked at Daisy, her eyes wide and scared. "I didn't do this."

"The police will figure it out. They will. Detective Willet and Detective Rappaport are good detectives."

Yet she knew the police could miss important clues. She knew they sometimes focused on the wrong person. She knew sometimes they got it wrong. Hadn't Zeke missed evidence during the last murder investigation?

After patrol officers were stationed at both exits, the detectives came over to Stella and Daisy. Daisy, as well as Jonas, had stayed clear of Zeke until today, but now she had to interact with him. She thought about Jonas's and Zeke's friendship that had blown up in their faces. She hurt for both of them, but neither would make a move toward the other.

Daisy wanted to call Jonas. Still . . . would that be the best move right now?

Detective Rappaport studied Daisy. It was obvious that he could see she wasn't as wet as Stella. A patrol officer came from a little room in back of the pool area carrying two towels. They were bath sheets.

Daisy knew the officer . . . his name was Bart Cosner.

She took the towel from him and swung it around her shoulders. The white terry cloth was like a cloak that could protect her from all of this somehow.

Stella seemed to be frozen, staring at the towel, not knowing what to do with it. Daisy took it from her hands, shook it out, and swung it around Stella's shoulders.

Detective Rappaport told Daisy, "We have to separate the two of you."

Daisy understood all too well what was going to happen next. She'd been through it before.

The detective went on, "I'm going to question *you* in the laundry room. Detective Willet will take Mrs. Cotton to that corner of the pool. Are you two all right with that?"

Daisy didn't have a problem with talking to the detective, but she was shaken up, just as Stella was. Yet she knew the detective needed their statements while memories were fresh. They'd want every detail.

Detective Rappaport let Daisy precede him into the laundry room. He left the door open. There was a cafeteria-sized table in the room along with two folding chairs. He pulled one out for her and she sat. He settled about a foot away from her on the same side of the table.

She studied him to distract herself.

The detective was probably nearing sixty, though it was hard to tell exactly how old he was. His hair was still thick, blond-gray. Grooves along his mouth were deep as well as the other lines on his face. Morris Rappaport was from Pittsburgh and had had a challenging time getting used to living in Amish country. But he was learning there were advantages to living in a rural town with specialties such as whoopie pies. Today he wore a dark-brown wool sports jacket and a tan shirt with a brown tie.

Daisy tried to compose herself when she felt his gaze on her, examining her.

Turning his chair slightly toward her, he ordered, "Tell me exactly what happened. Why were you here?"

She took a deep breath and hoped her tightened throat muscles would let her explain. "The principal and the guidance counselor had planned an appreciation tea for the teachers. I was here with staff serving it."

When she paused, he prompted, "Go on."

Daisy felt her insides turn queasy and she held her breath for a moment. Then she puffed it out. "Althea was here with the other teachers . . . and Stella and Megan."

"Megan?"

"Megan Pratt, the principal."

"Did anything unusual happen?"

Daisy considered the exchange between Claudia and Althea. Should she tell the detective?

"What are you thinking about, Daisy? You know by now you should tell me everything."

She still hesitated but Rappaport's coaxing stare led her to go on.

"Althea had been seated at a table with Claudia Moore. Althea resented Claudia because Claudia had been hired for a position that Althea thought a friend of hers should have gotten."

"A teaching position?"

"Yes."

"Why do you think Claudia got it instead?"

Daisy was kind of surprised that Rappaport wanted to hear about this. She thought he'd just want to hear about the crime scene. However, he was already searching for a motive.

"Megan told me that Claudia had fresher ideas and more energy. After Claudia was hired, Althea tried to find everything wrong that she could about Claudia."

"How old was Althea?"

"Near retirement age. This might have been her last year and why she felt she could speak so freely about everything."

Rappaport scribbled in his small notebook. "So tell me what happened with the tea service. Who on your staff were here?"

Daisy ticked off her servers. "Foster, Tamlyn, Cora Sue, and I each had a table. Cora Sue was covering hers and mine when I had to manage the whole tea service or go to the van for something."

As usual, the detective didn't miss anything. "Why did you have to go to your van?"

"I was having trouble with the refrigeration unit, and I wanted to make sure that the tarts were the proper temperature. They were and I was bringing boxes of them back when I heard a horrific scream."

In line with the way he investigated, Rappaport checked his notebook as if he'd already taken preliminary notes. "So you spilled those tarts all over the hall?"

"I guess I did. I don't even remember that part."

"What happened next?"

Not hesitating, Daisy let her thoughts rush out of her mouth. "I ran through the doors and found Stella in the pool, trying to pull Althea out. I helped her do it. But as soon as I unraveled that rope and felt for a pulse, I realized there wasn't any. Althea wasn't breathing. I knew she was dead."

"You say Stella was *in* the pool?"

"She was. Althea was tall." Daisy's voice shook. "Stella was pulling her to the edge and trying to drag her up the steps."

In investigator mode, Rappaport kept the conversation going. "Tell me what you know about Althea Higgins."

Not feeling quite as shaky now, Daisy felt anger raise its head at that question. After a hostile tension between them when they'd first met, she and the detective had settled on an unusual friendship. But sometimes he took advantage of that. "I'm not an encyclopedia about everybody I serve."

Detective Rappaport didn't seem to be affected by her outburst. "I know that. Still . . . you did preparation for the tea. I thought maybe you heard teachers talking. I thought maybe you talked to Althea yourself. Besides that, I know the tea garden can be a bevy of gossip. Maybe not for tourists who drop in, but for locals."

Daisy sighed because she knew Rappaport would get this out of her one way or another . . . at one time or another. "Althea spoke her mind and was often blunt. She came into the tea garden the other day to ask if I'd made arrangements for gluten-free treats, and if I used organic produce. I didn't mind her asking. People who hire me often ask those questions. If I know ahead of time, I can make gluten-free offerings. But then . . ."

"Then what? Did she hurt your feelings?"

The detective's voice was low and gentle, not sarcastic. He meant it as a fair question. "No, she didn't hurt my feelings, but she might have hurt my *business*. She told a woman her perfume was too strong and that she should consider not wearing it when she went out because she could cause someone to have an asthma attack."

"So she was tactless."

"For me that was just an annoyance. But for someone else it might really cause trouble."

"What else?" He was scribbling again.

"I really don't know much else, Detective. She's been a teacher at the high school a long time. She taught me English when I was in high school. She lives on a farm. That's the only thing I know about her private life."

"You don't know if she has any relatives?"

"Some of the teachers were around her every day and probably know that better than I would."

Rappaport closed his notebook and stuffed it back into his jacket pocket. He twiddled his pen between his fingers. "Daisy, I don't like that you're involved in this again."

"And do you think I do? One body was enough. Two—" She shook her head and shivered until her teeth chattered.

"You'll have to come into the station tomorrow. We'll do this again and sign a statement."

"I know the routine," she responded in a monotone.

Just then Zeke Willet stood at the door. His blond hair was as short as ever and his jaw even more square. Lean and fit, he looked ready to arrest someone. He nodded to Daisy and asked Detective Rappaport, "Are you done with her yet?"

"I am. She needs to get out of those wet clothes. She'll come down to the station tomorrow, and I'll record her and have her sign her statement. What about Mrs. Cotton?"

"I need to talk to her more thoroughly. She's going to come down to the station tomorrow, too, and we'll go over anything I didn't cover today. The crime scene is a mess . . . all those teachers in there before we cleared them out."

"Everyone was just trying to help," Daisy protested.

"Yes, well, in helping," Willet said in a disgusted tone, "they destroyed evidence. I'm letting Mrs. Cotton leave because there are so many other teachers to talk with too. I want to get more background."

Rappaport nodded. "Me too. We'll have to divvy up everyone."

Daisy stood and Detective Rappaport did too. He placed his hand on Daisy's shoulder. "Do you need me to call someone for you?"

"No, I'll call Jonas. Do you mind if I stay here to do it? As soon as I walk out there, I'm afraid there are going to be people asking me questions."

A patrol officer bumped Zeke aside, then came into the laundry room. He laid something onto the table. "Is this yours, Daisy?"

The officer was Bart. He had carried in her phone. She could identify that sparkling case Jazzi had chosen for her anywhere. "It must have slipped from my apron pocket when I dropped the tarts."

"Yep, it was lying just to the side of those." Bart said to Rappaport, "I'm between interviews. I'll take the music teacher to the squad car."

"That must be an awful place to be interviewed," Daisy murmured.

Both Bart and Zeke exited the room to continue what they had to do.

Daisy picked up her phone. She texted Jonas instead of calling. It seemed easier than talking right now. Something awful happened at the school. Althea Higgins is dead. The police are questioning everyone. Can you come?

He must have had his phone nearby because he texted right back. On my way.

Daisy wanted to stay in this room. She wanted to avoid everybody outside. But she had to meet Jonas. Perhaps all the teachers would be tied up with their own interviews and wouldn't even notice her. She doubted it.

Daisy had two choices—either wait in the hall outside of the pool room or outside in the March breeze. She chose outside because she wanted to see Jonas as soon as he arrived. Hopefully most of the other people who had been at the tea would be gone or were being interviewed down the hall in one of the rooms.

Slipping into the hall, she peered left and right and saw no one. She hurried to the door that led outside. She was about to cross to the left corner of the portico where she'd be out of the way and partially hidden, when Claudia approached her from the other side. She looked upset. Daisy guessed everyone who had been here was troubled, concerned, and worried. She thought she saw streaks of tears down Claudia's cheek.

"I didn't do it," she said vehemently.

"No one suspects you," Daisy protested, wondering why Claudia was telling her this.

"The police do. They know Althea and I didn't particularly get along. They know she didn't want the school to hire me." The detective and patrol officers must have already gathered a good bit of information.

"That's not a reason for you to commit murder," Daisy said evenly, beginning to shiver. Tightening her towel around her, she realized she really didn't want to have this discussion now. However, Claudia seemed to need to talk.

"I left the tea service," Claudia reminded Daisy. "I just wandered the halls for a bit, then I heard Stella scream."

"Did you tell the police that?"

"I did. It was Officer Cosner. He had this serious expression like he wanted to nail me. He didn't look as if he believed me. He wanted to know which hall, if the lights were on, did I go into any of the classrooms."

Ignoring her own discomfort, Daisy put her hand on Claudia's shoulder. "Take a breath. Did the detectives want to question you further?"

"Yes. I have to go to the station tomorrow."

"I do too."

Claudia's eyes widened. "Really?"

"I have to go over everything again and then I have to sign my statement. They'll expect all of us to do that, at least any of us who had left the tearoom. I found Stella and Althea, so of course I'm under suspicion."

As if Claudia hadn't noticed it before, as if she'd been in her own world of dismay, she saw the towel wrapped around Daisy and her wet clothes. "Oh, my gosh. You must be cold."

"I'm just glad it's not still winter," Daisy said. "I'll be okay until my ride gets here." She would. Jonas would turn the heat on in his SUV and she'd warm up. She'd go home and get changed into dry clothes and everything would be fine.

If she kept telling herself that often enough, maybe it would be so.

Claudia said, "I reminded Officer Cosner that there's an outside door to the pool. They might be barking up the wrong tree if they think one of the teachers did it. Anybody could have come in from outside."

"That door is supposed to be locked from the outside," Daisy remembered.

"With teachers coming and going, someone could have come in unnoticed, hidden in a classroom or closet, then followed Althea into the pool area. They could have pushed their way out the door afterward. No problem."

It wasn't out of the question that what Claudia was saying was true. However, if it was, someone had at least planned to meet Althea. Since the weapon of choice had been that rope that separated lanes in the pool, Daisy doubted the murder was premeditated. But that would be for the police to decide.

Studying Claudia in the light from under the portico, she saw that something else was on her mind. "Do you have an idea of who might have done this?"

"I just know that the same way Althea irritated the teachers, she irritated people outside of school too."

"Someone specific?"

"I heard that a former student of Althea's, Harry Silverman, vandalized her outbuilding because she ruined his chances for a scholarship."

"He was in her class?" Daisy wanted to understand the specifics.

"Yes. He was a senior last year—a football player who'd let his grades decline. She wouldn't give him extra credit to bring up his grades, even when his parents and the principal pleaded with her. So I don't think he even went to college. Imagine how angry he must be about that."

The door beside Daisy suddenly opened and Lawrence

Bishop pushed through. Spotting Daisy and Claudia, he stopped. He was somewhat wet because he'd checked Althea along with Daisy.

Lawrence, a science teacher in his late forties, was a town council member. He was more flexible in his thinking than the other members and had agreed with Daisy on a few points when she'd attended a town council meeting about the construction of a homeless shelter in Willow Creek.

Now, he pushed his hand through his brown hair, which was starting to be highlighted with gray. "This is awful. Absolutely awful. Willow Creek has had too much crime in the past two years. Tourists aren't going to want to come here."

Daisy knew that Lawrence took his town council duties as seriously as his teaching duties. She admired him for that.

"The police have got to get this solved quickly," he went on. "It's the only way to mitigate the gossip and the story and how much is actual news."

Daisy protested. "Quick isn't always better. The detectives need to follow all their leads and put the puzzle together. If they don't, they could end up arresting the wrong person."

She glanced at Claudia and saw Claudia's pursed lips and the fear in her eyes. Why all that fear? Had Claudia had something to do with the murder?

Waving his hand toward the pool inside, Lawrence stated, "Stella found Althea's body. What does that tell you? She was soaking wet in the pool with her. Chances are good there won't be any fingerprints on that rope. The chlorine in the water would have eradicated them."

"That doesn't mean Stella did it," Daisy said evenly. "She was trying to save her."

"So she says." Lawrence's face was tight and stern. "She had a raging argument with Althea last week about the school uniforms. I had to practically pull her away from Althea."

"Did you tell the police that?" Daisy asked.

"Of course I did. I'm not holding anything back, and no one else should either."

Claudia suddenly didn't look quite as terrified. The expression on her face eased, and the grip on her purse lightened.

Wind blew and Daisy couldn't stop shivering. Adrenaline, anger, worry, and sheer willpower had kept her from being too cold up until this moment. But now she felt her defenses were down, and fifty-degree temperatures felt like thirty.

As Jonas's SUV rolled up in front of the school entrance, Zeke Willet emerged from the school. Jonas climbed out of his vehicle and spotted Daisy right away. He stopped when he saw Zeke. Both men just stared at each other.

Then Zeke abruptly turned away, walking toward his car.

Jonas rushed to Daisy and wrapped his arm around her. "You're all wet! What happened? Gossip is racing through the town already."

"I got wet . . ." She took a breath. "I got wet trying to help Stella pull Althea out of the pool. Can we wait and talk about this when we get home?"

After a long steady look, Jonas nodded. "Of course we can. Come on. Let's get you into the SUV. I'll blast the heat."

Daisy briefly touched Claudia's hand in a reassuring gesture before she left. She tried not to think about Althea's body and all the questions Detective Rappaport had asked. She tried not to think about another murder in Willow Creek.

Chapter Five

Turning the CLOSED sign to OPEN on the front door of the tea garden Monday morning, Daisy noticed Stella Cotton hurriedly walking toward the door. School was in session today so Daisy wasn't sure why Stella was here. She opened the door wide to let the school guidance counselor inside.

Stella didn't even give her a chance to say good morning. "The police finished with the crime scene but the pool and the outside entrance are blocked off. Megan is having the pool checked and making sure everything is clean. There was fingerprint powder everywhere."

Daisy motioned to Stella to come in and took her to a table in the spillover tearoom so they'd have privacy. Iris, who stood at the sales counter—she was filling it for the day—nodded to Daisy that she'd take care of whoever came in along with the rest of the staff.

Stella sank down into a chair as if the blue-, yellow-, and cream-striped cushion could swallow up some of her fatigue. She had dark circles under her eyes and Daisy wondered if she'd slept the past few nights. "How are you?"

"I'm scared silly," Stella said, close to tears. "I signed

my statement and all, but those detectives are acting as if they don't believe me."

Cora Sue came into the tearoom to see if they needed anything. Her bouncy, curly red hair bobbed from her topknot. She raised her brows at Daisy as if she was afraid to speak, which was unusual for Cora Sue.

Daisy studied Stella and then asked, "Tea and a scone?"

Stella put a hand to her stomach. "I can't eat anything, but tea sounds good. I like that oolong tea you served at the tea before . . ."

Daisy told Cora Sue, "Two cups of oolong and maybe a couple of sugar cookies. They should go down easy."

"Milk and lemon?" Cora Sue asked.

Glancing at Stella, Daisy answered, "A little bit of everything."

Nodding, Cora Sue took another look at Stella and then left for the kitchen.

"Why do you think the police don't believe you?" Daisy asked.

"It's the way they asked their questions. I had to verify every detail."

"That's the way of a murder investigation. They probably asked the same questions of everyone else."

"I didn't tell them I had an argument with Althea last week. It was about those doggone uniforms. Do you think I should tell them?"

From her experience in murder investigations, Daisy knew what she should say. "Everything comes out in the end, Stella. It's really better if you don't hold anything back."

"I don't want them to know how much I disliked Althea."

On every occasion before this, when Daisy had spoken

with Stella, she'd been calm and reasonable with a sense of peace about her. But this woman didn't seem to have any of those qualities today.

"Nothing much ruffles me," Stella insisted. "After all, I work with teenagers. I'm used to every scenario possible, from smoking those e-cigs in the bathroom, to practically coming to school naked, to telling me a parent has a drug problem. But Althea . . . She just pushed my buttons. She knew exactly what to say to make me feel defiant and rebellious, and everything those teenagers feel."

"It was probably her authoritarian attitude. Vi got along with her. I got along with her when I was in high school because I didn't open my mouth or stand up for myself. On the other hand, back then, I respected her."

"I respected her," Stella admitted. "She was a good teacher. A little strident sometimes but her students came out of her classroom knowing exactly what they were supposed to learn."

"I heard there was a problem with Harry Silverman last year."

Stella shook her head. "I can't talk about any of Althea's students. Confidentiality is everything between me and the kids."

Daisy wondered if that meant there was something to tell. She wouldn't question Stella further about it. However, the police might.

"You know, if the police come up with other subjects to question you about and some of them are about students, you might have to answer."

"I can't break confidentiality."

"Then I'd advise you to discuss it with a lawyer."

"A lawyer?" Stella seemed aghast at the thought. "Do

you think this will go that far? Don't you think the police will catch whoever did this?"

"I'm sure they will . . . eventually. But the case can take time to nail down. They'll be digging into Althea's life."

Running her hand across her forehead, Stella sighed.

With a jaunty spring to her step, Cora Sue returned, bearing a tray with two teacups, a teapot, a small pot of honey, a crystal nappy with sparkling sugar, and a blue-and pink-flowered plate with a selection of cookies—snickerdoodles, lemon teacakes, and sugar cookies.

Kindly, Cora Sue said to Stella, "Whatever you don't eat here you can take along."

"Thank you, Cora Sue," Stella said, gratefully returning to the calmer woman Daisy usually knew. "Maybe I need a job at your tea garden. I could simply serve tea, baked goods, soups and salads all day. It wouldn't be like sitting in my office listening to everyone's problems, or trying to find colleges that suit students as well as their parents."

"Tell me something, Stella. Do you really think I don't listen to people's problems all day?"

Finally a smile, at least a small one, broke across Stella's lips. "I suppose you and your staff are more like bartenders."

"If you mean we hear things we shouldn't, and some of our customers become chatty with confidences, you're right about that. You can come serve tea anytime you want, just for a break."

Stella spooned honey into her tea and stirred. Daisy did the same.

After both women had taken a few sips, Stella set down her teacup. "That's beautiful china."

"My aunt threw me a surprise party a while back, and

everyone who came gave me a teacup for my birthday. I kept some of my favorites at home but brought the others in here. Jonas gave me a teapot that had cats decorated on it."

"That's right. You like cats. That's why I sent Jazzi to talk to Tara Morelli, because a cat sits in on counseling sessions."

After Jazzi found her birth mother, she'd needed someone objective to talk to. Stella had provided the name of someone who had a yellow tabby named Lancelot who sat in on the sessions. Tara and Lancelot had helped Jazzi considerably.

"We have two cats and since Vi moved out, they keep Jazzi company almost all the time. Sometimes I think animals are more intuitive than people."

"You can be right about that, although I like to think *I'm* intuitive." Stella said this with a hint of humor. And Daisy was glad this conversation seemed to be relaxing the counselor.

Stella picked up one of the snickerdoodles and took a bite. "Mmmm. These are delicious. I know your baked goods are. I really should come in here more often."

"Yes, you should," Daisy agreed with a straight face.

This time Stella actually laughed, but then she sobered quickly. "I just joked about being intuitive, but sometimes it takes so many sessions to get a student to open up. People are so afraid to share private thoughts and what they're really like, yet they'll go on social media and say practically *anything*."

"I doubt very much that Althea was on social media, but I could be wrong about that. I don't know anything about her private life."

"She never talked much about her private life . . . or her daughter. I got the feeling they didn't always get along. I do think Althea was fond of her grandson, though. She mentioned he came to the farmhouse to help out, but other than that—"

"Do you think she was lonely after her husband died? That wasn't too long ago, was it?"

"Two years."

Thinking back to a time that could make her melancholy, Daisy confided, "Even though I had my girls, I was terribly lonely after Ryan died. Lonely in a way I never had been before."

"When spouses are really partners, that's what happens." Stella looked sympathetic. "I was in love with my husband, but after ten years we just couldn't make it work anymore. I knew all the signs. I knew it was coming. Still when it did, it was a shock. I missed him, even though I knew it was best that we split up."

"I'm sorry."

"I'm well past it now. I have been for ten years. But I don't know if I'd be in a hurry to ever marry again."

Daisy knew exactly what Stella meant. "It's an element of trust that's hard to develop again," she murmured.

"Yes, it is."

They each nibbled at a lemon teacake.

After another sip of tea, Daisy said, "I know you have to leave, but I did want to talk to you about something."

"What?"

"Jazzi asked me for a favor. She wants to bring Brielle Horn home for spring break and the week after that. She said Brielle's parents are going to Geneva. Brielle doesn't want to go along because she's hoping her parents will bond again and not bicker so much and maybe not divorce."

Stella's eyes widened. "Jazzi told you all this?"

"Apparently she and Brielle confide in each other."

"That's an odd pairing," Stella decided. "Jazzi and Brielle. But who knows what makes good friends? Are you asking me if you should do it?"

Since Portia had planned a visit the first weekend in April, at least Daisy didn't have to be concerned about Brielle staying with them when Jazzi's biological mom visited. Still, she needed to know all she could. "I guess I'm asking you if there's anything about Brielle I should know if I *do* invite her to stay."

"I can't talk to you about Brielle without Brielle and her parents giving permission."

"If that's what it takes, then I'll get it. I need to know what I'm stepping into if I have a houseguest for two weeks."

Stella went silent and her face looked troubled again. Was that worried expression about Brielle . . . or about Althea Higgins's murder?

At closing time Daisy's last customer—and she used that term loosely—was Detective Rappaport. He crossed to the spillover tearoom away from the customers in the main tearoom.

Daisy knew what that meant. He didn't merely come for an iced tea and a scone. He wanted to talk about the murder.

She knew the drill. He wasn't going to give her any

information. Instead he wanted information she knew or had gathered. Maybe he'd gone over her statement and that had generated even more questions. She doubted it because he'd been thorough.

Tessa had been checking over the list of baked goods to make for the following day. She and Daisy had agreed on rice pudding, blueberry coffee cake, and cinnamon scones to start the day. Iris would handle the cookie making.

Daisy bumped Tessa's shoulder and nodded to the spillover tearoom. "Detective Rappaport's in there and I think he wants to talk to me."

"No problem. Most of these customers will be leaving shortly and I'll start cleanup with Cora Sue and Eva. Iris is inventorying the walk-in."

Daisy went to the kitchen and prepared oolong iced tea with plenty of sugar syrup, grabbed a few chocolate whoopie pies from the walk-in, and put it all on a tray. Then she carried it in to Rappaport's table.

As she placed the iced tea in front of the detective, he asked, "Are you telepathic now?"

"That depends. Did I get it right, or would you deign to try a cup of *hot* tea?"

"If I got through the winter without it, I don't need it now. This is just fine, especially those whoopie pies. Are all three for me?"

"You can eat them here or if you want to delay gratification, you can take them along with you."

"I'll decide after we talk."

After Daisy was seated, she asked, "And what are we going to talk about?"

She and Detective Rappaport had a history. At first it had been an adversarial one. Then they had come to respect each other. Their burgeoning friendship sometimes made them both smile.

Nevertheless, the detective wasn't smiling now. "I didn't ask you one important question. Did you notice anyone who was wet after you found Althea?"

Daisy took a moment to think about it. "Lawrence Bishop got wet because he helped Stella and me turn Althea over. Of course, Stella was wet most of all because she'd knelt down beside the pool and then went down the first few steps to reach Althea."

"Anyone else?"

"Claudia was wet because she'd spilled a glass of water on her dress."

"Did you see that happen?"

"She stood quickly and spilled a glass of water," Daisy said thoughtfully. "But that doesn't mean anything, does it?"

"I'm not sure. Think about it. I didn't get the autopsy report yet, so I don't know anything for certain. Give me your scenario of the events."

Truth be told, Daisy had put some thought into exactly what had happened with Althea. "Do you believe I think like the murderer?"

"No, but you have an analytical mind. You knew Althea Higgins. What do you think would have been the setup for this murder?"

After a pensive pause, Daisy told him. "My guess is someone called or texted or showed up and pulled her aside and maybe asked her to step into that pool area to talk."

The detective's bushy brows raised at least a half inch. "So was it somebody she knew and maybe trusted?"

"Somebody she knew. As I said, I didn't know her well so I don't know how easily she trusted."

"Then what?" he prompted.

"I'm not sure. But Althea had a habit of pushing the wrong emotional buttons. She could easily make someone angry. Those ropes for lane separation hang on hooks on the wall with the floats, weights, and noodles."

"Noodles?" Rappaport looked perplexed.

"They're long and light pool equipment, sort of like Styrofoam in bright colors. You can bend them under your arms to float, or you can use them to exercise in the pool."

Rappaport looked a little sheepish. "I don't go swimming."

"They're almost as light as a feather and couldn't do anybody any harm. I noticed they'd been knocked aside and were lying in a pile near the wall. So my guess is whoever reached over for the rope knocked them askew."

"So Althea would have seen the person coming at her?"

"Possibly. She could have backed up and fallen into the pool. But I doubt that because then the killer would have had to jump in the pool to strangle her. I rather think maybe Althea turned to leave and had her back to the killer. That would have been much easier for him or her to go over Althea's head to wrap the rope around her neck. Then he either pushed her into the pool or she fell."

"You used the term *he*."

"Althea was about five-seven. She was thin. Maybe she weighed about a hundred and ten. Someone taller than her could easily have strangled her. If not taller than her, heavier than her. If she was surprised, there are many ways anyone could have gotten that rope around her neck."

"I think you're getting too good at this," the detective grumbled.

"At what? Thinking through a murder? From what I understand, the outside door to the pool could have been ajar. Someone could have come in from the outside to do it."

"We do have to consider that someone not related to the teachers at the tea could have murdered her. How likely that is, I don't know."

"Is Zeke Willet going to stay on this case?" Daisy asked.

"Zeke is on the case. We want to get this solved as quickly as possible. But I believe he's still off his game."

After Rappaport eyed the whoopie pies, the detective took one from the plate and ate it in two bites. Then he took a few swallows of his iced tea. "I didn't just come here to go through that murder scene with you."

"Why else did you come?"

"To ask you if you can't do something about two stubborn males."

That surprised her. "Me? I have no influence over Zeke Willet. I'm not even sure Jonas and I are all right. He's pretending to be fine, but he's more guarded than he was before Zeke's announcement at the bonfire. Brenda's betrayal rocked him, though he's trying to hide it. And Zeke won't admit to anyone that he betrayed Jonas's friendship, that maybe *he* was the cause of Brenda getting herself killed because she was thinking about him instead of herself. After all, that triangle could have gotten pretty sticky."

"Both Jonas and Zeke are blaming themselves for what happened," Rappaport determined. "Neither of them was at fault. Brenda's killer was. He didn't even know Brenda and Jonas. He just wanted to run. He aimed his rifle at them as if he were doing target practice. At least that's the way it seemed to me from Jonas's description of the event."

With a resigned expression, the detective studied her and then continued, "Don't you think you have enough pull with Jonas to get him to talk to Zeke?"

"I've prodded, Detective Rappaport. But I don't want to pry so much that Jonas shuts down with me completely."

After Detective Rappaport ate the second whoopie pie in two bites, he said, "I know what Zeke's problem is. He does blame himself. My guess is that he's sure that Brenda had him on her mind the night she told Jonas she was pregnant. She also knew she'd betrayed Jonas. She was probably wondering what Zeke would do . . . if he wanted a DNA test. If Jonas ever found out, he'd probably demand a paternity test. All of it was a huge distraction. I'm sure Zeke believes if she hadn't been distracted, she wouldn't have gotten killed."

Daisy watched as the detective took a few swallows of his iced tea to wash down the whoopie pie. Then she revealed, "Jonas and I haven't talked much about this, which is part of the problem for him. If he'd get it out of his mind, maybe some of it would go out of his heart. I'm sure he blames himself too. He *has* told me . . ." She stopped. "I shouldn't be sharing this with you."

"You don't have to tell me, Daisy. I know Jonas's background. His dad was killed in action. As a law enforcement officer, Jonas didn't want to leave children fatherless, so he decided not to have any. My guess is he didn't react so well when Brenda told him she was pregnant. Being a cop, I know how that works. He blames himself for her distraction. He blames himself for her death. At least he did. But now, I suspect he doesn't know what to think."

Morris Rappaport eyed the third whoopie pie on the plate. He gave a shrug, picked it up, and ate it. "Good stuff you serve here," he said when he'd finished chewing.

"I hope so. That's why I opened the tea garden. I have a lot of elderly customers who come in and take home soup and salad. Of course, with a few goodies thrown in. But they're getting something wholesome. I wish we could start a Meals-on-Wheels."

Rappaport shook his head. "As if you aren't busy enough."

"Idle hands and all that," Daisy reminded him with a smile.

"You know, the Amish have many proverbs that sounded silly to me when I first came here. But now I realize most of them are good wholesome truth. That's a rare thing these days."

After eying Daisy once more, Rappaport stood and pushed back his chair. Then he put his hands on the table and leaned down to her once more. "I still think you can make a difference with Zeke and Jonas. Give it some thought."

As Daisy watched the detective leave, she knew she'd give his suggestion *much* thought. She would do anything to help the two men heal. The problem was—they would not want her to interfere.

Still . . . she might have to do it anyway.

Later that afternoon, Daisy had arranged an appointment with someone she'd never met before. Foster and another young man came into the tea garden right on the stroke of three. On time. That was a good sign, Daisy thought.

Foster grinned at Daisy as he crossed the room to her. "This is Ned Pachenko. Ned, this is Daisy."

Foster was right on time for his shift, and Ned . . . She was going to be talking to him about music, a very special kind of music.

"Hi, Ned, it's good to meet you. Why don't you come into my office so we can talk?"

Ned's hair was blond and curly. The curls dipped well over his T-shirt's band around his neck. Foster had told her he was in classes with Ned and Ned was in his early twenties. The musician carried an acoustic guitar with him as he followed Daisy to her office.

Once inside, she sat on the corner of her desk and motioned Ned to the chair in front of it. "I've planned teas before for children," she explained. "Never one involving music. When Foster told me that you were good at interacting with an audience and writing silly songs, I thought that would be wonderful entertainment for our children's tea. Do you like kids?"

His wide grin was charming. "I love kids. I come from a big family. I have four younger brothers and sisters. I got into the habit of playing the guitar and making up songs with them to keep them out of trouble."

Daisy laughed. "That's a good idea."

"I do it all the time at the dorm too," Ned said. "At Lancaster's Ice Cream Festival, I had a permit to sit in the square to play and sing and make up songs with kids that were around. They usually liked it."

"You sound perfect."

"Why don't I give you a little demonstration." His

smile could definitely melt young women's hearts, as well as kids'.

She motioned to his guitar. "Go ahead."

He started strumming and seemed to make up lyrics as he played. "There was a pretty woman whose tea garden was a hit. She not only brewed tea, but made cookies out of choc-co-lit."

Daisy couldn't help but smile. Ned had a good voice and the silly lyrics with the intentional rhyming would make kids giggle and laugh. "You've sold me. Of course, I'll pay you for the afternoon. What do you usually charge for a gig?"

He told her and she thought the price was low. They settled on a date and a sum that made both of them happy. Daisy thought he'd leave after that. She already had his contact information. But he said, "Foster told me that you're the one who found Mrs. Higgins in the pool at the school."

If Ned was a good friend of Foster's, she could see why Foster would have talked to him about it. "I did . . . along with the guidance counselor."

Ned rested his guitar on the floor, still holding it by the neck. Then he shook his head. "It's terrible to think some-one disliked Mrs. Higgins so much. I know she was strict. I had her in high school. But she was a good teacher."

Daisy had wondered if Althea's students respected her or made fun of her. Daisy had respected her but there had been other students, students she didn't get along with, who had called Althea names and joked about her appearance.

"I know Mrs. Higgins had kids in class that would have done anything to get *out* of her class. They just wanted an easy teacher so they could make a decent grade and move to the next level. Especially the football players. I still cheer for the home team when they play."

Not that Daisy was collecting information for any investigation, but she had an inkling who Ned was talking about. "Do you have someone particular in mind?"

"Harry Silverman."

"Is he the student who missed out on the college scholarship because of Mrs. Higgins?"

"Yes, he was. A scout was going to come and watch the game but he'd failed too many exams. Mrs. Higgins reported him and he couldn't play."

"Do you know what he's doing now?" Daisy asked.

"He's working for a storm door company in Lancaster. I ran into him at one of my gigs. He's still bitter."

"I've learned holding on to a grudge only hurts me, not the other person," Daisy said.

"I know what you mean. If you hold on to a grudge it gets bigger instead of smaller. If Harry blames Mrs. Higgins for his life, rather than looking at his own choices, he'll never be able to be a success."

Daisy could see that Ned was sincere and wasn't just spouting advice he might have heard from someone. Foster had chosen a good friend. She hoped Ned could make the children's tea a huge success.

After Ned left, Foster came into Daisy's office. "What did you think?"

"I liked him. I think he'll be good with kids."

"With tourist season on a roll, we need to really advertise this event. We need to play up the kids' music day on our website. Can I experiment with it?"

"Sure you can, if you have the time."

"I have time. If the day's a success, it will be a good draw for the future too. We can do it again in the fall."

Foster was adept at social media. She had no doubt he could help her promote the event. "That's a good idea. How did you and Ned become friends?"

"When I first met him, he came over to the house. He and my dad jammed."

"Your dad plays the guitar?"

"Yeah, he does. He doesn't play a lot anymore. He says he doesn't have time. But I think it's more about my mom. He used to play for her. I think when he plays now, it reminds him of that. Emily and I convince him to get out his guitar at least at Christmas."

Daisy hadn't seen Gavin Cranshaw much since Christmas. When they *had* seen each other at Vi's and Foster's apartment, Sammy had taken all of their attention, as a grandchild should. Someday, maybe Gavin would play his guitar for all of them.

Chapter Six

That afternoon, Daisy left the tea garden to drive into Lancaster. She would be meeting Brielle's parents at their law offices. She didn't know *what* to expect.

When she arrived at the address, she saw that the building was five stories of granite and shadowed glass. She found a parking spot a half block up the street on the other side of the building instead of parking in the public garage. All that concrete gave her the heebie-jeebies. She wasn't sure why, but she just didn't like those garages.

Her lilac duster flapped against her cream slacks. According to the calendar, spring was on its way. Nevertheless, the breeze hadn't forgotten winter. Her chunky chocolate clogs clicked on the porcelain tile after she passed through the electric doors that had parted at her approach. Although she'd memorized the suite number, she checked the roster board under glass beside the elevator. The law office of Horn and Horn was located on the fifth floor.

Was that the penthouse floor?

As the elevator whisked her upward, Daisy wasn't sure what she wanted to ask of Brielle's parents other than the question if they were on board with Brielle staying with her. *She* had asked for this meeting, which had seemed odd. Wouldn't Brielle's parents have wanted to question *her*?

Apparently the law offices took up the entire top floor. Exiting the elevator, she went through another glass door. To say the reception area was classy would be an understatement. A leather sofa in the palest gray sat perpendicular to several black leather club chairs. The floor looked like terrazzo.

Daisy crossed to the receptionist, who sat behind a sleek granite-topped desk with a computer station, printer, and other electronic devices. The receptionist looked to be in her twenties. Her blond hair fell in a geometrical cut, one side longer than the other. Her makeup was flawless. She wore a wine-colored pantsuit, a gold choker necklace, and dangling gold earrings.

Without a smile, she asked, "Mrs. Swanson?"

"Yes. That's me," Daisy responded with a smile. "I have an appointment with Mr. and Mrs. Horn."

"Yes, I see it's on their schedule."

Suddenly the door behind the reception desk opened. A woman who looked to be in her mid-forties walked out. Her suit was severe and black. The jacket had long narrow sleeves and the skirt was pencil slim. Daisy could see an older version of Brielle in the woman's face—her hazel eyes, her petite nose, and her perky chin. This woman, however, must be on a strict diet. She was thin . . . skinny, really. Her brown hair was caught in a perfect bun at the nape of her neck. She wore black onyx button earrings, a black onyx necklace, and a long onyx ring on her index finger. The diamond on her wedding ring finger was a solitaire big enough to rival the shine on a Maglite. Stiletto black pumps completed the outfit.

As the woman walked toward Daisy, Daisy could see the red soles on her shoes. Oh my. The price of those shoes could keep the lights on in the tea garden for a few months.

"Hello, Mrs. Swanson," the woman said, extending her hand. "I'm Nola Horn. Come with me and you can meet my husband."

There really wasn't anything to say to that, was there?

Daisy followed the woman down a hall and into an office that was as spacious as the spillover tearoom at the tea garden. The room was sectioned into two spaces—a work area with the glass-topped desk, and a sitting area. Two black leather chairs faced the desk on the red and gray rug. It had a distressed Persian look. The charcoal leather furniture around a coffee table was reminiscent of the lobby. There was a refrigerator and a wet bar in that area too, and Daisy supposed the couple served drinks. She wondered if snacks went along with them.

Mr. Horn rose from behind the desk and came over to the sitting area, motioning to the sofa. His long nose was patrician, his cheekbones high, his stubbled jaw sharp and pointed. It looked to her as if his black hair might have been touched up. She could only imagine how much his custom-fitted blue pin-striped suit had cost. "Sit down, Daisy. It's all right if I call you *Daisy*, isn't it?"

"You can call me Daisy if I can call you Nola and . . ." She trailed off waiting for him to give her his first name.

He forced a smile. "Elliott. My name is Elliott."

Nola asked, "Would you like a sparkling water?"

"No, I'm fine. Thank you."

Elliott said, "You asked for this meeting. What would you like to know?"

So they were going to be blunt. She could be blunt too. Already she seemed to understand why Brielle rebelled a bit with her piercings, dyed hair, and a sometimes defiant attitude. "I'd like to know if you're comfortable with Brielle staying with me . . . if that's what we decide to do."

"We were surprised," Nola acknowledged, "when Brielle came to us with this request. So, of course, we did a background check on you."

That startled Daisy. She might have guessed they would do that. They were lawyers.

"And?" she asked.

"And you checked out. No record. Not much outstanding debt. You're a widow with two daughters just as Brielle said. She told us a lot about you."

"I'm not sure that was from personal experience," Daisy said. "I just met her once."

"Oh, I think your daughter has filled her in. You run a tea shop, you go to church, you're dating a store owner, and you own the tea place with your aunt. Does that about cover it?"

Apparently that covered what this couple wanted to know. It didn't nearly cover who Daisy was, how she felt, why she would let Brielle stay with them. She decided to throw a different question their way. "My daughter Jazzi found her birth mother. Portia might stay with us a couple of days while Brielle is there. Is that a problem?"

The couple exchanged a look. "We could look into her background," Nola said.

"I'd rather you didn't," Daisy protested. "She's not a

drug dealer. She's married with children. She and Jazzi get along well."

"And how about *you* and this woman?" Nola asked.

"Portia and I are getting to know each other. I admit it's an odd situation and awkward sometimes. But we're making it work. Jazzi deserves that from both of us."

Nola looked a little embarrassed for a moment but then said, "Yes, our children deserve everything we can give them."

"If Brielle stays with me, will I be able to get in contact with you if I need to?"

"We always have our phones on. You can text us, e-mail, call. But I doubt if that will be necessary. Brielle doesn't have any medical conditions that could flare up or anything like that."

"Good to know," Daisy agreed.

Elliott was already checking his watch. "I presume that's all you need from us?"

Daisy did not particularly like this couple. She had to admit that was rare for her to think. She tried to find the good in everybody. But these two and their attitude toward Brielle . . .

"Yes, I think that's all I need to know." Daisy stood. "I'll be happy to have Brielle stay with us."

After she said her good-byes, after the receptionist gave her a nod and she left the couple's offices, after she rode down the elevator and left the building, she'd already made the assessment that this couple's careers were more important than their daughter.

Everyone needed love, laughter, and compassion in his

or her life. Hopefully Daisy and her family could give that to Brielle for a little while.

Daisy had returned to the tea garden and called her mother. After rocky communications for most of their lives, she felt she could talk honestly with her now. Her mom had shared a secret that had made all the difference in the world. When she told her mom now about the meeting with Brielle's parents, Rose Gallagher had said, "Think of Brielle, not her parents, and you'll do right."

After Daisy ended the call, she thought about the advice her mother had given her. She was right.

Thinking of her mom now with a smile instead of a frown, Daisy looked up when Eva Conner, the tea garden's dishwasher and girl Friday, stood in the doorway of Daisy's office.

"Can I talk to you for a few minutes?" Eva asked.

Eva was around forty-five, single, and intuitive as far as what Daisy needed to have accomplished in the kitchen. Tessa depended on her to make the kitchen run smoothly and it did. Eva's medium brown hair was boyishly short. Daisy suspected she kept it that way for her kitchen work so she didn't have to worry about it when she was around food. She usually stayed in the background, making sure she fulfilled all of her duties precisely.

"Sure. Come in," Daisy invited, hoping her aunt and Cora Sue could take care of the customers and their end-of-the-day closing procedures. "What can I help you with?"

Eva looked relieved at Daisy's invitation. "I don't know

if you want to talk about this . . . about Althea Higgins. I imagine finding her like that was traumatic."

"It was," Daisy agreed, trying not to let the pictures of that day run through her mind.

Eva took a few steps forward, closer to Daisy. "The thing is—Althea Higgins was my teacher."

Eva was older than Daisy, but Daisy realized that Althea Higgins had been at that school a long time. Her students had had children and grandchildren.

"I didn't know that," Daisy said.

"Who talks about their high school teachers?" Eva let out a breath. "But in this case, I want to. I liked Mrs. Higgins."

Daisy tried to keep her surprise from showing. She knew some students respected Althea. But actually liked her?

"I more than liked her," Eva admitted. "I was grateful for her. Mrs. Higgins monitored me in homeroom as well as taught me in English class. She could easily see that my mother couldn't make ends meet. When she and my dad divorced, he was long gone. When I was in school, we had trouble paying bills and just meeting everyday expenses like clothes and school supplies. I tried to stay in the background so nobody noticed, but Mrs. Higgins did."

Thinking about it, Daisy revised her estimation of Althea. In past murder investigations, she'd found that murder victims and even their killers weren't always all good or all bad.

"Did she help you with your school supplies?"

"More than that," Eva said, clasping her hands together. "She brought us food. There were times when she even sewed skirts and blouses for me. She was an excellent seamstress. The clothes looked store-bought. She did it so nobody made fun of me. I can't tell you how much that meant. I suppose girls' cliques and mean girls are worse now, but back then we had them too."

Daisy had been fortunate that her high school days had been mostly positive. She'd had good friends like Tessa. Her self-esteem had been built up when Cade Bankert, a real estate agent in Willow Creek now who had sold her the tea garden and her house, had asked her to the prom. She'd concentrated on her studies. Her grades had seemed to surprise some of her teachers who'd thought she might not have brains under that blond hair and behind her blue eyes. But for the most part, she remembered high school fondly. Eva, however, must have had a totally different experience.

"I know a lot of people didn't appreciate Mrs. Higgins," Eva admitted. "She could be sharp and forceful, persistent, and downright authoritarian. But I saw her other side. I saw the side of her that wanted to help whoever she could. And for that reason, I owe her."

"I understand why you feel that way," Daisy said. "But what does that have to do with now?"

"I want you to try to find Mrs. Higgins's killer. I'll help you any way I can. It's been on my mind since I first heard about it. Please, won't you help?"

"Eva, I'm not a private investigator. I'm definitely not a detective. This murder belongs to the police to solve."

"I know they'll try," Eva agreed. "But that doesn't mean they'll find who did it. Time passes and the clues run cold. You've had success. You've found the right person five times. That's not coincidence. It's not an accident. You're good at this, Daisy."

Daisy felt taken aback with that analysis. And Eva apparently could see that because she said, "I don't for a minute think Mrs. Cotton had anything to do with it. She was the one who found Mrs. Higgins. I know she helped Jazzi and I've heard only good things about her. What if the police settle on her and not look at anybody else? You know that can happen. It happened to Tessa. *And* it happened to your aunt."

Daisy's aunt Iris and her best friend, Tessa, were the reasons she'd gotten involved with investigations to begin with. "You're right, Eva. That's why I got involved. But back then I didn't have a relationship with the police department. Detective Rappaport and I were at odds. Now we're not."

"That's even more reason why you can find things out and share them with him. All I'm asking is that you make an effort to dig a little, discover who the suspects could be, and then share that information with the police department. I've seen Detective Rappaport in here. He listens to you."

Daisy noticed that Eva wasn't mentioning Detective Willet. He was a whole other case entirely. She didn't want to make a promise to Eva that she couldn't keep. She also didn't want to interfere with Detective Rappaport or with Zeke Willet. It was much better if she flew below the radar.

"Are you going to Althea's funeral? I can give you the time off."

Eva shook her head. "I don't know her family. I'd feel odd there."

"I'll tell you what. I'll be attending the funeral. One thing I can do for you is to keep my ears open. At funerals, people often say things they wouldn't say other places. If

I hear anything incriminating, I'll be sure to share it with the police. How about that?"

Eva didn't look particularly happy, but she nodded. "That's a start. I know you, Daisy. One clue will lead to another and you'll figure it out. Anytime you want my help, just ask. I'll do anything."

To inspire such loyalty, Althea Higgins must have had a good side. Maybe at the woman's funeral, Daisy could find out more about it.

Althea Higgins's farmstead was in decent shape, at least on the outside. Daisy and Jonas walked toward the graveyard to the rear of the property on Wednesday. They passed the farmhouse, as well as the barn and out-buildings. Daisy wondered exactly who did do the upkeep. The red paint on the barn had peeled away until the barn looked almost brown. The white trim had peeled too. The barn itself, however, looked sturdy enough. In fact, on the side there was a new unpainted single door that led inside.

Daisy wondered if there were horses in the barn or if the building was empty. Hard to know without peeking. A few goats were penned near the chicken coop. Someone would have to feed the animals and collect the eggs each day. Dried pampas grass at one corner of the coop was overgrown and way high, at least five feet. That should be trimmed back so it would regrow again over the summer.

"The farm is functioning," Jonas said to Daisy, "but it could use some work." He took her elbow as they stepped from the mown section into longer grass that led them to the family burial plots. Split-rail fencing that had broken down with mold and lichen designated the Higgins burial area. A picket gate stood open. Mourners, many of them teachers, were already gathered at the farthest end of the burial ground.

Stella crossed to Daisy through dead grass and spring sprouts, almost tripping. "I'm so glad you're here," she said, righting herself. "Reverend Kemp hasn't arrived yet."

Already Daisy could see some of the oldest tombstones in the row nearest the house. Some were faded from age, others were covered with moss or lichen. She read the inscription on one—

Beloved Wife Theresa Clark Higgins
Born December 2nd, 1813
Died February 5th, 1884
Aged 71 Years Two Months Three Days.

There was a tall square stone with a cross on top. The white marble had been shadowed and blackened from years of wear and weather.

Daisy noticed tombstones positioned around an area that was bigger than the other plots. One tall monument read—

Mary, Jenny, and Albert
Children of George and Suzanna Higgins.

Further down it read *George Higgins* and his birth and death dates. Then *Suzanna wife of George Higgins* and her dates. The whole family was buried there. Suzanna had died in 1909 and her husband, George, in 1921. The children must have all died before they did.

Influenza outbreak? Measles? Any childhood disease that had now been wiped out with a vaccine?

Apparently Stella noticed Daisy studying the tombstones. "I know this isn't a place you want to be today."

Thinking of Ryan and the burial plot in Florida, she recalled his tombstone that read *Beloved Husband and Father.* She felt her throat grow tight. "No, not a place I want to be *any* day."

Jonas wrapped his arm around her and squeezed. She knew he understood because he'd gone through the death and the grief and the loss of people he'd loved too.

Suddenly a young man came through the gate. He was dressed in jeans and a sweatshirt. His work boots were muddy. He would have been a handsome young man, but his expression now was practically a scowl. His russet hair, longish and mussed, inched over his forehead and along his cheeks.

Jonas was wearing a charcoal suit and Daisy could see other men wore suits too. Those men were probably teachers. She'd worn a deep purple pantsuit. The jacket was a little light for the cool March weather, but she'd resisted wearing a shawl or cape over it. Other mourners mingled who wore casual clothes—jeans or khakis with sweaters or button-down shirts. Everybody seemed to be dressed better than this boy.

To Daisy's surprise Stella stopped him. "Lucius. I'd like to introduce you to this couple."

Lucius didn't look particularly happy to be stopped, but he nodded as Stella said, "This is Jonas Groft. He owns

Woods downtown. This is Daisy Swanson. She co-owns the tea garden with her aunt Iris. Daisy had your grand-mother as a teacher. Daisy and Jonas, this is Lucius Higgins, Althea's grandson."

"Nice to meet you," he said with a twitch of his lip that was meant to be a small smile. It didn't quite make it. "I'm sorry I can't talk with you. Reverend Kemp just came and he wants me to snag men for pallbearers."

"If you're short, I'd be glad to help," Jonas said. "I didn't know your grandmother, but on a day like this, everybody should pitch in."

Lucius's eyes widened a bit as he took a better look at Jonas. "I'd be grateful." Then he strode away to the group of people at the other end of the burial plots.

Daisy said to Stella, "You said his name is Higgins. I thought Althea had a daughter."

"She did. Her name is Phebe. But when Phebe divorced, she returned to her maiden name."

Many women did that. It wasn't unusual, especially if a divorce had been contentious.

"The odd thing," Stella said, "is that Lucius is the one who inherited this property."

"Not his mother?" Jonas asked.

"Nope. Phebe has never wanted anything to do with the farm. Lucius helped his grandmother with upkeep here. Althea left it to him, expecting him to live here and keep it running."

"Do you think he'll do that?" Daisy asked, looking around the property.

"I don't know. I've heard rumors that he intends to sell it. I've also heard he didn't have the best attitude toward Althea but I have no idea why." Stella lowered her voice.

"I hope the police are exploring that option. It might guide them away from me."

"You seriously think Lucius could have harmed his grandmother?"

"Look at him," Stella said, waving to the young man who was now talking with Lawrence Bishop. "He's certainly tall enough, broad enough, and strong enough. And if he and his grandmother didn't get along, who knows what was in his head."

Indeed, who knew? Daisy told herself she was not going to explore and find out.

Jazzi had asked Daisy if she could go shopping with Brielle after school on Thursday instead of working at the tea garden. Brielle's mom needed clothes for her trip and she was going to shop too, though probably not in the same stores. Park City Center, outside of Lancaster, was a perfect place to go their separate ways and then meet up again when it was time to drive home.

Since Daisy wanted to get to know Brielle better before she was a houseguest, she said, "Why don't you have Brielle's mom drop you both off here. Brielle can stay for supper and then I'll take her home later. Maybe I'll get a few minutes to talk with Brielle's mom that way."

It wouldn't hurt to see if Brielle's mom was as stiff as a board on her free time as well as when she was in her office.

It had all been set, so Daisy had thought. However, things hadn't gone as planned. Daisy had fed Marjoram and Pepper and was chopping vegetables to prepare a stir-fry for supper. That would be healthy for all of them, and she hoped Brielle would enjoy it. She'd brought home cucumber salad from the tea garden along with lemon teacakes for a light dessert. It was a simple meal, but the food was less important than the conversation they might have around the table.

When Brielle and Jazzi swept in the door around seven thirty, Daisy was folding laundry. Exiting the laundry room, she entered the living room to see Brielle and Jazzi dropping packages onto the sofa.

Crossing to them, Daisy asked Brielle, "Is your mom going to come in for a few minutes?"

Brielle shook her head and exchanged a look with Jazzi. Daisy looked to Jazzi for an explanation.

With a sigh, her younger daughter placed the last of her bags onto the sofa. "Plans changed, Mom. Connie, Brielle's housekeeper, took us shopping. Or rather she dropped us off, and then she picked us up again to bring us here. Brielle's mom had a last-minute meeting."

Brielle kept her eyes downcast on the packages she'd brought in.

"I'm sorry to hear that," Daisy said. "I was hoping to talk to your mom again. Are you hungry? The stir-fry fixings are ready."

Brielle brightened up and Daisy wondered if she'd thought Daisy would be cross because of the change in plans. She wished Jazzi had texted her to tell her about it.

"Can we show you our clothes first?" Jazzi asked. "I got some different things, sort of like Brielle wears sometimes."

"Show me," Daisy said, sitting down on the armchair.

The thing was . . . as Jazzi showed Daisy, Daisy couldn't hide her dismay. The first outfit Jazzi brought out was a crop top with spaghetti straps that would show more than her belly button. The yellow and white patterned shorts could hardly be called shorts. They might be called mini-shorts. Daisy bit her tongue while she saw what else Jazzi had bought. The fuchsia romper was cute with cold shoulders and hems long enough to be appropriate for school. But the swimsuit Jazzi produced next made Daisy shudder. She would not have her daughter parading around in strings with tiny pieces of cloth between them.

Jazzi saw her mother's expression. "What? Don't you like what I bought?"

Not knowing exactly how to handle this with Brielle present, Daisy took a few moments to put on her tactful mother hat. "Where would you wear the first outfit, Jazzi? To sunbathe?"

"Sunbathe? No, Mom," Jazzi protested. "It's to wear to school."

"The romper would be appropriate for school. I really like it. It's a beautiful color and style. But the first outfit . . ." She shook her head. "That has to go back."

"Mom . . ." Jazzi drawled, exchanging a look with Brielle that said her daughter was embarrassed.

Daisy had known this would happen, but since Brielle had been an influence for these outfits, she might as well see what the consequences were.

"I can use the bathing suit to sunbathe," Jazzi said hopefully.

Instead of shaking her head vehemently or protesting, Daisy gave Jazzi something to think about. "Tell me what you think Colton would say if you wore that bathing suit when you visited him and Portia."

Jazzi's face flamed as she thought about it. "I'd never wear that around Portia's husband."

"Exactly. You could wear it in the backyard if you wanted to sunbathe, but I imagine with the price you probably paid for it, it would deserve more wear than that. Am I right?"

Brielle suddenly jumped in. "Mrs. Swanson, I told Jazzi how great she looked in that bathing suit. I mean . . . look at her. She's got a figure any woman would want."

"She does," Daisy agreed. "But it looks just as good with clothes as without clothes. That bathing suit is almost like not wearing any clothes. Do you get my drift?"

"Are you saying you have to approve of my clothes before I can wear them?" Jazzi asked, with a bit of defiance she usually didn't have in her voice.

"It's never been an issue before," Daisy said. "Now it might be. You know, don't you, that the school is thinking about incorporating uniforms."

"But you said you weren't *for* that."

"I'm not, but I *am* for appropriate dress in school. Can you think about it? Brielle, do you want to show me what you bought?"

"I don't think I'd better," Brielle mumbled.

Jazzi looked at her mother accusingly.

"Did you buy a bathing suit like Jazzi's?" Daisy asked, hoping to lighten the atmosphere.

"No way. I just bought capris and a T-shirt, but the capris are leather and tight. The T-shirt has black lace inserts."

Daisy didn't know whether to laugh or to pretend they had never had this conversation. Daisy looked from Jazzi to Brielle and neither of them looked happy. "How about if we table this conversation for now and have supper?"

"Mrs. Swanson, do you still want me to come and stay with you over spring break?" Brielle asked hesitantly.

"Of course I do. Are you sure you still want to come?"

Brielle grinned at her. "I do. I want to see what your family is like."

Because she doesn't like the dynamics in her own? Daisy wondered. Having Brielle as a guest might be an experience that would keep her on her toes.

Chapter Seven

Daisy's thoughts swirled in her head as she served a new lemon-lime oolong tea to customers on Friday morning and watched as they tasted it. They seemed to like it. For the upcoming summer, the combination made sense.

Daisy had just refilled cups at a table for four when Trevor Lundquist entered the tea garden. Daisy liked Trevor, even more so now that he was dating Tessa. The odd combination of the artiste and the journalist seemed to work to everyone's surprise. Today, however, Trevor had that gleam in his eye that he wanted something. Daisy knew exactly what that would be.

She showed him to a table for two in the spillover tearoom and put up her hand before he could ask her anything. "Before you start questioning me, I don't know any more than what was reported in the news."

"I doubt that," he countered with a grin. "But I'll accept that for now. I've been doing a bit of digging myself. Actually, I've been interviewing Althea's former students to put together my memorial article since she taught at the high school for so long. But I can never stick to one topic . . . like only Althea's good qualities."

"Trevor, what are you going to do?" She didn't think Willow Creek was ready for an exposé.

"Oh, nothing for the memorial. I have quotes. Nice ones from some students. I'll tone down the others. But while doing this, I discovered something else."

If Daisy asked the question, she'd be getting involved. Did she want to step further into this?

She remembered that pool rope around Althea's neck. That seemed personal and rage-filled. So she asked the question. "What?"

Trevor leaned closer to her. He wore cologne that was pleasant, not overpowering like some. He'd dressed in khaki pants and a light beige sweater. He was a good-looking man and she could see why Tessa was interested in him.

He lowered his voice. "Althea found a deal with a uniform company. If the school decided to initiate a uniform policy, she would receive a kickback."

"Really? She could have done something like that?" Daisy had always considered Althea a by-the-book woman.

"Anything is possible."

Eva came over to them and asked what they'd like to drink. Trevor chose the lemon-lime-infused oolong tea and Daisy oolong hot tea with clover honey. The local honey was supposed to help with allergies but she didn't know if there was scientific fact to back that up.

After they were both sipping tea, Trevor asked, "Did you know Althea has a grandson who helps on the property?"

"Yes, I met him. From what I could see at the funeral, there's a lot to take care of. I could see goats standing outside a pen as well as a chicken coop. I don't know if horses were in the barn."

Trevor took a few swallows of tea then swiped his mouth with a napkin. "Althea wasn't taking care of all that herself. She has a neighbor who is a good bit of help along with her grandson."

"I think his name is Floyd Hirsch. I only caught a glimpse of him at the funeral. I didn't talk to him."

"I understand that between the three of them, they kept the place running," Trevor noted. "I'm going to try to go back there when someone's there and ask a few questions."

Trevor's alarm went off on his watch. "I'd better get going. I have a meeting at the paper." Pushing back his chair, he stood, his hands still on the table. "If you find anything out, will you let me know?"

"I'll let you know. Maybe this one will be solved quickly. That would be best for everyone."

After a two-fingered salute, Trevor went to the counter to pay. Daisy gave Iris a signal that Iris knew meant Trevor's tea was on the house.

He glanced over at Daisy, nodded, and mouthed a *thank you*.

As he was leaving the restaurant, Eva came over to Daisy. "I couldn't help but overhear some of what you and Trevor were talking about. Althea had a head on her shoulders for finances. She was always looking for a way to extend every penny and to pick up more pennies. Do you know what I mean?"

"I *do* know what you mean. But I don't think of Althea as a person who would go behind everybody's back for her own benefit."

"She had a kind side," Eva said. "But she also had a ruthless streak in her. Heaven help anybody who crossed her. That's why she was so strict with the football players. At the beginning of the year, she laid down the law and she told them exactly what she expected from them. She told them she'd be clear the whole way through the year on what they had to do to make their grades and stay on the team. But I guess some just didn't take her seriously. Kids now have a sense of entitlement, and they think their parents can get them out of a tough situation. But Althea wouldn't let that happen. I do admire her for that."

Eva might admire Althea for the strict way she lived her life, but Daisy could easily see how others might not like it . . . how someone could consider that strictness a motive for murder.

Although Althea Higgins's murder often disturbed Daisy's thoughts, something else did too. Morris Rappaport thought that Daisy could make a difference between Zeke's and Jonas's relationship. Was he right about that? Should she try? Friendships were too valuable to throw away. If one could be saved . . .

What if she visited Zeke on her lunch break? She decided everything about this situation with Zeke and Jonas was better kept private if it could be. When Zeke had moved to Willow Creek, Jonas had told her where he lived. He rented the first-floor apartment of a Craftsman-style home. A porch ran across the front with brick pillars that stretched to the ceiling. Daisy had noticed stairs along the side of the house that rose to the second-floor apartment.

On her lunch break, she walked to Zeke's. Her PT Cruiser as well as her van were recognizable. She didn't want to start any gossip. Rappaport had told her that Zeke usually had Fridays off if he worked the weekend. She'd taken a chance he'd be at home today. Climbing the porch steps, she noticed the sidelight windows around the door. She knocked on the door and glimpsed movement inside.

Zeke opened the door wearing sweatpants and a gray T-shirt. He hadn't shaved. She wondered if he'd slept in late. That's what days off were for, right?

His eyes widened in surprise when he saw her. "I never expected to see *you* here."

"I thought we might have a talk. Can I come in?" she asked calmly.

He backed up, motioned her inside, and closed the door. "No customers at the tea garden today?" he asked facetiously.

"I'm on my lunch break."

"That means this will be a short conversation." His voice was clipped as if he hadn't wanted to invite her in.

"If you want it to be," she agreed.

"I can't offer you a cup of tea. I'm out. I have water and beer. Would you like either?"

"Zeke." She said the word as if she were talking to a teenager rather than a grown man.

His face flushed. "Sorry. My defenses are on overdrive." He motioned her to the right to a living room that was small but comfortably furnished with a tan faux suede sofa and a recliner in dark brown leather. A flat-screen TV hung on the wall.

She sat on one end of the sofa and he sat on the other.

"Do you have information about the murder?" he asked.

"No, I don't. Althea Higgins's murder isn't why I'm here. I'd like to talk about you and Jonas."

She could see Zeke's face shut down just as Jonas's did when he didn't want to have a conversation about something.

Nevertheless, she continued. "Zeke, you and Jonas were friends. He feels betrayed by Brenda and betrayed by you. If the two of you could talk about this—"

"There's nothing to talk about," Zeke snapped. "It's like you said—I betrayed him and so did Brenda."

She didn't know if she should ask, but she did. "What happened?"

He rubbed his hand over his face and suddenly didn't look so closed off.

"What happened is an old story. Jonas, Brenda, and I are a cliché."

"I don't think it's that simple," Daisy protested. "Clichés are clichés for a reason. There's truth in them. Tell me about your truth."

Zeke collapsed against the sofa back as if he was tired of holding everything inside, tired of being bitter, tired of letting it all interfere with his life.

"The three of us were friends, really friends. I liked Brenda a lot but Jonas started dating her. I didn't think he ever would because they were partners. But the heart wants what the heart wants. Somebody said that once. And Jonas and Brenda were really good about separating their personal relationship from their professional one. I watched them. Maybe I was watching for that first chink in their relationship. I don't know."

"You had feelings for her, and they didn't go away just because Jonas began dating her."

He nodded. "Because we were all friends, Brenda often came to me to talk about a professional problem when Jonas was too busy. Paperwork seemed to multiply each year we were on the job. Jonas had seniority. Sometimes the captain asked his advice and pulled him in on matters that Brenda wasn't a part of."

"Did that bother her?"

"Sometimes. But I don't think she had as much ambition as Jonas or I did, and I found out why."

Daisy leaned toward Zeke. "Can you tell me?"

"Sure. You'll probably understand. She wanted a husband and she wanted children."

"But I thought she and Jonas had an agreement."

"*Jonas* thought they had an agreement," Zeke explained. "Apparently they had an agreement for a while because Brenda had an IUD put in."

"And then?"

"She didn't tell me and she didn't tell Jonas that she'd had it removed. Becoming pregnant was on her mind. One night Jonas got pulled into a task force meeting. Brenda stopped over at my place. I had a bottle of wine and we shared it. I don't have to tell you what happened next."

Zeke's cheeks had turned redder and Daisy could see that he felt embarrassed, not only for what had happened, but because he was having this conversation with her. She remained silent to let him think through what he wanted to say and how he wanted to say it. Maybe this was the first he'd told anyone the whole story.

"She told me she was pregnant before she told Jonas,"

Zeke said, and let out a long breath. "She said she wanted to be honest with me . . . that she didn't know who had fathered the baby. But she was going to tell Jonas she was pregnant and she wanted to marry him and have a family with him. She was cutting me out. I had been a mistake." He rubbed his hand down his face. "Isn't that what guys always tell women? In this case, it was the opposite."

"What were you going to do? Be honest with Jonas? Buy into her plan?"

"I didn't know *what* I was going to do. I guess I was going to wait around and see if their relationship fell apart. Yet deep down I knew that wouldn't happen. When Jonas found out Brenda was pregnant, he'd step up. He always did. That pregnancy might change his life, but he'd take responsibility for it. There wasn't any chance he'd walk away. There'd be no chance for me."

At that moment Daisy felt sorry for Zeke.

After a glance at her, he continued. "Somehow I learned that Brenda had told Jonas she was pregnant before the shooting. Jonas was still loopy when he came out of surgery and he told one of the other guys. He had lots of friends on that police force and they all cared about him. I knew Brenda had been distracted by the whole situation. If she told Jonas before they left that night, his mind was on her and that baby rather than what they were doing."

"If that's true, and I don't know if it is," Daisy said, "do you blame him?"

A resentful look passed over Zeke's face and he fisted his hands. "I blame him for dating his partner. I blame him for getting involved with her in the first place. It was *wrong*."

"You can tell yourself what you want," Daisy suggested. "But that shooter that night was the one with the rifle. He ambushed them. Nothing they did could have prevented that."

"Is that what Jonas told you?"

"Do you have something to tell me that's different?"

Zeke hung his head and looked down at his bare feet. "I tell myself they should have parked farther away. I tell myself that if they were in sync, they would have stayed in the car and watched first. I tell myself that if I'd been in that car with Brenda, she wouldn't have been killed. She wouldn't have died."

"You tell yourself all those things. But do you believe them? Tell me something, Zeke. Why aren't you angry with Brenda rather than Jonas?"

Zeke didn't answer her. He didn't have an answer for her because he was idealizing Brenda. He didn't want to admit Brenda had betrayed them both.

Daisy picked up her purse from the sofa and rose. There was nothing else to say here except for, "If you want your friendship back, if you want to save it, one of you has to make the first move. Maybe you should be thinking about that instead of thinking about what can't be changed."

Zeke didn't move. He gave Daisy one long look, then she left.

Had she done the right thing? She didn't know. But she was sure she'd find out soon.

When Daisy returned to the tea garden, she was surprised to see Stella Cotton waiting for her. Had she taken another personal day? Spring break wasn't until next week.

Cora Sue intercepted Daisy. "Mrs. Cotton has been waiting for you. She came in about fifteen minutes ago. I brewed her tea and supplied her with a couple of snickerdoodles."

"Thank you, Cora Sue." Daisy checked her watch. She had about fifteen minutes until her hour break was over. She liked to follow the same rules as her servers. In this instance, she might have to take a little extra time.

Daisy asked Cora Sue, "Will you tell her I'll be there in five minutes? I want to take my purse to the office, get rid of my jacket, and wash up."

"No problem," Cora Sue said. "I'll take a cup of tea to the table for you. Oolong?"

"That seems to be what I'm craving these days." Daisy needed a bit of bracing after that conversation with Zeke. She was mightily concerned about its repercussions.

Five minutes later she sat next to Stella at a round table in the spillover tearoom. "Cora Sue said you wanted to talk to me."

"I guess you're wondering why I'm here on a school day. Since the police talked to me twice, I made an appointment with Marshall Thompson and took the afternoon off and started spring break a little early. He advised me on what to do if they call me in again. He said he'd go with me."

"Good. Marshall is a fine attorney. He helped me and Aunt Iris."

"You were both suspects?"

"We were. Aunt Iris had been dating the murder victim. The police thought I might be helping her cover up her crime."

"I'm sorry to hear that. Everything turned out all right?"

"Everything turned out all right. The detectives try

really hard to find the truth. Sometimes they just need a
little help."

Stella sipped her tea, then she put down the cup and
added more sugar. "I think I just need sweetener in my
life these days."

"So your meeting with Marshall went well?"

"It did. I told him that Althea was accused of plagiarism
in her self-published book."

"Had you told the police that?"

"I had. Since then, I learned even more."

Daisy considered whether she wanted to know or not,
but she didn't have to ask any more questions because Stella
went on. "The author of the book lives in Philadelphia. She
filed a complaint against Althea with the Department of
Education. It's on the teachers' information loop. Her name
is Tatum Beatty. From all the comments that have been
posted, she's young, smart, and assertive . . . a go-getter.
I'd like to know more about her, but I think the police
are watching me pretty carefully. I probably shouldn't associate with anybody who has anything to do with Althea.
That's why I wanted to see *you.*"

"I don't understand."

"I'd like you to help me. Not investigate or anything
like that. I don't want you to get into trouble with the
police. But I thought maybe you could talk to this
Tatum Beatty. Philadelphia's not that far away. What do
you think?"

Daisy thought the idea was crazy!

However . . . Brielle would be starting her stay with
them tonight. Maybe, just maybe, Brielle and Jazzi would
appreciate a visit to the Philadelphia Museum of Art

tomorrow. While they were there, Daisy could possibly meet with Tatum Beatty. *Was* it a crazy idea?

Daisy was still wondering that on Saturday after she dropped off Brielle and Jazzi at the Museum of Art. Last evening, she'd called Tatum Beatty and arranged for a meeting at one o'clock.

After finding a place to park, which wasn't that easy, she walked to the address that she'd typed in on her phone. It was a row house, two stories, and it looked as if it had history behind it with its rough brick, black shutters, and white trim. She held the black wrought iron railing as she went up the four steps to the door. Daisy realized that the knocker, in the form of a pineapple, replaced a doorbell. She used the knocker.

Tatum Beatty answered the door. Daisy knew it was her because she'd viewed Tatum's profile picture on her website. Tatum was chubby with a round face, short red-brown hair that spiked up on the top, and large black-rimmed glasses. She was wearing black leggings and a bateau-neck black shirt.

Smiling at Daisy, she extended her hand. "I'm Tatum, and you're Daisy. I looked up your tea garden on your website. Very polished."

What would people do without websites? Daisy had read on Tatum's that she taught Shakespeare in high school and had a specialty for creating strategies to capture students' interest. Tatum had written a book about it. Daisy had learned that a chapter in Althea's book seemed to copy a section of Tatum's work word for word.

"I know you like tea," Tatum said as she showed Daisy into the living room with sleek black lines, chrome and glass. The white leather couch hardly looked used. The red leather club chair with a hassock might have been. A legal pad lay on the hassock with a pen clipped to it.

Tatum continued, "I have water and milk. Would you like either?"

"No, thanks," Daisy said, slipping her purse under her arm. "I brought my daughter and a friend to the Philadelphia Museum of Art and I'd like to join them for some of the tour."

"I read on your website that your daughters help you out at the tea garden."

Daisy didn't feel as if she wanted to share her personal life with this woman without even knowing her, but if she shared a little, maybe Tatum would too. "Jazzi still helps out there. I suppose we should change some of the text on the website. Vi has a baby now."

Tatum motioned Daisy to the sofa. "Make yourself comfortable."

Tatum sat in the club chair and leaned forward with her elbows on her knees. "I'd like you to be honest with me."

"And I'd like you to be honest with me," Daisy returned, setting her purse on the sofa.

"Yes, people say that but I don't know if they mean it." Tatum ran one hand through her spiked hair and it didn't move. "I want to know if you were Althea Higgins's friend."

Daisy relaxed a bit. Now she understood some of where Tatum was coming from. She wanted to know if Daisy was here to defend Althea Higgins.

"Not a friend," Daisy assured her. "Althea was my teacher when I went to high school. I respected her but was mostly just afraid of her as were a lot of her students. Recently the high school hired my tea garden to serve a tea service in appreciation of the teachers. That's how I came in contact with Althea again."

"I don't understand then why you wanted to see me. What does her death have to do with you?"

"I found Althea's body along with the school guidance counselor. Stella feels she's the number one suspect because she found Althea first. She wants me to help prove she had nothing to do with it."

"In other words, she wants to make *me* a suspect?" Tatum had caught on quickly.

"That's not really my purpose for being here. I told Stella I would talk to you, but I mostly want to gather information. The police and I sometimes have a working relationship. I've helped with other investigations."

Tatum adjusted her glasses and studied Daisy more carefully. "So you're not just a blonde with a pretty face."

Instead of being offended, Daisy smiled. "No, I've had to counteract that impression more than once in my lifetime. Tell me about what happened between you and Althea," Daisy suggested.

Tatum sat back in her chair and put her legs up on the hassock. "It's pretty cut and dried, really. I didn't know Althea Higgins. My focus is on teaching and teaching well. Shakespeare is a wonderful subject. I want students to realize his plays aren't outdated. They're simply written in a different language. By that, I mean poetry, and I can teach them to understand it if they come along on the journey with me. I wrote a book about it. Mrs. Higgins copied one of my chapters almost word for word and put it in what she called *her* book."

"Althea Higgins wasn't stupid," Daisy said. "I can't imagine how she thought she'd get away with it."

"That's easy," Tatum quickly responded. "The e-book market is glutted. There are so many books on the same subjects that who would think to compare two? But that's just the point. Althea Higgins might not have been stupid, but she didn't understand the Internet and the far-reaching search capabilities of it."

Daisy could see that.

"Her credits in her book of course included the school where she was teaching. It didn't take me long to send her an e-mail and fight the fact that she'd plagiarized me. But she wouldn't admit it. I wasn't going to let her get away with it. I hired a lawyer and we introduced a lawsuit. Her book was pulled from Internet sales outlets because of my efforts. It's quite possible that Althea plagiarized other parts of her book with authors other than me. They possibly have no clue she did it."

"So what happens now?"

"I'm in talks with the lawyer settling her estate. I really can't discuss that."

"And you reported her to the Department of Education?"

"I did. So Althea's reputation most likely would have been ruined. If the word got out, and I assume it would have. Teachers gab and gossip just like the rest of the population."

Tatum didn't seem to hold any bitterness or resentment. But was she telling Daisy the whole story? On the other hand, had Althea plagiarized someone else who also had Tatum's drive and knowledge of social media and the Internet?

That was an answer the police should explore. But would they?

Chapter Eight

When Jonas strode into the tea garden on Monday morning with a determined, stony expression on his face, Daisy knew she was in for trouble. They'd both been busy over the weekend. She'd been tied up with Brielle beginning her stay at her home, and Jonas had driven toward Waynesboro to gather more reclaimed wood.

She heard the click of Jonas's boots on the tile, spotted the tension throughout the straightness of his shoulders, noticed the nerve thumping on the left side of his cheek where his scar was the most prominent. Instinctively, Daisy knew she was going to have to meet him head-on.

Crossing to him, she asked, "What's wrong?" She probably knew full well what *was* wrong.

He didn't raise his voice. He usually didn't. But there was an edge to the question he posed to her. "Can we talk in your office?"

For this discussion she almost wished she had blinds that closed on the Plexiglass where she looked out from her office over to the kitchen. Hindsight was twenty-twenty.

"Of course we can." The sweetness that was usually in her voice when she talked to Jonas, because she was always glad to see him, had vanished. What could she say to him that would explain what she had done? How could she prove to him that she was on *his* side?

He beat her to her office. It wasn't that he rushed, but his strides were longer. Today she wasn't sure she wanted to keep up. She wasn't sure if she wished she could veer off to the right into the kitchen instead of into her office. However, *she* was the one who had prompted this confrontation. *She* was the one who had forced this subject out in the open where Jonas and Zeke didn't want it.

He paced back and forth before he said anything, as if he was debating with himself about each of the words he might utter.

She closed the door.

"What were you thinking?" His voice was even but his green eyes blazed. She didn't think she'd ever seen Jonas this upset. Maybe she *had* done the wrong thing. Maybe interfering was the last action he'd expected from her. Maybe Detective Rappaport had been all wrong and she had no influence at all.

Trying to slow this down, she asked him, "How did you find out?"

"Oh, Daisy. You knew full well I'd find out. Zeke mentioned to Rappaport that you'd paid him a visit. Rappaport dropped that bomb on me. You knew he would, didn't you?"

"The way you and Zeke have been closemouthed about everything concerning the situation, I didn't think anyone would talk about it."

"And just what would talking about it accomplish?"

Keeping her voice calm, hoping he'd let her explain, she said, "You were dead set against speaking with

Zeke. I thought maybe I could influence him to talk with
you. You need to hash this out. You need to look at what
happened—"

Cutting her off, he countered, "You don't know *what* I
need. If you did, you never would have done this."

"Jonas, please. Let's sit and have a cup of tea and talk."
She couldn't keep the pleading note from her voice. If he
wouldn't discuss this with her, she was anxious about
what would happen next.

"We're already talking. Tea won't help this. You know
what I really needed from you, Daisy?"

She was afraid to ask, but she did anyway. "What?"

At that moment, he looked more disappointed and sad
than he looked angry. "I needed your loyalty. I needed to
be able to trust you. God knows I couldn't trust Brenda. I
couldn't trust Zeke. Now I don't even know if I can trust
Rappaport. I thought you and I were getting somewhere.
I thought we both understood how important trust is."

"I *do* understand, Jonas. I do."

He backed up a few steps. "No, you don't. If I don't
want to talk to Zeke for the next twenty years, that's *my*
business. If he doesn't want to talk to me, that's *his*."

Here she could have inserted that Detective Rappaport
had spoken to her, that the detective had thought the whole
situation was affecting Zeke's performance as well as
Jonas's well-being. But she wasn't about to throw Detective Rappaport under the proverbial bus.

Hoping to soften Jonas's attitude, she took a step closer
to him, took in the spicy scent of his aftershave, wanted
to touch his jaw that was so set. But the look in his eyes
made her heart practically stop. He was so offended, so
resentful, so . . . betrayed. Now she took a step back

too, knowing she couldn't approach him . . . she couldn't explain . . . she couldn't do anything but listen.

Still, she offered, "I never intended to upset you like this. I never intended to break your trust in me." Her voice caught on the last word, and she felt as if she couldn't swallow.

He had to see how much she cared about him. He had to see in her eyes that she loved him. He had to see that she was only trying to make things better.

Apparently he didn't. After another long look at her, he shook his head and then left her office. She wanted to run after him. She wanted to say she was sorry. Hadn't she said that? She should have.

As he strode through the tearoom then out the door, she sagged against the doorframe to her office trying to breathe in a gulp of air . . . trying not to cry.

Just what had she done?

Daisy was still in her office fifteen minutes later. Sitting at her desk, she'd propped her elbows on the blotter, her head in her hands. She had ruined everything. Thinking she had been doing good, she'd done the opposite. Jonas would never forgive her. They'd already had a rocky road. The trust they'd starting putting in each other had been golden. Now she'd tarnished it. She knew she had to let her thoughts and emotions settle. She knew she couldn't go after Jonas because he wouldn't listen to her. Talking to anybody else about this would simply be more betrayal in his eyes.

She didn't know how long she stared into space, trying to empty her mind instead of fill it with thoughts.

Suddenly, however, there was a rap on her office door. She looked up expecting to see Iris or Tessa, who were possibly wondering where she was and what she was doing. They'd surely noticed Jonas coming and leaving. But neither Iris nor Tessa had rapped. The person at her door was Eva.

Daisy had noticed a change in Eva ever since Althea had been murdered. Always efficient, always ready to help, she still was. Her smile, however, had faded and her expression had been melancholy.

She asked, "Can I come in?"

Daisy pulled her thoughts away from Jonas. She tried to compartmentalize and set aside what had just happened in her office. Her employees and her business deserved her attention.

"Come on in, Eva. Is there a problem?"

Eva sank into the chair in front of Daisy's desk. She clenched her hands together and then looked up at Daisy. "There hasn't been any progress to find Althea's murderer, has there?"

"I'm not privy to the police investigation," Daisy reminded her.

"But they haven't arrested anyone, have they?"

"Not that I know of. I know you're upset about Althea's death. Would you like time off?" She'd miss Eva. She depended on her and so did Tessa. Helping to run the kitchen smoothly was Eva's job. But if she needed time to grieve . . .

"I don't want time off. I want to do something to help solve the murder. Aren't you doing that? Didn't you say you would help Mrs. Cotton?"

At this moment, Daisy wasn't sure what she had said or how she could help.

She let out a sigh and leaned back in her chair. It squeaked. "A murder investigation isn't as simple as it looks on TV shows. One clue doesn't always lead to another. There are many loose ends that have to be tied up, witnesses who have to be interviewed, statements that have to be compared."

"But you don't have to do all that. You don't have to do a dance around witnesses or play a game. You can ask questions of whomever you like."

"Yes, I can. But I've had harrowing experiences because of it. Is there somebody in particular that you'd like to question?"

"There is, and I'm not afraid. Mrs. Higgins wouldn't have been afraid. She was a role model for me, and I have to do something for her." The certainty in Eva's voice let Daisy know Eva would do something on her own if she had to.

"Who do you want to talk to?"

"I want to ask Harry Silverman questions. He's the athlete Althea kept from securing a scholarship. Maybe we could do it together."

Daisy sat forward again, stared Eva in the eye, and warned seriously, "You have to be very sure you want to get involved. Zeke Willet threatened me more than once with obstruction charges. No one will like it if they think we're trying to do this."

Eva brushed her hair away from her face and straightened her spine. "I don't care what anyone thinks. I want to do this for Mrs. Higgins. I'm not afraid."

Daisy thought about her after-work plans. Instead

of coming into the tea garden today after school, Jazzi and Brielle were going shopping with Vi for clothes for Sammy. He was already growing out of everything. Vi and Sammy were both doing well, and Jazzi wanted to keep her friendship with her sister strong. Daisy supported that idea in every way. Even if it meant Brielle and Jazzi were shopping together again. Vi would keep them in check and probably search for baby clothes at the thrift store, A Penny Saved. The bottom line was that Daisy was as free as she could be after work today.

"Do you know where Harry Silverman lives?" she asked Eva.

"I do. I looked him up on the computer. There are sites that help you find addresses quickly."

"Where does he live?"

"I checked Google Maps. He lives in an apartment on Fern Avenue above an insurance office."

"This could be a wasted trip. We don't know if he'll be there."

Eva shrugged. "We won't be any worse off then, will we?"

"I suppose not. All right. After we close, I'll drive us over there and we can see if we can find out anything."

Eva smiled, the first smile Daisy had seen on her in a while. Maybe pursuing this investigation would lift both of their moods.

At the end of the day, Daisy and Eva came together in the parking lot. They climbed into Daisy's purple PT Cruiser and Daisy headed for Fern Avenue. She easily found a parking place and saw that the insurance office was closed for the day. At least the blinds were pulled and a CLOSED sign hung on the door. After they exited her car, they headed for the stairs leading to the second floor.

Eva asked her, "Are you nervous?"

"I'm always nervous when I intend to question some-one I don't know. Just be prepared. He might shut the door in our faces."

"That's if he's even home," Eva said as if she might be wishing that he wasn't going to *be* home.

"We can still turn back," Daisy told her.

"Not a chance. Let's do this."

Maybe false bravado was better than no bravado, Daisy thought as they climbed the wooden stairs to the second-floor deck.

The wood deck was only big enough for the two of them to stand still. A molded plastic lawn chair sat beside the door. There was no doorbell. Daisy motioned to the door as if asking Eva if she wanted to do the honors.

Eva opened the wooden screen door and rapped on the main door. "If he works for a storm door installer," Eva said in an aside, "you'd think he'd put a new storm door on here."

"He's renting, remember? It's up to the landlord to do that."

Suddenly the door was pulled open and a young man stood there, not looking too happy to see them. He was wearing a T-shirt, jeans, and flip-flops. He had terrifically broad shoulders and muscles in his arms that looked as if they'd seen many workouts. His high forehead made his short-cropped hair look as if he were wearing a dark brown cap. But that cap was shaved from neck to above the ears on the left and the right and probably the back where Daisy couldn't see. His black T-shirt read *Go Harley*. It was possible that he owned a Harley-Davidson instead

116   *Karen Rose Smith*

of a car. Harleys were popular in the area because the factory was in York. Even used, they were pricey.

Harry's eyes, dark brown in color, seemed small under his heavy brows. His nose might have been broken once or twice. His lips were fixed in a tight line. Obviously, he was not happy to see anyone on his landing.

Daisy and Eva hadn't figured out who was going to ask the questions. Daisy waited a tick but when Eva didn't speak, she did. "Harry Silverman?"

"Who's asking?" he growled.

"My name's Daisy Swanson. This is my friend Eva Conner. We knew Althea Higgins and would like to talk to you about her."

The scowl that had begun when he'd opened the door turned fierce now. "I don't want to talk about that—" He stopped before he said a word that might not be acceptable to them.

"Harry," Eva started.

Daisy realized it seemed natural for Eva to call him by his first name since he was only nineteen. Mr. Silverman just didn't seem to suit.

Eva proceeded quickly. "Althea Higgins was kind to me when I had her as a teacher. She brought me food and clothes when my family couldn't provide them. I'd like to figure out who would harm her." She pointed to Daisy. "We both would. Could you give us a minute?"

Daisy had to admit Eva's tone and expression were coaxing.

Eva was holding the screen door open but Harry didn't make any move to shut the main door. His voice was tight when he said, "She might have been kind to you but she

wasn't kind to me. She kept me from a career in the NFL."
His face had flushed and he was obviously angry.

"What did she do?" Daisy asked.

His eyes narrowed. "You must have heard something
or you wouldn't be here."

"We did," Daisy confirmed. "But I know rumors zoom
around this town faster than snow in a blizzard. That's why
we wanted to talk to you. Could you tell us what happened?"

Harry's eye twitched as if the telling of what had
happened affected him physically. "I didn't do my English
homework. I didn't give a fig about it, not about the cruddy
Shakespeare or vocabulary or grammar. Mrs. Higgins had
this bee inside that high-neck blouse of hers that we all
had to conform to some kind of rules in order to get jobs
and succeed. I didn't need to know how to talk or spell to
play football. I was good. I was the best that school had
ever seen."

Eva said, "I heard you won the games for them . . . that
you made the whole team proud."

"I did," he agreed, his chin lifted high. "I had two
scouts coming to see me. I could have had a full scholarship."

"If you had a bad grade, didn't Mrs. Higgins give you a
chance to do extra credit or take a test over?" Daisy asked.

Now he didn't look so proud. He looked down at the
toes of his flip-flops and back up at Daisy. "She did for
the first test."

"Then?" Eva prompted, acting as a perfect tag-team
partner.

"I didn't think it mattered," he blurted out, raising his
voice and clenching his fists. "That stupid subject didn't

matter. Second to last game of the season and Mrs. Higgins
went to the principal. She told him I was a slacker. She
told him there was no way she could approve me for the
team. I couldn't make up everything I'd screwed up in a
week. I had no chance with the scouts because of her."

He took a step forward over the threshold, flushed, and
looking as if he could punch his fist on the deck railing.
He barked, "And if you two find out who killed her, you
tell them *thank you* from me. Got that?"

Daisy had dealt with bullies a time or two. She wasn't
going to let this teenager bully her. "Harry, we're not your
enemy. We're just trying to do what's right. I'm sorry you
lost a chance at a football career. What kind of work are
you doing now?"

Daisy's compassion and her question seemed to calm
him down. "I'm working at an aluminum siding and storm
door company in Lancaster. I install storm doors. We're
contracted out to housing developments and for renova-
tion projects."

"Do you like the work?"

"It's okay," he said with a shrug.

"Room for advancement?" Daisy asked.

"I guess," he mumbled.

"I didn't go to college," Eva said. "Daisy owns the tea
garden and I wash dishes, set up tea services, do plating.
But I'm taking courses at a community college at night."

That was a surprise to Daisy.

Eva went on, "I hope to do more with my life with a
degree. You made the choice to slack off in high school.
Mrs. Higgins was just following the rules. But you don't
have to slack off now. Learn what you have to do to rise
in the ranks, or find out what you really want to do. If you

still love football, how about coaching? There are all kinds of teams that don't have to be in the big leagues. The important thing is to do something you love to do."

Daisy was aware that Harry could have turned off Eva's suggestions, but he seemed to be listening. Maybe he didn't have any role models to give him the advice he needed.

Seemingly embarrassed because he'd listened, Harry checked his watch. "I've got to get going. I'm working tonight. We're expecting a couple of deliveries."

Daisy said, "Thank you for talking with us."

Before Eva could say good-bye, Harry closed the door in their faces. They turned together and walked down the steps.

Following Daisy, Eva asked, "Did we really learn anything?"

Daisy stood still when she reached the ground. "We learned that Harry Silverman can be volatile. But whether he was angry enough or volatile enough to commit murder, I don't know."

Eva sighed. "It's always like this, isn't it? You don't get any real answers."

"No real answers for us. But maybe the police are finding some."

Chapter Nine

Brielle had been staying with Daisy and Jazzi for a few days when she approached Daisy. "Jazzi said you'd like to meet my grammy. I think you'd like her."

Brielle had been fairly quiet since she'd arrived at Daisy's home, except when she was with Jazzi on the second floor. Then Daisy could hear the girls chatting, giggling, and even having a pillow fight. She'd been serving plain but wholesome food, and Brielle had been helping with cleanup.

So when Brielle had asked about visiting her grandmother, Daisy had responded, "If you and Jazzi help at the tea garden tomorrow, we can leave when it closes and visit your grandmother."

On Wednesday, as Daisy followed Brielle's directions to her grandmother's house, Daisy realized the property was located in the same area as Althea Higgins's farm. In fact, Glorie Beck owned the property *beside* the Higgins's farm. Sometimes life was a circle of connections, less than six degrees of separation between residents in a small town.

According to Brielle, the Beck property encompassed

only two acres, whereas the Higgins property might be quadruple that. The small plain house Brielle's grandmother lived in was nothing like the large farmhouse where Althea had resided.

Brielle had called her grandmother, so Glorie knew they were coming. As they drove along the gravel lane, Glorie stood on the small front porch and beckoned to them.

The house was white clapboard and looked to be in good condition. The porch with its little roof was painted gray as were the floorboards. The window trim had been coated with the same gray.

Brielle let information flow freely as they slowed on the gravel lane. "My mom and dad pay to have the house painted every two years. They want Grammy to move to an assisted living place, but she's having none of it. She says she's lived here for seventy years and she's not moving now. This was her home when she was a little girl. When she got married, she and my grandfather lived here. It has heat, electricity, running water, and not much else. Mom says as soon as she and Dad get back, they're having air-conditioning put in. It gets awful hot in there. We visited one summer and Dad couldn't stand it. We all went to a hotel in Lancaster but Grammy wouldn't go with us. Though she did let my mom bring her a fan. She can be pretty stubborn."

Daisy smiled at that conclusion. She knew her mom and even Aunt Iris could be pretty stubborn too. Maybe stubborn wasn't the right word. Maybe they just knew what they wanted. Women in Glorie Beck's generation, and even her mother's and Aunt Iris's, had taken a back seat for most of their lives. They'd let their wants and needs either be trampled or swallowed up by what other people thought they should do. Daisy had even felt that way as a young girl. But after she'd moved to Florida with Ryan and become a mother, she'd learned a strong woman didn't have to sit back. A strong woman could use resolve to get what she wanted.

Glorie Beck was a diminutive woman. Her curly light brown hair was streaked with gray. It looked like a cloud around her face. She was wearing jeans and an oversize royal blue T-shirt that practically swallowed her up.

Brielle said in an aside to Daisy, "Grammy has different colored T-shirts for every day of the week. She doesn't usually wear much else unless she has to go to the doctor. She still wears her jeans, but Mom bought her a couple of blouses online. Grammy insists they're too fancy."

As soon as they climbed out of Daisy's car, Brielle ran up the steps to hug her grandmother. It was obvious there was affection between the two of them.

"I'm Glorie," the little woman said. "And you are Daisy . . . and you are Jazzi. I love those names."

"And I like yours," Daisy said.

Glorie Beck's face was well lined. Those lines were made deeper by a tan that Daisy bet never left her cheeks. She suspected Glorie enjoyed being outdoors.

Glorie took a step back and reached for her cane, which had been propped against the wall.

Brielle asked, "Is your hip bothering you again?"

"Mostly when I get up from a chair," Glorie told her granddaughter. "Don't you worry none. You'll get permanent wrinkles from it. C'mon in, everyone." Using her cane, she went up the steps and inside. Daisy and the girls followed her. "I brewed tea when I heard you were coming. Brielle said you like it. You have some sort of tea shop or something?" Glorie asked Daisy.

"My aunt and I run Daisy's Tea Garden," Daisy responded, glancing around the little house. The many-colored rag rug on the floor was a larger size than Daisy was used to seeing. It was about eight by ten and lay under the sofa, armchair, wood rocker, and coffee table.

Her gaze must have lingered on it too long because Glorie noticed. "It's a little shabby."

"The rag rug? It's beautiful," Daisy told her.

"I made that about twenty-five years ago, before Brielle's mom went to college. Phillip—my husband, God rest his soul—insisted I put all kinds of colors into it. I did, including old dresses that belonged to Brielle's mom, a couple of Phillip's threadbare shirts, and an apron or two of mine. I can look at those materials in the rug and re-member lots of things. Sort of like with a memory quilt."

"Do you quilt too?" Daisy asked.

"Oh, no. That's one craft that's beyond me. But I do sew. I made the slipcovers for those sofa cushions. And those curtains on the windows. Believe it or not, I still have a treadle sewing machine."

The slipcovers were a green plaid that had obviously faded from the sun shining in the window above the sofa. The curtains matched. The stuffed armchair looked like it might be a Chippendale, though the burgundy fabric was worn. A wooden rocker was reminiscent of so many of the handcrafted rockers with carvings on the back that Daisy had seen in the area. Her friend Rachel used one of them in her living room.

When Daisy glanced toward the kitchen, she noticed white metal cabinets that had been popular in years gone by. These looked well maintained. The counter was a gray-speckled Formica that had seen better days. A white gas stove looked old too, as did the refrigerator with its rounded top. A square pedestal table with four oak chairs that were probably antiques sat in the center of the kitchen.

It was easy for Daisy to guess that a small bedroom and a bathroom had been built to the rear of the living room. A screened-in porch led off of the kitchen into the backyard.

However, what she really appreciated was a flight of stairs that led up to a loft.

Brielle pointed up there. "That's where my mom slept when she was little. I stay there when I come over. We don't think Grammy should go up there anymore because the steps are steep. But she says she has to clean it."

Glorie mumbled, "They'd run my life if I let them." Then she brightened. "I have some of those chocolate sandwich cookies that Brielle likes so much. I haven't baked much lately. Would you like those with your tea?"

"That would be great," Jazzi said. "Most of the time, I only get to eat Mom's cookies . . . or Aunt Iris's."

Daisy laughed. She couldn't help it. Most kids didn't have access to homemade baked goods and would choose them. Jazzi would eat store-bought cookies if anyone would let her. But Daisy liked a chocolate sandwich cookie that wasn't good for her either.

Glorie held on to the counter as she opened the cupboard and tried to reach a higher shelf for mugs. They were Pfaltzgraff in brown and off-white, a heavy ceramic that had been around for years. The pottery was a staple in the area. Or at least it had been. The company had been founded in the 1800s in York County. The family of potters carried on the business, each generation taking up the craft. The company had a long history selling to specialty stores, then department stores, but it had been sold in the early 2000s. Now the pottery was sold online.

Daisy said to Glorie, "Let me help you."

At first, Glorie looked at her askance, but then she agreed. "Today I'll let you. If I'm prideful about it, I'll probably drop everything."

They were all seated at the table eating cookies and enjoying tea with honey, when Brielle said, "Grammy likes it here. I do too. When I'm in one room and she's in another room, we can call to each other, and actually hear each other."

Grammy shook her head. "The house my daughter and her husband bought is so big they could get lost in it. A suite for a housekeeper. Can you imagine!"

"What if you moved into the suite, Grammy . . . instead of going to one of those assisted living places," Brielle asked with a hopeful expression.

Glorie gave her granddaughter a warning look. "I'm not going anywhere. I have my garden. I can take a walk to my springhouse. I can even walk through the field to the Higgins's property if I want. Why would I want to move anywhere?"

Instead of delving into that push-pull fight that Brielle and her parents probably had ventured into with her grandmother many times, Daisy made an observation. "I saw on the drive here that Althea Higgins was your neighbor."

"Indeed, she was. I'm almost ten years older than she

was. Would you believe I babysat Althea when I was a teenager?"

It was hard to think of Althea Higgins as a child, let alone Glorie babysitting her.

"I know Althea's neighbor on the other side too, Floyd Hirsch," Glorie explained.

Althea's neighbor had been pointed out to Daisy at the funeral, but she hadn't paid much attention. Now, however, she listened as Glorie went on. "Althea's husband, Charlie, took Floyd under his wing and almost treated him like a son. I think Althea was jealous of that. Charlie didn't seem to relate well to their daughter, Phebe, and Althea never had more children."

"Do you think she *wanted* more children?" Daisy asked.

Glorie's expression became distant . . . as if she was remembering. "Oh, yes. I think she did. I got the impression that she and Charlie—" Glorie abruptly stopped. "I probably shouldn't say anything. You know the Amish believe gossiping is a sin. I try to adhere to that. After all, who is there for me to gossip with? Maybe that's why I'm babbling to you. I only talk with Mrs. Green, who comes over to help once in a while. That's Brielle's mother's doing too."

Jazzi took another sandwich cookie and said to Glorie, "It's not exactly gossiping if you just talk to my mom about Mrs. Higgins. She's trying to figure out who murdered her."

"Jazzi!" Daisy said before she could stop herself.

"Well, it's true," Jazzi maintained. "You're trying to help Mrs. Cotton so the police don't think she did it."

"Stella Cotton?" Glorie asked.

"Do you know *her* too?" Daisy asked with some amusement.

"Sure do. Phillip and I used to have a farm stand that we built out front. Lots of local folks stopped and bought our produce. The Cottons were good people. So is Stella from what I understand. Her mom stopped in here once in a while. She told me Stella had gotten a divorce. That's such a shame." Glorie and Brielle exchanged a look.

Brielle gave her grandmother a sidelong glance. "I know you don't want Mom and Dad to get a divorce. But sometimes I think it would be better."

"What would be better, young lady, is the two of them working out their problems," Glorie concluded. "That's what folks my age used to do. A commitment was a commitment. A vow was a vow." After a few moments of silence, Glorie asked Daisy, "So you're really hoping to find who murdered Althea?"

"I'm just collecting information. I know the detectives on the case. If I can help them, I will."

Glorie took a few sips of tea and carefully put down her mug. "You know, don't you, that Althea's grandson was the one who helped her out the most. And Floyd helped *him*. Althea had a lot more property over there to take care of than I do . . . along with livestock. The fence often needs to be repaired."

"So Althea got along with this Floyd? Even after her husband died?"

"Oh, yes. I don't know what she would have done without him. Her grandson helped her out with the chores but I'm not sure how interested he was in doing them. Floyd, on the other hand, has always wanted to make his farm a success. He raises soybeans one year, corn the next. He changes the crops like the Amish to help the land rest in between." Obviously thinking about Althea's grandson again, she continued, "I think Lucius has been living over there since Althea died. I was sorry I couldn't make it to her funeral, but my arthritis was just too painful that day to go trudging over there. Althea and I said our piece when she was alive, so I didn't think it mattered if I went over there when she was dead."

After Brielle and Jazzi finished the last of the cookies, Brielle asked, "Do you have your list, Grammy?"

"What list?" Jazzi asked.

"When Grammy has things that need to be done around here, she makes a list. Then when I come over, I help her do them."

Grammy pointed to a drawer near the sink. "It's in there."

Brielle scooted from her chair and opened the drawer. When she pulled out the list, Daisy saw the paper was on a small notepad. Brielle tore off the top sheet. "You need a lightbulb changed in your bedroom and the trash can that has all the catalogs emptied."

"I don't know how those companies find my name and address," Grammy grumbled. "I've been receiving phone calls that are nothing but computers talking to me. It's awful."

"You need to buy a landline phone that talks to you and sign up for caller ID, Grammy," Brielle directed. "Then you could hear who's calling you and you wouldn't have to get up to answer. Or you need a cell phone to keep with you all the time."

"Your mom bought me a cell phone and set it up before

she left," Glorie said. "I have it in the drawer next to my bed."

"Do you have my number in it?" Brielle asked.

"Your mom said I did. She has yours and Mrs. Green's in there. I just have to go to that little picture that has the big C on it."

"You have to carry it around in your pocket, Grammy. If you fall, then you'd have it right with you."

"I'll think about it," Glorie muttered with a stubborn look.

Daisy suspected the woman would only carry it around when she was good and ready.

Daisy was arranging the teapots on the shelf in the spillover tearoom the next day when Foster came up beside her. She was on a stepstool and, for a change, she was taller than he was.

She glanced down at him with a smile. "How's Sammy today?"

He grinned back at her, not looking as serious as he usually did in his black-framed glasses. With his hair brushed to the side and styled with gel, he looked more mature. Daisy had liked Foster when she'd hired him to work at the tea garden . . . before he had become her son-in-law. As her son-in-law, he'd helped Vi through a difficult period of postpartum depression. Now Daisy hoped the couple was on the other side of it and enjoying their baby in a new way.

"He's almost sitting up on his own. Vi insists he already did and I just missed it."

Daisy chuckled. "She wants to be the one to experience his firsts."

"I guess," Foster agreed with a nod. "Tessa said she's going to make cabbage sausage soup today. I hope it tastes better than it sounds."

Daisy grinned. "Potatoes are a main vegetable in it too." She knew Foster liked potatoes of any kind. When she stepped down from the stepstool, Foster was again taller than she was.

"I came over to tell you something else too," Foster explained. "A woman just came in who would like to talk with you."

"Really? Did she give you her name?"

"She said her name is Phebe Higgins."

"Tell her I'll be right there." She hadn't expected Althea's daughter to search her out.

Daisy pushed the stepstool under a serving stand and made sure the teapots were arranged exactly the way she wanted them to be. Then she crossed to the main tearoom and spied Foster at a table with a brunette about Daisy's age who had just bitten into a snickerdoodle. A two-cup teapot decorated with yellow and green flowers sat on her table.

Daisy crossed to her. "Foster said you'd like to speak to me?" Daisy had simply glimpsed Phebe at the short funeral service.

The woman half rose from her seat but Daisy motioned for her to stay seated. Her hair looked home-cut, but then Daisy chided herself for thinking that. These days anything went. Phebe wore bangs that were a bit uneven and straight hair that fell about to her chin with no layering or style. She wasn't wearing makeup. She was tall and her long nose reminded Daisy of Althea.

Phebe said, "I'm Phebe Higgins. Althea's daughter."

At that Daisy gave a nod to Foster and he knew she'd like a cup of tea too. She sat at the table across from the woman and said sincerely, "I'm so sorry about your mom." Daisy hadn't had a chance to speak with her after the graveside service.

Phebe lowered her eyes to her teacup and murmured, "Thank you."

Daisy felt awkward and didn't know where this conversation would be headed. She filled in with conversation of her own. "I had your mom as a teacher in high school."

Phebe's hazel eyes came up to hers. "Really? So you knew her before . . ."

When Phebe couldn't seem to finish, Daisy did. "Yes, I knew her before we started planning the tea at the high school. She also stopped in to make suggestions for the menu."

"I'll bet she did," Phebe determined with a grimace.

Daisy wondered if Althea had been as difficult with her daughter as she had been with everyone else.

"What did you think of my mom?" Phebe asked.

Daisy pulled her thoughts together quickly. "I respected her as a teacher. I really didn't know her well past that."

Phebe's sigh was drawn out. "I didn't come here to talk about my mother. I heard you have an inside track with the police."

At that moment, Foster brought Daisy's tea . . . the oolong that she'd been drinking lately. He quickly left, obviously noticing that the two women were having a serious discussion.

Daisy took a moment to spoon honey into her tea and stir it. "I do know Detective Rappaport, and I've had contact with Zeke Willet. They don't share much with me. I do tell them if I find out anything concerning the person who was murdered . . . or any suspects." She motioned to the people in the tea garden. "My staff and I hear a lot of gossip and rumors. I don't pass on rumors, but I try to find facts."

"I need to know something." Phebe leaned forward.

"What's that?"

"I need to know if my son, Lucius, is in the clear."

Althea's grandson. Was there a particular reason why Phebe would think he was a suspect? "Does anything make you think he's not in the clear?"

Phebe again looked down at her hands and Daisy realized how difficult this conversation was for her. She seemed much more reserved than Althea. Because of Althea's big personality?

"If I tell you something, will you tell the police?"

"I don't know. If I believe it has anything to do with the murder, I might."

When Phebe bit her lower lip, her gaze was troubled. "I suppose they're digging into everybody. Lucius was close to his grandmother."

"That's good to hear. One of Althea's neighbors—Glorie Beck—told me that Lucius helped Althea with chores."

"He did. Once upon a time, he used to do it more willingly."

There was a story here and Daisy wondered if there was motive too. "Used to do it more willingly?"

"My mom was going to pay for Lucius's college tuition.

Then she decided to pull her funds. She said he'd have to get loans and do it himself."

"Can you tell me why?"

"I'd rather not. Lucius did something she didn't like and that was my mother's way. She either approved . . . or she didn't."

"I see," Daisy said even though she didn't really see.

Phebe looked around, then went on in a low voice. "After my divorce from Lucius's father, Lucius acted out some. He became defiant. My mother didn't like that. I just wondered if you could find out if he is on the police's suspect list. He's a good kid. And now he's doing most of the chores on the farm. The neighbor on my mom's other side—Floyd Hirsch—helps too."

If Lucius had become defiant, if he'd acted out, Daisy suspected that meant he may have gotten into legal trouble. Would that be the reason Phebe suspected he was on the suspect list? Immediately she thought maybe Jonas could find out. Then she remembered how Jonas had walked out. Maybe she'd talk to Detective Rappaport instead.

Phebe wiped her hands on her napkin and stood. "That's all I wanted." She handed Daisy a piece of paper. "That has my contact information on it. If you find out anything that concerns Lucius, could you please let me know?"

There didn't seem to be anything wrong with Daisy answering in the affirmative. "Yes, I can let you know. But as I told you, the police keep me out of the investigation as much as they can. They keep their information close to the chest."

Phebe was going to pick up her check and go to the

sales counter to pay, but Daisy put her hand on Phebe's. "This is on the house."

Phebe gazed into Daisy's eyes and didn't argue. She just said, "Thank you."

Daisy watched as Phebe left the tea garden, her shoulders slumped. Was she grieving for her mother or just worried about her son?

The school board meeting that evening was being held in the high-school cafeteria. Up for discussion had been after-school meetings, service hours for students, and fundraising for school trips. Then the hottest discussion had begun—the subject of school uniforms. To say the discussion was contentious was definitely an understatement. Those teachers who had backed Althea seemed to have a renewed vigor in defending her choice to make uniforms mandatory. But there were just as many teachers and parents who had felt like Daisy. Self-expression was important but so were guidelines at school. Damien Resnick, the chairman of the school board, had decided the best thing to do was to form a committee who could establish rules and guidelines at the next meeting. Then they would take a vote and decide yea or nay on the uniforms.

Damien, who was in his forties, a parent and an electrical contractor, brushed his auburn hair over his forehead and told the group with a smile, "Now, I don't want all of you who aren't interested in technology to leave. Lawrence Bishop is going to demonstrate the interactive whiteboards that we'd like to put in every classroom. They are an innovation that has been slow to come to Willow

Creek. But if we want our students to have the best chance to learn, we have to provide innovation. Lawrence is going to demonstrate how the interactive whiteboard can be used."

Daisy heard the door at the back of the room open and close. Detective Rappaport had entered with Jonas. Her heart sped up. She wondered if Jonas would speak to her. But as Detective Rappaport came forward and took a seat next to her, Jonas stayed standing in the back of the room, his arms crossed over his chest. His gaze met hers briefly, but then he looked away. There would be no forgiveness in the air tonight. She was sure of that.

The detective gave her a sideways glance. "I understand the two of you quarreled. Word about altercations travels fast around town. At least Jonas is in the vicinity," he said in an aside to her.

She glared at the detective. She knew *she* was the one who had made the mistake in going to see Zeke, but Rappaport had had a part in that too.

Rappaport leaned close. "Jonas is here because he's thinking of using one of these whiteboards to explain furniture designs to his clients." He paused a moment. "Just in case you wanted to know."

So that's why Jonas was here. Not for her. That hurt.

As Lawrence Bishop used his clicker, a special "marker," and even his finger to show people what a whiteboard could do, Detective Rappaport's attention seemed to be centered on Claudia Moore, who was seated two rows ahead of them.

As per his demonstration, Lawrence quickly handed out clickers to everyone in his audience to show them how quizzes could be given on the interactive board.

Rappaport elbowed Daisy. "Claudia was against the uniforms, right? Did she raise any fuss earlier?"

Daisy hadn't had her attention focused on Claudia, but as she remembered the discussion about the uniforms, Claudia had only made one comment to the school board. "No fuss," Daisy said in a low voice to Rappaport. "Why?"

He didn't answer.

As soon as the demonstration was over, Daisy looked over her shoulder and saw Jonas leave the cafeteria. He wasn't staying for her to detain him. He wasn't staying to have a conversation. He obviously didn't want to talk to her.

Lawrence wound up his explanation of why the school board should provide funds in the budget to buy interactive smartboards for the classrooms. Then the school board chairman closed the meeting. As members of the community began to depart, Rappaport stayed seated, his gaze still on Claudia as she spoke with another teacher.

Daisy asked Rappaport, "Do you have any idea how I can break through the stone wall that Jonas has surrounded himself with?"

The detective had the grace to look sheepish. "Daisy, I'm sorry I suggested you go visit Zeke. I didn't realize . . ." He tossed his hands into the air. "Stubborn is as stubborn does. He and Zeke are making me want to bang my head against a wall. But don't you give up. Just give Jonas time."

"Time could make things worse."

"Time could also persuade Jonas that he was being foolish to take this out on *you*. He's upset with himself. He's upset with Zeke. And he's upset with everybody around him. From what I gather, all he's doing is working. I told him he should get a dog."

That almost made Daisy smile. Almost. "And what did he say to that?"

"He said I should mind my own business."

"Do you think a dog would soften him up?" she asked.

"I think *you* could soften him up. But not yet."

"Why?" she said almost indignantly. "He's like a roast in the oven and I have to do it at the right time?"

The detective frowned at her. "He'll miss you. He'll miss Jazzi. He'll miss what he could have."

Was that true? Would Jonas miss a future with her?

To turn her thoughts away from Jonas, as well as her feelings about him, she asked Rappaport, "So why are you studying Claudia so closely?"

She knew how he was going to react and added, "Don't give me one of those dismissive glances. If you're going to insert yourself into my personal life, I can insert myself into this investigation." That was a bit of bravado that she wasn't really feeling, but she'd see if it would work.

Apparently it did. Maybe the detective was feeling sorry for her. Maybe he just felt he owed her the truth. "I'm trying to deduce if Claudia is strong enough to have strangled Althea and drowned her."

"What makes you think she might be?" Daisy asked.

"Witnesses have informed me that Claudia works out in the weight room at the school. Those muscles in her arms are real ones."

Claudia was wearing a short-sleeved top with a skirt tonight. The muscles in her upper arms were well-defined.

Could this teacher have strangled Althea and pushed her into the pool?

Chapter Ten

On Friday at a quiet moment, Tessa took Daisy aside into the spillover tearoom. She'd fixed a tray with oolong tea, blueberry coffee cake, and the accoutrements to go with all of it.

Daisy protested, "I really shouldn't."

With a shake of her head against Daisy's protest, Tessa determined, "The kitchen is under control. Come on. You and I haven't had a good talk in a while."

To keep the conversation light, Daisy asked, "And you think I'm going to have a heart-to-heart in five minutes?"

With a serious expression, Tessa sat at one of the round tables for two and pointed to the other chair. "We're going to try."

Both Daisy and Tessa fixed their tea in the way they liked it. To Daisy's relief, Tessa started out easy. "So everything is working out for Brielle to stay with Jazzi?"

"It is. I spoke with Brielle's mother last night and told her Brielle is a wonderful houseguest. She couldn't believe it."

Tessa laughed. "Where was she calling from?"

"Geneva. She sounded stressed and rushed. If I went to Geneva, I'd want to be relaxed and in a Zen mood."

Tessa asked, "Do you think you'll ever go to Geneva?"

"One never knows, does one?" Daisy's remark was offhanded but Tessa caught the sadness underneath.

"I didn't bring you over here to talk about Brielle. What's going on with you and Jonas?"

Although Daisy and Tessa had been friends for years and had always confided in each other as she became a grandmother and her relationship with Jonas had revved up, she and Tessa hadn't had as many heart-to-heart talks lately. She didn't know if she wanted one today. Her hesitation and silence said it all.

"Have you contacted him since your blowup?"

Obviously, Tessa knew about the blowup since it had happened at the tea garden. In a small voice, Daisy murmured, "I can't."

"Why not?"

"Because I was wrong, I suppose. And whether I was or not, he feels betrayed and hurt. What am I going to do about that?"

"Apologize."

"I have apologized."

"Sincerely . . . as if you meant it?"

"Tessa," Daisy warned.

"If you're waiting for him to get over it, he might not unless he has the help from you."

"My 'help' landed us in this mess."

The door to the tea garden opened. After a minute or so, Daisy took a glance in that direction. She almost did a double take. At first, she didn't recognize the woman walking in but then she did. It was Tatum Beatty!

At Daisy's expression, Tessa asked, "What?"

"That's Tatum Beatty, the teacher from Philadelphia who Althea supposedly plagiarized."

"Do you know the man who's with her?"

The man who had pulled out a chair for Tatum at one of the tables was dressed in a navy suit, crisp white shirt, and blue-and-red-striped tie. He looked like a politician ready to go onstage to convince somebody to vote for him. He might be in his fifties. His black hair streaked with gray looked professionally cut. It was swooped back over his forehead in a style that said a stylist had done it.

Daisy rose. "I'd better see what they want."

Tessa tapped Daisy's arm. "Don't think our discussion is finished."

Daisy just gave her friend a *don't-push-me* look and went to the main tearoom.

Stopping at the table Tatum had chosen, Daisy smiled. "Hello, Tatum. This is a surprise."

"I expect it is," Tatum agreed. She motioned to the man around the corner of the square table. "This is Donovan Santos. He's my lawyer."

Since Tatum and Daisy had been fairly honest with each other at Daisy's visit to Tatum's row house, Daisy asked, "You needed to bring a lawyer with you to the tea garden?"

Tatum chuckled. "No, but I did need to bring him to a settlement conference. Why don't you sit with us?"

"Can I get you anything first?"

"Iced tea," Donovan said, and then added, "It's good to meet you. Tatum told me about you."

That was interesting. Daisy looked at Tatum. "Iced tea for you too? Any particular kind?"

Tatum waved her hand at the board above the sales counter. "One of those tisanes—pineapple and green tea or something like that."

"I'll be back," Daisy told them, then hurried to the kitchen. What did these two have to tell her? A settlement conference? Maybe that had happened in order to probate Althea's will.

She soon hurried back into the tearoom with a tray laden with two glasses of pineapple green tea that was iced and slices of blueberry coffee cake.

Mr. Santos looked at the coffee cake. "I couldn't resist this if I tried."

"I can even smell the blueberries," Tatum agreed.

Daisy let them enjoy their tea and coffee cake without asking any questions. Tatum made comments about the tea garden, how pleasant it was, what a unique atmosphere. She pointed to the teapots and teacups on the shelf. "Are those for sale?"

"They are."

She said, "Donovan here has been by my side through this whole plagiarism fiasco. We met with Althea's lawyer today. Donovan asked for damages for the money Althea made on her book. The last time we spoke I told her lawyer that I would go to media outlets and ruin Althea's reputation for good if we couldn't come to an agreement."

"What did he say?"

"He said he'd have to talk to her grandson then get back to me. Her grandson seems open to the idea. I'm hoping we can settle this. If we don't, probate's going to take much longer and that might be our leverage."

Tatum suddenly stood. She motioned to the baked goods case. "I'm going to go over there and buy goodies to take along. I imagine they're as delicious as that coffee cake."

When Tatum was out of earshot, Donovan looked at Daisy. He shook his head wearily. "Sometimes Tatum has too much determination and energy."

"I don't understand," Daisy said.

The lawyer stared down at his empty dish and then rotated his glass of tea. "Tatum told me she was honest with you."

"I believe she was. I think that's the way she is."

Donovan gave Daisy a wry smile. "You pegged her right."

Tatum might be honest, but had she wanted revenge?

Not long after Tatum left, Daisy's phone played its tuba sound and she saw on the screen that Vi was calling.

"Hi, honey. What's up?" She went through the doorway that led to the hall to her office on the left. Going inside, she pulled out her chair and sat at her desk.

"Foster's taking my car."

Vi sounded upset, more upset than she should if Foster had taken her car to run an errand.

Daisy joked, "He's bringing it back, I hope."

"Not for a while," Vi moaned. "What am I going to do if Sammy needs something?"

"Slow down and tell me what's going on."

"Foster's car broke down. It's old, needs a part, and the part won't be in for two weeks. So he wants to use mine. We can't afford a new car, Mom, you know that."

Yes, Daisy did know that. She had sat down with the couple and made a budget for this year after Sammy was born. Gavin had looked it over too. Daisy was giving them this first year to live at the apartment rent-free, which helped with their finances a great deal. Foster was working at the tea garden, going to school, and building websites in his *spare* time. In the past month, Vi had been helping Otis at Pirated Treasures, an antiques shop, with his books and inventory list. When she could, she stopped in at the store to help him too. But the job was only part-time.

Vi said in a rush, "If Sammy gets sick, what am I going to do without a car? And I promised Otis I'd stop in there this weekend. Foster has class today and is working at the tea garden Saturday and Sunday."

"What worries you most?" Daisy kept her voice calm even though Vi's was rising now and then.

"Sammy. If he gets sick or I need something for him, what am I going to do?"

"You know I have your back. If Sammy needs something, just call me. I'll take you wherever you need to go. So will your gram and Aunt Iris, and even Tessa. Among all of us, we have you covered."

"You can't be my chauffeur," Vi said, and Daisy realized her daughter felt as if her independence was being taken away. "No, we can't. But we can make do until Foster gets his car back."

"What if it's too expensive to fix?"

"You're borrowing trouble. We'll worry about that when the time comes."

"We don't want to keep relying on you and Gavin."

She and Gavin had done a lot for them and felt as if the couple now had to stand on their own. But they wouldn't mind car rides and helping with Sammy when Vi and Foster needed the assistance.

Daisy worried that maybe Vi was just feeling claustrophobic and needed to get out of the apartment again. Like many young mothers, she was there with Sammy most days. Even when she went to Otis's shop, she took Sammy along.

"How about this," Daisy said. "Why don't you call Gavin and see if he can take care of Sammy tomorrow for a few hours. You know he and Emily feel they don't get enough time with him." Emily, Gavin's daughter, seemed to have a special affinity toward Daisy's grandbaby.

Daisy went on before Vi could comment. "I'm taking Jazzi and Brielle to Rachel's tomorrow. She's having a work frolic to get ready for church on Sunday."

"And she wants you to help? Don't you feel out of place with all the members of her district helping?"

"I've never felt out of place with Rachel if she wants me there. And a few more hands will make the work go faster. They're going to be having church in the barn and set up tables outside for the meal afterward if the weather is fit. You could come along, get out, breathe in fresh air, spend a little time with us. Then afterward I could take you to Pirated Treasures for a while. You'll get a lot more done there if Sammy's not with you."

When Vi had her baby with her, her attention was still mostly on him, not on everything else she wanted to accomplish.

Vi's tone was hesitant. "You don't think Rachel will mind if I come?"

Daisy considered Rachel Fisher and her family, who'd always welcomed Daisy with open arms. "I already asked her about Brielle and Jazzi. I'll stop over at Quilts and Notions before I go home and ask her about you. You get along well with her girls and we're like family."

"I guess that's what happens when you know each other since childhood."

"It is. So you're going to give Gavin a call?"

"I could let Foster do it."

"Vi, he's *your* father-in-law. If he's busy, he'll tell you, then we can work out something else."

"Okay. It's just I don't want Gavin to think I'm a bad mother to Sammy or a bad wife to Foster."

"I don't believe he thinks that. If you really want to know, ask him sometime. Gavin is as honest as Jonas." The thought of Jonas made her heart hurt. She was trying not to think about him . . . trying to figure out what to do next.

"All right," Vi agreed. "I'll text you to let you know what Gavin says."

"Sounds good. I'll call you later to work out times. But tell Gavin the work frolic starts early."

Daisy was hoping if she filled her days with activities, she'd have less time to think about Jonas. The work frolic tomorrow was just what she needed.

As Daisy drove down the lane to the Fisher farm on Saturday morning, Brielle and Jazzi were on their phones in the back seat, their heads together. Daisy had already told them that once they were at the farm, no cell phones. The Fisher family was New Order Amish. Rachel had a cell phone for work and emergencies and the family had a phone in the barn.

Daisy always enjoyed entering the farm's environs. Peace seemed to wash over her when she did. Maybe it was the fields planted with soybeans or corn or timothy grass. Maybe it was the pasture where the horses were turned out this time of year. Maybe it was the white barns with their black trim, the clothesline on a pulley that led from the house to one of the barns, or maybe it was the white clapboard house with its porch that Daisy knew would be welcoming. Childhood days with Rachel flitted through her mind.

On the Esh farm, Rachel's family home, she and Rachel had rambled through the cornstalks. They'd hiked through the sweet grass to catch sight of deer or even a bunny. They'd dressed very differently, and their lifestyles had seemed contradictory, but their family values had been very much the same. When Rachel had married Levi and they'd moved into his family home, Daisy had always felt at home there. Daisy's parents had taught her that hard work was essential while they ran their nursery. Rachel's parents had taught her that hard work was essential when running a farm. Where Rachel's faith was strong, so was Daisy's.

Daisy drove around to the parking area in the back of the Fishers' house. Buggies were already lined up near the hitching posts. The horses grazed in the pasture or gathered around hay bales that had been tossed there. Men and women in Amish dress milled about, already busy.

Brielle stared openmouthed out the window. "The Amish really do dress like this?" she asked in an awed voice.

"If you mean, do the women wear long dresses with black aprons, and the men work trousers with suspenders and long-sleeve shirts and straw hats, *yes*, they do dress like this."

"What about in summer?" Brielle asked.

Jazzi answered that one. "Pretty much the same. That's why Mom told us to wear jeans and conservative blouses today so we wouldn't stand out too much."

Vi, who had been sitting next to Daisy in the front seat, added, "It will be good to see Rachel's daughters again. I've missed them. I never thought I'd be married before they would."

Daisy knew one of Rachel's daughters was courting and would be married in the fall. But Vi was right. Who would have thought?

Before Daisy entered the mudroom through the back door of Rachel and Levi's house, she waved at Rachel's oldest brother and his wife. They lived and farmed on the Esh property, the farm next door. In this house, Levi's *ma'am*—his grandmother—lived with him, Rachel, and their children.

Rachel's brother motioned to the inside of the house to Daisy. "Go on in."

Daisy waved back that she would.

Brielle glanced around the mudroom as if she hadn't seen anything like it before.

Jazzi leaned close to her and whispered, "Don't say anything rude."

Brielle nodded.

Although delicious smells usually emanated from the Fishers' kitchen, today Daisy caught the scent of vinegar and lemon. Inside Rachel and two other women from her district smiled at Daisy. One was taking a mop to the floor. Rachel and the other woman were washing down the walls.

Seemingly amazed, Brielle just stared.

Jazzi explained, "Amish church services are held every two weeks. The service sites alternate from one family in the district to the next. Rachel and Levi host the church service about once a year."

Daisy said, "The service itself is located in the barn because that's big enough. Everyone will meet outside afterward when lunch is served. All the women in the district help prepare the food."

Brielle peeked around Daisy into the kitchen. "Then why clean in here?"

Once again Jazzi answered. "Because the bishop and deacons stop in and everyone is in and out readying food and serving it. Mom and Vi and I have helped them get ready before. My guess is they'll need our help cleaning the living room. All we have to do is go to one of the women and ask and they'll show us what needs to be done next. It's teamwork at its best."

Although Jazzi and Vi had only been influenced by Rachel and her family for the past few years since they'd been back, the lessons had taken. It was indeed teamwork. That's what this Amish community was all about and it spread over to the other residents of Willow Creek if they were willing to absorb the lessons.

Rachel hurried over to Daisy, obviously happy to see her. "Did you bring Vi along?"

"I did. She saw your daughters outside."

"I'm glad they'll have time to gab as they work, ain't so?"

The women in the kitchen were speaking in Pennsylvania Dutch. Taking Daisy's elbow, Rachel led her back to the mudroom. "Before I forget, Levi would like to speak with you."

That was unusual. Usually it was she and Rachel who did most of the talking. "I'd be glad to speak with him."

"I think he's in the barn, directing the men where to put the benches."

"Do you think it's all right if I go in there?"

"I told him you'd be coming and he'll probably be watching for you. He'll come outside to meet with you."

Daisy was accustomed to Amish ways and customs. It wouldn't be appropriate for her to walk into a barn that was filled with Amish men, look for Levi, and take him aside. That would cause gossip. She wouldn't do anything to hurt Rachel's or Levi's reputation.

Seeing the doubt in Daisy's eyes, Rachel said, "I'll go along with you." Daisy felt relieved at that. "I suppose it's safe to leave Brielle and Jazzi inside?"

Rachel peeked into the kitchen and around the living room. "They already have mops in their hands. They'll be fine for a short time."

After Daisy and Rachel walked outside, Daisy spotted Vi under a tree with one of Rachel's daughters. She and Rachel kept along the path that led to the biggest barn. The livestock barn was farther along near the chicken coop. This barn was mostly used for equipment, which had obviously been moved out for the weekend.

Apparently watching for them, Levi exited the barn and came toward them. He motioned to a tall elm and they headed that way. After greetings, Levi said, "I'm curious. What will happen to Althea Higgins's land? Rachel thought you might know."

"From what I understand, Althea's grandson inherited it, but he might want to sell it."

Levi looked interested. "I know an Amish family interested in buying it. Would that be possible?"

"There wouldn't be any harm with them getting in contact with him, or even Althea's lawyer. I can give you the information."

"That would be *wonderful gut*," Levi decided, nodding. "Have you heard if the police are close to finding her murderer?"

"They don't tell me where they are in the investigation. Do you think there are a lot of people who would want that property?"

"Possibly. Even her neighbor," Levi said. "But that's an odd situation between them."

"How so?" Daisy asked.

"Althea's husband took the neighbor Floyd Hirsch under his wing, sort of like a father would. He loaned Floyd a substantial amount of money so he could purchase additional land to farm."

"So they were close?"

"Close enough. Mr. Hirsch helped Althea's husband with chores, especially toward the end of his life. I understand he grieved like a son would when Mr. Higgins died."

"Had he lived next to them long?"

"Mr. Hirsch started with a smaller property than the Higgins's farm and added to it over the past decade or more. It was in awful shape when he bought it and he fixed it up, piece by piece. A few years ago his barn was hit by lightning and burned down. Many in the community helped him raise it again. I don't know how he's fixed financially now but Hirsch might be thinking of buying the Higgins place. I know several people who might want it and that could certain sure cause a bidding war."

"A bidding war would be good for Lucius but not for anyone else."

"So true," Rachel said, adding her comment to the conversation.

"I knew you would tell me what was happening. I didn't want to listen to gossip or rumors," Levi explained.

"If I hear anything else about the investigation or about what Lucius intends to do, I'll let you know."

"*Danke*," Levi said. "It's all in God's plan. We have to remember that while we let Him do His work."

One of the men in the barn shouted to Levi. He waved his arm that he was coming.

Rachel decided, "And that's enough talk about murder today. We'll have a fine time cleaning, cooking, and catching up, ain't so?"

"We will," Daisy seconded, glad she'd come today, glad she could reconnect with Rachel . . . and maybe forget for a short while about everything else that was complicating her life.

Chapter Eleven

Daisy, Brielle, and Jazzi were tired when they returned home from the Fishers' farm. Daisy had dropped Vi off at Pirated Treasures earlier in the afternoon, then gone back to the farm to continue helping. After Aunt Iris finished at the tea garden, she was going to pick up Vi at the antiques shop and bring her home.

There had been plenty of food at the work frolic and none of them were hungry as they changed their clothes and got ready to relax for the evening. Rachel had insisted that Daisy bring home shoofly pie, a container of potato salad, and slices of ham. Everyone had brought so much food to share for lunch at the frolic that, as usual, there was an overload. If she and the girls were hungry later, they could pick on that if they wanted.

In her bedroom, Daisy glanced at her phone charging on her dresser. She so badly wanted to call Jonas. She thought about him every spare moment that she wasn't thinking about something else. Considering Tessa's advice, she picked up her cell phone. She texted, Can we talk?

Sitting on her bed, her phone in hand, Daisy waited for a response, even though she knew that was silly. Jonas might not be near his phone. He might have it turned off. He might simply not want to answer her.

Five minutes later she was still staring at it, wondering what else she could do. Then she thought about what Levi had said concerning Althea Higgins's land and who might end up with it. He'd said, "It's all in God's plan. We have to remember that while we let Him do His work."

Should she just let go of Jonas? Or should she let go of the worry about Jonas? Letting go and doing nothing felt like throwing everything they'd shared into the wind and watching it blow away.

Her phone still in hand, she rose from the bed and went to her closet. After she pulled out a cardigan, she hung it around her shoulders. The evening had grown chilly even in the house. Spring might have arrived but winter's tail still caused night temperatures to dip. Maybe she should light a fire. The girls might enjoy that.

She was just opening her door to the short hall that led to the kitchen when Brielle came rushing toward her. The teenager looked close to tears. "What's wrong, honey?"

Her phone in her hand, Brielle kept it pasted to her ear. "Keep talking, Grammy. I want to know you're okay."

To Daisy she said, "Grammy went down to the basement, tripped and fell. Now she's having trouble climbing the staircase. She doesn't want to fall again, and I don't want her to. Thank goodness she had her cell phone with her. What can we do?"

"Tell her we'll be there as soon as we can. Does she want me to call emergency services?"

Brielle asked but her grammy replied, "Definitely not."

"Grab your backpack and phone and tell Jazzi to do the same. I'll meet you at the front door."

Brielle responded, "I'll keep her on the phone while we drive. Is that okay?"

"Absolutely." Daisy had often done that with her girls.

Ten minutes later, they'd arrived at Glorie Beck's house. A light glowed in the living room. Before they went inside, Daisy caught Brielle's arm. "If she shows any signs that her breathing is labored or her head hurts or any symptoms at all from this fall, I'm calling 9-1-1."

Brielle nodded soberly that she understood.

Once inside, Daisy told Jazzi and Brielle, "You stay up here for now. I'll go down and check her."

Frozen in place and wide-eyed, the girls watched as Daisy carefully went down the raw wooden steps.

Glorie was seated on the second step from the bottom, leaning against the railing, her hands circling it in a tight grip. Her hair was disheveled and her face pale. Her eyes were bright, however, with regret and maybe embarrassment.

"I didn't want to cause any trouble," she murmured.

"You didn't cause us any trouble. It's just a quick ride out here. Now tell me how you're feeling. Be honest with me."

"I'm fine," Glorie grumbled.

"You're not fine if you can't climb the stairs. Do you mind if I take your pulse?"

"Go ahead," Glorie said with a sigh.

As Daisy took hold of Glorie's wrist, she noted that the older woman's pulse was fast but strong. "Did you bump your head?"

"No. My ankle turned over and I grabbed onto the railing. It's these shoes. I shouldn't wear flip-flops to come down here."

That was certainly true. Daisy noticed that Glorie seemed to be breathing normally. "Let me look at your foot."

Glorie's ankle was already swelling and Daisy couldn't tell if it was broken or not. She knew some older women were diagnosed with osteoporosis, which made fractures more likely. But whether Glorie had fractured her ankle would have to be left to the doctors.

"Will you let me call the paramedics?"

"No, no, no," Glorie protested vehemently. "I just want to make it upstairs and put ice on this ankle. I'll be fine in the morning."

"What if I take you to urgent care?"

"Not tonight. Please. Just abide by my wishes. Help me up the stairs, maybe make me a cup of tea, and I'll be fine until morning."

That was Glorie's scenario but not Daisy's. They'd discuss what she had in mind if they could move Glorie upstairs.

Daisy called up the stairway, "Brielle? Could you come down and help me?"

"There's a walker in my bedroom," Glorie said. "I use it sometimes when I go outside. Maybe Jazzi could get that for me."

And so it went. Daisy and Brielle carefully helped Glorie up the stairs where she could use her walker. She pushed it into the living room and sank down on the sofa. Her face told the story of obvious pain.

Brielle retrieved an ice pack from the freezer and Daisy covered Glorie with the afghan from the back of the sofa. "The girls and I will stay the night to make sure you have everything you need. You'll probably need help going to the bathroom and finding something to eat. Did you have supper?"

Glorie shook her head. "I'm not hungry."

Brielle jumped in. "You have to eat, Grammy . . . to keep up your strength." She looked at Daisy. "Are you sure you can stay?"

"I'll call Vi and she can stop over at the house and feed Pepper and Marjoram. They'll be fine until morning."

"I'll try to call Rowena Green," Brielle told her grammy.

"I tried to call her first so I didn't have to bother you, but I kept reaching her voice mail."

Turning to Daisy, Brielle explained, "Rowena is the woman who helps Grammy a few times a week. I'll try to call her later and maybe she can stay here for a few days."

"That sounds like a good idea."

While Jazzi found an extra pillow and made sure that Glorie was comfortable, Brielle went with Daisy to the kitchen to make tea. "I can't believe you'd disrupt your life like this to stay here."

Daisy turned toward Brielle and put her hands on the girl's shoulders. "Your grammy needs help. We're available. It makes sense, don't you think?"

"Thank you," Brielle said with a catch in her voice.

Daisy hugged her because the teenager looked like she needed a hug. Then they set about making tea and finding something in the refrigerator that Glorie Beck might like to eat.

On Monday, Daisy was flying around the tea garden full force. Tourist buses, three of them, seemed to line up one after the other, and many of the tourists visited the tea garden.

Daisy thought about the day before as she served tea, soup, blueberry coffee cake, and salads. Yesterday morning, Glorie had still insisted that she didn't want to go to urgent care. The swelling on her ankle had been down considerably and she could put some weight on it. Maybe a twist was all that had happened. Daisy had made sure that Rowena Green, the woman who often looked after Grammy, was able to come and stay for a few days. She assured them all she'd take good care of Glorie. She'd cook, straighten up, and clean. All Glorie would have to do was sit, sip tea, and read her Bible if she wanted to.

When Daisy and the girls had returned home Sunday morning, they'd had another surprise. Vi had stayed the night with Sammy. She and Foster had had another argument about the car. Foster had wanted to look around for a used one. Vi just wanted to get the old one fixed. Stalemate, at least for now. Vi had taken Sammy home after Daisy and the girls had had lunch with her.

With the busyness this morning at the tea garden, everyone's breaks were scattered. As Daisy bustled about, she thought about the town council meeting tonight and what might happen there. The meeting was sometimes monotonous, yet other times it could be informative.

Daisy had just seated a table for four when Jada, who had been on break, rushed back into the tea garden. Jada was one of Daisy's part-time servers. She didn't want to work full-time because of her college courses, but she often asked for extra hours. Her mocha skin was flawless and her dark brown eyes sparkled. High cheekbones and full lips gave her oval face a sculptured beauty. She was in her early twenties. At five-foot-one, she usually wore her braids in a high ponytail. She was an asset as a server because she usually wore a smile. More important . . . she knew her tea.

Jada wasn't smiling now, however, as she pointed to Daisy's office. Daisy didn't know what to think. What had happened?

It didn't take long to find out. Jada spoke so fast that, at first, Daisy could only catch the words "murder" and "Claudia."

"Slow down," she advised Jada. "What's going on?"

"Rumors are flying about Claudia Moore," Jada said. "People are saying Claudia murdered Mrs. Higgins."

"Where did you hear the rumor?" Daisy asked calmly.

Jada pointed down Market Street. "In the yogurt shop. There was a table full of customers and they were talking about it, and then it spread to another table."

"Is there a specific rumor?"

Nodding vigorously, Jada explained, "One of the women claimed that Claudia was angry with Althea because Mrs. Higgins was blackballing her with the other teachers. Mrs. Higgins kept her from working on the committee to choose a play for next year.

"And," Jada went on, "Mrs. Higgins was against Claudia's idea to encourage students to act in the community's little theater summer production."

It sounded as if Althea hadn't wanted to give up any control. She had been chair of the English department and guided the productions as well as recommendations to the students.

"Was one person spreading these rumors?" Daisy asked.

"That was hard to tell," Jada answered. "I just sat at the bar and listened. Four or five people were talking about it. But if most people at those tables went out and talked about it in shops or at the farmers' market or someplace like that, anybody could hear. What if people believe them?"

What if? That was such a great question.

Daisy received a partial answer to it later in the afternoon when Claudia herself came into the tea garden. The young teacher was practically in tears.

Daisy took her by the elbow to a more private table in the spillover tearoom. The tour buses had all left and business had slowed. Apparently Iris had noticed and brought two iced teas and a plate of snickerdoodles to the table. Then she left them to talk.

"What's wrong?" Daisy asked. Claudia's eyes were red and puffy and she had dark circles underneath them.

"I don't know what to do," she admitted with a little hiccup. "A friend of mine called me today and told me she was in the convenience store and she heard a couple talking about me . . . that I was probably the one who had killed Althea."

Daisy could see that Claudia was agitated. Her hands never stopped moving. She was turning her glass around and around in a circle and looked as if her thoughts were traveling in that vein too.

Daisy advised, "Stop and take a breath."

Claudia let her shoulders sag as she sat against the chair back. Her lip quivered and Daisy knew the young teacher was filled with worry and anxiety, let alone embarrassment and fear at what was going to happen next.

"I want to know who's starting the rumors," she said angrily.

"Would that help stop them?" Daisy asked reasonably.

Claudia put her elbows on the table and dropped her head into her hands. She mumbled, "Probably not." After a minute or so, she looked up at Daisy and admitted honestly, "I had many grievances against Althea, but I wouldn't kill her. If we could figure out who spread the rumors, would that mean we found the killer?" Claudia asked.

"Have the police called you in for more questioning?"

Claudia absently picked up a cookie and took a bite. "No, but that doesn't mean they don't suspect me."

"No, it doesn't mean that. Do you have any enemies who would start this kind of rumor? I've heard about some of it. Did you tell anyone that you thought Althea was blackballing you?"

"I never used that word. I told a couple of the other teachers that she was preventing me from giving my input. But if they're spreading this, I really don't understand why."

Claudia was young, attractive, full of ideas and energy. She could have rivals she didn't even know about. "What about friends who aren't teachers? Did you talk about Althea to any of them?"

"I have friends I go bowling with in Lancaster. I might have mentioned my troubles."

"All I can tell you, Claudia, is that if I hear anyone in here discussing it, I'll put a damper on it. Gossip will run itself out."

"Unless someone keeps stoking it. Pretty soon the

superintendent might tell me I don't have a job next year. Daisy, you've got to help me."

"How?"

"By doing what you've done before. Find the person who murdered Althea Higgins."

More than anything, Daisy hoped Jonas would be at tonight's town council meeting that was held in the high school cafeteria. She sat waiting and watching, hoping he'd come through the door. The room filled up. Tonight's meeting was supposed to reveal the progress the council had made in setting up plans and an agenda for a homeless shelter in Willow Creek. It had been months since the idea had first been proposed but the men who had proposed it had had no idea of what they were proposing and the services a shelter might need.

While Daisy still kept her eye out for Jonas, the mayor introduced himself, though he needed no introductions. He began by explaining who was on what committee for the planning of the shelter. Daisy was sitting on the end of a row and the seat beside her was empty. She'd been saving it for Jonas, she realized, when it finally hit her that he wasn't going to show up. Because he'd believed she would be here? She knew he had volunteered for one of the committees but all the committee work was completed off-scene in private homes or at the mayor's office.

Daniel Copeland, an assistant bank manager, took the microphone next as Gavin came up the side aisle, eyed the seat beside Daisy, and she nodded. Of course he should take the empty seat.

Gavin was lean and tall with sandy brown hair and a

square jaw. A contractor, he was tan from often working outdoors. He comfortably lowered himself into the folding chair beside her, then said, "It's good to see you here. I hear you have company."

"I do. Jazzi has a friend staying over for two weeks, but it's going well. What do you think we should do about Foster and Vi and the car?"

Gavin gave her a long, steady look. "I think we should let them figure it out. What about you?"

"I know we should," she said with a sigh. "Why is it that I want to fix their problems?"

Gavin gave a low chuckle. "That trait seems to come with parenthood. We've done enough for them. I know you're chauffeuring as well as Iris and even your mom. I am too. But I think it's best if we just show them they have a support system. They'll figure out something."

From the podium up front, Daniel was explaining how the town council was accepting bids to build the shelter.

Gavin said in a low voice, "My company will be submitting a bid to build it. I don't know if we'll get it. I have a feeling that if we do, the deal will come with a mountain of headaches. But I'm willing. We need projects to draw this community together and maybe this one can."

Considering what Gavin had said, Daisy thought the shelter could either bring people together or push them apart. Many residents were opposed to the idea. But the plot of land had been donated, churches had been contacted for meal outreach, and job training apprenticeships and internships would be next to help get the people on their feet who needed the shelter.

Tilting her head close to Gavin's, Daisy asked, "Did

the architect's plans include a women's section and a men's section?"

"I heard there were cons against it because of the cost," Gavin said. "But, yes, that's the way I drew up the plans. It's the only sensible thing to do."

At least it was the only sensible thing to do in Willow Creek. Propriety was all-important to many people.

At the podium, Daniel was explaining, "We have a list of possibilities for the position of fundraiser. We're going to bring a professional in to do this. The fundraising will begin this summer with a community gathering in the social hall at the firehouse. More about that in the weeks to come."

There were a few general questions about fundraising and outreach and how the town in general could help. The specifics of all of that would be finalized in the coming days.

Gavin tapped Daisy's elbow and stood. "I need to leave. I have to pick up Emily at a friend's. It was good to see you. Take care and if you need anything, call me."

Daisy nodded that she would and watched as Gavin left. The mayor and the councilmen had left their seats at the table. Lawrence Bishop came down the aisle and Daisy stood, eager to speak with him.

"Do you have a minute?" she asked.

He lowered his voice. "Is this about the murder?"

"It's tangentially connected," she said honestly.

Since the row had emptied, they took the two seats she and Gavin had occupied. Lawrence knew the politics inside the school. He was well aware of gossip and which teachers were rivals. "Have you heard the rumors about Claudia?"

"Heard them?" he scoffed. "I think they started at the school. It seems everyone I've spoken to has heard them."

"Do you have any idea where they started?"

"There's supposition about that too. I believe Stella started them to throw suspicion on Claudia rather than herself."

Daisy was shocked. "Do you really believe that?"

"Imagine if you were a suspect in a police investigation. If you were desperate, wouldn't you do anything to put yourself in the clear?"

Daisy had been a suspect and she'd never thought about throwing suspicion on someone else. That was one of the times she decided to find out who had committed the murder. She just couldn't believe Stella would do that.

However, if she would, did that mean Stella murdered Althea?

Chapter Twelve

"Oh, no," Daisy gasped into her cell phone on Saturday. Then she thought about Ned instead of what was supposed to happen at the tea garden that day. "I'm so sorry you have the flu. That fever sounds wicked. I'm glad you went to the doctor. We'll be fine."

She said it, but she wasn't sure of that at all. Ned was her entertainment for this tea that her patrons had paid money for. Just what was she going to do?

After she finished with Ned, she walked to the sales counter and her expression must have shown her dismay.

Foster, who was nearby, approached her. "What's wrong? You look . . . upset."

The thought of her being upset seemed to disturb Foster. Trying to slow her breathing, she calmed her voice. "We have a problem. Ned has the flu. Our customers are going to start arriving in an hour. What are we going to do, Foster? I promised entertainment for all those children."

Foster looked as if he was going to suggest something, stopped, and studied her again.

"If you have an idea, tell me," she demanded.

"Let me call my dad and see if he's free."

"Your dad?"

"Remember, I told you he played the guitar? He's pretty good. I don't know if he can do what you want him to do, but I can find out."

After Daisy thought through the idea for about two seconds, she asked, "Do *you* mind calling him? Because if he doesn't want to do this, I think he'll be honest with you. He'd fudge with me, and I don't want to put him in a position he doesn't want to be in."

Pushing his glasses up to the bridge of his nose, Foster agreed. "I understand that. I'll call him right now. Can I use your office?"

"Sure."

Daisy practically counted the beats of her heart until Foster exited her office. He was wearing a smile. "He said he'll be here in half an hour. Ben and Emily are coming along. Is that okay?"

"Yes, that's okay. Does your dad know what he's taking on?"

Foster laughed. "He knows all about the tea. Vi and I filled him in. This will work out, Daisy, I know it will."

She could see that Foster had pride in his father. He also exhibited a bit of pride that he'd thought of this idea, as if he'd solved the problem for her. And he had. She knew he felt as if he wasn't doing enough for himself and Vi and their whole situation, but she admired the way he was handling it.

Right there, in the tearoom, she gave him a big hug. "Thank you, Foster. I'm glad you're my son-in-law."

Beaming, his face reddened. He mumbled, "I'll get back to serving customers and setting up for the tea."

Daisy filled in everyone that there was going to be a

change of plan and Gavin would be taking Ned's place. Her aunt Iris arched her brow. Tessa smiled and shrugged. Eva, Jada, and Cora Sue didn't seem to think anything about the change and went toward their customers with their usual smiles.

Not long after, Gavin arrived, guitar case in hand. Daisy went to the door to welcome him.

"It's acoustic," he said. "I'm old-school."

"I don't care what school you are. Thank you so much for agreeing to do this. Are you really going to be okay with it?"

They moved to the spillover tearoom and Gavin set his guitar case on the table. "I'm fine with this, but I don't know how good I'll be at doing it. I used to make up songs for my kids. Annie would give me a line now and then or an idea. It was my way of connecting with them when I was working so many hours. Once I tune my guitar, we'll be good to go."

It wasn't long before Daisy's tea service guests began arriving. At the door, Cora Sue took tickets from parents while Eva showed them to tables. An hour later, the kids were engaged and Gavin was on a roll. He had a light style, a huge smile, and a talent for guitar playing.

Daisy was helping to serve small glasses of iced herbal tea or milk to children and hot tea to their parents when Gavin asked for volunteers. He beckoned several children to come up around his chair. They watched enamored as he played and sang. From "Row, Row, Row Your Boat," which involved the whole room, to "Eensy, Weensy Spider," which involved hand movements. Daisy remembered them from when she'd taught her girls. She found herself beside Gavin, smiling, making the movements with her fingers as the spider crawled up the spout. The kids were standing at their tables and following every movement. Daisy spotted Trevor in the back of the room taking notes for an article for the *Willow Creek Messenger*.

As the servers quickly set out tiered trays with tiny sandwiches, mini-cookies, and little whoopie pies, all her tea guests nibbled. When Gavin sang a silly song, making it up as he went, taking lines from those shouted out from the guests, everyone giggled and laughed. It was such a fun time that Daisy found herself forgetting about everything else for a change.

When Gavin motioned to her to join him, Daisy went to his side and sang along to "Twinkle, Twinkle Little Star." Soon he was making up a song about the planets and asked the kids for unusual names.

Suddenly Daisy caught sight of Jonas. He must have come in when she had her attention on the children and her guests. Now he'd reopened the door and was leaving.

She tapped Gavin on the shoulder. "There's something I have to do. I'll be back." Without another word, she rushed after Jonas. Had he come in response to her text? The thing was—they couldn't talk here. Maybe it was a sign.

After she exited the tea garden, she ran down the steps of the Victorian and up the street. Jonas's stride had taken him much farther than she'd expected. She called his name. "Jonas!"

He stopped immediately and turned. Seeing her, he looked . . . resigned. She didn't see hope or understanding or caring on his face. Simply resignation. That scared her.

She asked quickly, "Do you want to talk?"

"There's not much to talk about," he said.

"Jonas—"

After a short silence he said, "You and Gavin work well together."

"I told you once before, Gavin and I are friends and family."

"Sometimes it looks like more than that," he admitted.

"Have you forgiven me?" she asked, knowing all of her hope and caring was in her eyes.

His voice was gruff when he answered her. "I'm wrestling with forgiveness on many levels."

She imagined he was. Zeke, Brenda, and herself. "I told you before that Gavin and I *are* just friends. I'm not Brenda. If you can't trust me, then you have more than forgiveness to think about."

This time, *she* was the one who walked away. She practically ran back to the tea garden, hoping that if she immersed herself in this children's tea, she could forget about everything else once more.

On Monday, Daisy left the tea garden early to pick up Jazzi and Brielle at school because she wanted to visit Stella first. As she traversed the halls to Stella Cotton's office, she thought about everything that had happened over the weekend. Jonas possibly wasn't going to forgive her, no matter what she did or said. Would time heal his heart? Would time give them more opportunity to trust again? She didn't know.

After a call from Brielle's mother, Daisy had agreed to have Brielle stay another week. Jazzi seemed happy . . .

with Brielle for sisterly company as well as the news that
Portia would come to visit next weekend. Brielle understood that Jazzi would want to spend time with her birth
mother.

Instead of thinking about all that, Daisy considered
what she could do for Stella Cotton, who had in the past
been so helpful with concerns about Jazzi.

As she approached the guidance counselor's office, her
blue clogs squeaked on the tile floor. It was clean and
waxed just as it had been when she'd attended school here.
Bulletin boards still proclaimed school events even though
whiteboards might be taking over the classrooms.

When she reached Stella's office, she saw that the door
was closed. That was unusual.

Looking through the glass upper half of the door, she
saw Stella sitting at her desk, working on her computer.
Daisy rapped and Stella reacted as if she'd been startled.
Daisy hadn't knocked that hard.

Still, Stella jumped to her feet and came to the door.
As she opened it, she asked, "Has something happened?"

"No," Daisy was quick to assure her. "Nothing has
happened. Nothing unusual. I just came to see how you
were doing."

The lines on Stella's face cut deep over the V above her
brows, and her black hair wasn't styled as neatly as usual.
Her lipstick was pale and that was unusual too. Stella was
all about brightness, loud colors, big beads, red shoes. But
this Stella, in a cream sweater and beige slacks, didn't
look like herself at all.

Stella gave Daisy a *come-on* motion, gesturing her into
her office. She did it quickly. "Did anybody see you come
up here?" she asked Daisy.

"Not that I know of." Daisy felt perplexed by the question. Why did it matter?

Stella quickly closed the office door. Daisy knew she did that for conferences. She was surprised that Stella did it now.

Unzipping her jacket, Daisy sat on a chair in front of Stella's desk and put her purse on the floor. "What's going on with you, Stella? You don't seem yourself."

"How can I be myself when I found a dead body?" she asked in a voice that rose with each word. She was obviously agitated, anxious, and worried.

Daisy moved her chair closer to the desk so there wasn't such a long space between them. "I know how awful that is."

"That's right. You were there too," Stella murmured.

"Yes, I was, but I was thinking about another murder. I found the body that time."

"And were you a suspect?" Stella's eyes were wide with surprise.

"Circumstances prevented that," Daisy said. "But there have been other times that I've felt the eyes of detectives on me. So I know what it feels like. You're still in shock, going through some grief even though you and Althea didn't always see eye to eye. You jump every time a phone rings or there's a knock on the door. You don't feel safe anymore."

Stella's eyes had gone even wider. "I'm supposed to be the counselor, not *you*."

"It doesn't take a counseling degree to know what it feels like when something like this happens. That's why I came by. Although this bad stuff is swirling all around you, you have to take care of yourself too. Are you?"

"You mean am I sleeping? Am I eating? Not much of either. And when I'm in here, I can't really work. I feel like I've had ten cups of caffeine even though I haven't. My mind won't stay on one track. Even though I know it's normal with something like PTSD, I don't feel anything about this is normal."

"Has anything happened lately to make you more . . . afraid?"

"Not afraid, exactly, but worried I could lose my job. Meagan actually came to me and asked if I'd started the rumors about Claudia. I did *not*, but I can't prove a negative. I have no way of finding out who *did* start them. I don't know what to do." She shook her head, put her elbows on her desk, and leaned her chin into her hands.

Daisy gave her a few moments to compose herself. She knew there wasn't much she could say that would make Stella feel better.

Finally Stella raised her head. "Not many people know this because I keep my professional relationships to myself, but I befriended Althea more than the other teachers. They steered clear of her. I felt by interacting with her I would understand her better. I even had dinner at Althea's house with her and her grandson and her neighbor."

That was news to Daisy. "How did that go?"

"That evening it was just fine. I had seen Lucius now and then and he was sometimes surly. But that evening he wasn't. He and Floyd, that's Althea's neighbor, had a conversation about buying more goats. They talked about buying fancy chickens."

"Fancy chickens?"

"Yes, they have longer feathers or something. They're supposed to be good egg layers."

"And you and Althea joined in?"

"Althea and I talked about sewing, of all things. I didn't realize that she had sewing skills. She showed me a small room in her upstairs where she kept all her materials— threads, rickrack, and buttons. Her machine was quite complicated. It even did that fancy embroidery. She showed me a couple of samples."

"So you got along?"

"We did."

She thought about telling Stella about Eva and her experiences with Althea, but that was personal history. So she simply said, "I know someone whom Althea sewed clothes for when her mother couldn't afford them. Althea was definitely a complicated woman."

"Aren't we all," Stella muttered sarcastically.

"Tell me something, Stella. If you weren't here trying to work, what would you rather be doing?"

"To ease my mind, I'd like to go see Lucius. I heard he's staying at the farm. He has to live there if he wants to keep it or even sell it. But I just . . . I just can't make myself go alone. The truth is that I lost friends when my husband and I divorced. It's funny how that happens. You're no longer a couple, and so couple friends steer clear. Anyway, I don't have any women friends right now, certainly not a best friend."

Thinking about the tea garden, about Brielle and Jazzi, who she'd come to pick up after school, about Jonas, and about Stella's predicament, Daisy made a decision. "I'm going to take Brielle and Jazzi home. If you meet me there, I'll go with you to Althea's farm. Would you like that?"

When Stella's eyes misted over, Daisy felt so sorry for her. Then the counselor said, "I would like that very much."

* * *

Whenever Daisy drove to Glorie Beck's property, she felt as if she were stepping back in time. With Althea Higgins's farm, on the other hand, she felt differently. There was a sense of historic presence around Althea's farm from the graveyard to the barns to the farmhouse. However, she didn't feel the peace she felt at Glorie's house. Althea Higgins had been a perfectionist, at least with teaching. At the farm she'd obviously let parts of it get run-down.

Daisy parked on gravel and Stella pointed to a rattle-trap car near the barn. "That belongs to Lucius. I saw him driving it."

"Maybe he'll seriously think about updating and repairing the place."

"Or maybe he'll sell it to a developer," Stella said acerbically. "I don't think he wants to work at it. Farming is tough, even for those who have a love for it."

Broken stepping-stones led from the gravel area across the grass. There was a wooden gate that had fallen lopsided on its hinges. It wouldn't take much to knock the latch from it. Stella opened it and they closed it again behind them.

Going up the walk, Daisy noticed the rosebushes that needed to be trimmed, the arborvitae that had grown much too woody and tall. Althea had taken great pride in her dress and in her classroom. That's what was wrong with this property. Daisy couldn't see the pride in it.

There was a glassed-in front porch. They went up the two steps and Stella opened the door. Indoor-outdoor carpet there was curling at the edges. There was an assortment of lawn furniture but nothing matched. Not that matching mattered but the carelessness of it didn't remind Daisy of Althea at all. A rusty shovel and a hoe leaned against a wall.

The door to the inside of the house was open, but a screened storm door stopped them. Before they could mount the three steps to open it, they heard male voices coming from inside.

The voices were angry, raised, and distorted.

"That's Lucius, and maybe the next-door neighbor," Stella explained. She rapped sharply on the storm door. Daisy wondered if the men would hear the knock above the ruckus.

They must have because the yelling stopped. Seconds later, Lucius approached the door.

He was dressed pretty much the way he'd been dressed for Althea's funeral, in jeans and a sweatshirt. His work boots weren't muddy this time, but they were well-worn. His russet hair looked as if he'd run his hand through it and left it standing up. Maybe that was just a cowlick. Floyd Hirsch was well groomed, wearing a green flannel shirt with the sleeves rolled up and jeans secured with a leather belt. His boots were dusty but not worn through. He was taller than Lucius and fifty pounds heavier. His dark brown hair appeared to have seen a cut recently. It was layered, short, and had bangs that swept to the right. His dark brown eyes were curious as he eyed Daisy and Stella.

Lucius quickly introduced them.

Floyd nodded in greeting and extended his hand, obviously more mature than Lucius, probably around age forty. He knew the niceties. He said, "I'm glad to see Lucius has callers."

Stella looked Lucius in the eye. "I wanted to make sure you were doing okay."

"I have enough casseroles for a week," he mumbled.

Floyd smiled. "He has desserts too. Don't let him tell you otherwise—good Pennsylvania Dutch shoofly pie, fry pies, and even apple strudel. We just finished up some of that."

Floyd was making it sound as if he and Lucius had just had a social visit. Daisy wondered if that was true, or if what they had been arguing about was serious. Still, Lucius didn't flinch when Floyd placed his hand on the younger man's shoulder. "I'll help you go through that paperwork if you want me to. I'm right next door for whatever you need. I told Althea I'd watch over you and I will."

Just when had Floyd and Althea discussed that? Maybe Floyd was going to teach Lucius about farming? Is that what Althea had meant?

Lucius's neighbor said, "It was nice to meet you, ladies, but I have chores that won't wait and horses that need to be fed." With a nod at them, he went down the steps and out the door of the glassed-in porch.

As he strode away, Stella asked Lucius, "Has he been helping you?"

With an embarrassed frown, Lucius admitted, "I don't know what I'd do without Floyd with the chores around here. If I really want to keep this place, I'll have to hire somebody. The barn needs to be repainted. The fences need fixing. I can't ask Floyd to do all that."

Daisy wasn't going to step into treacherous territory

but Stella did. "We heard you and Floyd arguing when we came in. It sounded serious."

Lucius looked from one of them to the other. "Why don't you come in? I have more of that strudel left." He headed inside.

Daisy gave Stella a nod and said in a low voice, "This could be important."

"Sure," Stella responded to his invitation. "I haven't had good apple strudel in a long time."

Lucius seemed to be at home in Althea's kitchen with its old outdated gold-speckled counter, oak cupboards, and maple table for four. Curtains at the windows were printed with vegetables and Daisy imagined that Althea might have sewn them. They surrounded the window with a ruffled valance and café panels.

Once they were seated at the table with glasses of water and plates with apple strudel, Lucius just shook his head again. "I don't know what to do with all this." He waved over the kitchen and into the living room. "What am I going to do with a house and a farm? That's what Floyd and I were arguing about. He thinks I should keep it and run it. But I don't know the first thing about it."

"Maybe Floyd can teach you what you need to know," Daisy suggested. "You could have a life here if you want to be a farmer. Or you could breed horses or cattle."

Lucius was shaking his head. "Not the life I want. If I sell the place, I can go to college."

Stella said, "You could have applied for financial assistance and gone now."

Again Lucius was shaking his head. "I didn't want loans up the kazoo that I'd have to pay when I was out.

That made no sense. It's not like I want to be a lawyer or a doctor or a Wall Street guru and make lots of money."

"What do you want to do?" Daisy asked.

"I like computers. If I became a software engineer, there's no telling where I could get a job. I wouldn't have to go in just one direction. You know what I mean?"

Stella took another bite of her apple strudel and her expression said she was enjoying it. "I know exactly what you mean and that's smart. So what are your options?"

"I think I could get a good price on this place. There's an Amish family who's interested. I've also heard from a developer who would cut it up in sections for an over-fifty community."

"Would you want to see your grandmother's property cut up that way?" Daisy asked.

Lucius shrugged. "I need time to think about it. I spent a lot of time here as a kid, but some of those memories weren't all that happy."

"Take your time," Stella advised him. "Don't let anyone talk you into anything."

That was good advice but Daisy didn't know if Lucius would take it when he said, "Like they say, time is money. I want to get the best deal, but I do want to make the decision on my own."

Just what decision would this young man make?

Chapter Thirteen

"I don't want to intrude on your family dinner," Stella protested when Daisy asked her to come home with her.

"You won't be intruding. Every day something new happens. Brielle's parents were supposed to be home today but I received a call from them Saturday night that they'd been delayed. They won't be home until next weekend. Not much explanation. So Brielle is still staying with us. Jazzi and Brielle always have something interesting to say around the table. They can keep your mind off whatever thoughts you're having. Wouldn't that be better than going home and moping?"

"Moping, waiting, worrying. That's all I've been doing," Stella confessed. "I'm always such an up person and this murder investigation has simply driven me into the doldrums."

"Then come home with me," Daisy suggested again. "I have leftover chicken my mother sent home with me yesterday after a family dinner. I can put together a chicken pie. You can peel apples for baked cinnamon apples, and I might even have rice pudding for dessert if the girls haven't eaten it all. Sound good?"

"You're bribing me?" Stella asked with half a smile.

"When I mention good home cooking, I don't have to bribe."

Stella actually chuckled. "All right. We'll see what the girls think about having their counselor at their supper table."

At Daisy's house, Stella glanced around and then looked up the staircase and heard the teenagers' voices. "Brielle seems to have settled in nicely."

"Does that surprise you?"

"You are a guardian while you're taking care of Brielle. I imagine I can talk to you about this. Her mother told me anything you need to know, I should feel free to divulge. Brielle isn't as open with everyone as she is with Jazzi and with you. I *am* surprised. From what her teachers were saying at school, she keeps to herself, doesn't reach out to make friends, and is too . . . precocious for some of her teachers."

"About boys?"

"Yes, but just about anything. Her parents are lawyers and most of us agree she picked up the attitude from them."

"I'm not sure it has anything to do with being lawyers," Daisy suggested. "They could be architects, doctors, accountants. I don't see that that makes much of a difference. What does make the difference is the time they give Brielle. I don't think they give her much."

Immediately Daisy corrected herself. "I shouldn't have said that. I'm judging and I have no right to do that. If the assessment you're making is that her parents are cold, I agree."

"Don't feel bad, Daisy. An observation is what it is."

Trying to add a positive aspect, Daisy said, "On the

other hand, she loves her grandmother to bits, and her grandmother loves her. They get along well and Brielle has a different kind of energy when she's around Glorie Beck. She cares and it shows. It would probably be good for her to stay with her grandmother for a while."

"Do you feel Glorie could handle her?"

"I think she could. Brielle respects Glorie. I don't think she respects her parents."

Stella's brow creased as she looked thoughtful.

Brielle and Jazzi tramped down the stairs and surprise lit their faces. After a brief explanation that Stella would be joining them for supper, Daisy told Stella, "You can wash up in the powder room. I'll get started on supper."

It didn't take Daisy long to mix a double pie shell for the chicken pie. While she let the crust rest, she steamed carrots, peas, and potatoes, drained them, and then made a roux.

Jazzi came to her and asked, "Can we build a fire? It's going to be cold tonight and we'll be here until it goes out."

"Do you think you can do it?" Daisy asked. "You might have to bring in kindling."

"I know how to build a fire," Brielle said. "I was in Scouts for a short time and learned when we went camping once. We'll get it going in no time."

Daisy gave Brielle a nod. "Go ahead. I should have the chicken pie in the oven until you're finished. Then it will be about a half hour until supper."

Since Daisy already had the leftover chicken cut up, it was easy to mix it all into the gravy, pour it into the pie shell, then top the pie with the other shell. She scored triangle designs in the top crust to let steam puff out while the pie baked as Stella sliced apples.

Brielle and Jazzi both carried wood in their arms when
they came in the back door. Pepper and Marjoram greeted
them. Marjoram was eyeing Brielle with interest and the
small branches she was carrying.

"Why is she looking at me like that?" Brielle wanted
to know.

"Because Jazzi has started a habit when she brings in
the kindling. She'll often take a branch and play with it
with Marjoram. It's a way for the felines to exercise. Feel
free."

Soon Brielle and Jazzi were swishing thin branches
across the floor as Marjoram and Pepper jumped over
them, tried to catch them, and sat on them with satisfac-
tion. The girls were having as much fun as the cats.

Finished with the apples, Stella watched them. "Pets
are great to make kids feel grounded."

Suddenly a buzzing sound emitted from Stella's slacks
pocket. She pulled out her cell phone and frowned. She
murmured, "I better take this." She put it to her ear and
walked into the living room away from the fireplace . . .
away from the kitchen. A few minutes later she came back
to Daisy, her face pale, her hands shaking.

"What's wrong?" Daisy asked.

Stella took a deep breath and steadied her voice. "It
was a disguised voice telling me to confess." She kept her
voice low enough that the girls couldn't hear.

Daisy took her arm, "Oh, Stella, that has to be fright-
ening."

"It's happened before."

"Did you call the police? It could be the killer."

"No, I didn't. I just don't have the guts . . ."

"You *do*. You have to keep yourself safe. You also have

to let Detective Rappaport know what's going on. It's another clue that might help him put the pieces together. Do you have his number?"

Stella nodded. "I entered it into my phone after he questioned me."

"Call him."

Once again Stella stepped into the living room and paced. Daisy heard her say, "I'd like to speak to Detective Rappaport. I see. If he won't be back until morning, I suppose I can wait. All right. I could talk to him. Yes, I'll wait while you patch him through."

Daisy supposed the person Stella would be talking to would be Zeke. She wondered if Zeke was mad at her too, or if he'd gotten his head back in the game because he'd finally let his feelings out with someone. She just wished it hadn't been her. She wished it had been Jonas.

Stella must have been talking to Zeke. She glanced at Daisy, told Zeke, "Let me check." Her eyes were pleading when she asked Daisy, "Can Detective Willet come here? I told him I was here and he says he knows where you live. Would that be all right?"

It was easy to imagine that Stella didn't want to be alone with Zeke. She was still afraid. She was worried she'd say the wrong thing. She wanted support.

"It's fine if Zeke comes here."

"He said he won't be here for about an hour. He's driving back from Hanover."

"We'll be ready to eat soon. We'll probably be finished when he comes. It will work out."

"You sound like the Amish," Stella mumbled.

Daisy knew what Stella meant. The Fisher family believed

God's will was in everything. What He deigned would happen. Daisy wasn't sure she believed exactly that.

An hour later when Zeke arrived, he wouldn't look Daisy directly in the eye. For their sakes as much as Stella's, Daisy sent Brielle and Jazzi up to their rooms.

Zeke looked tired but as handsome as ever in khaki pants, a pale blue shirt, and a plaid blazer. He'd loosened his tie, though, and opened the top button of his shirt.

Daisy offered, "I can go into my bedroom if you need privacy."

"You don't have to go, Daisy," Stella said. "Does she? Can't she stay here?"

Now Zeke did glance at Daisy. "You can stay as long as you don't interrupt."

"No problem," Daisy assured him, and took one of the armchairs in the living room.

Stella sat on the sofa and Zeke in the other armchair. After Stella revealed what the anonymous caller had said, Zeke asked if she'd give him her phone so they could trace the call. She thought about it for a few moments and then said, "Here. It's been nothing but a distraction anyway." He took it and dropped it into the inside pocket of his blazer. "Now tell me again exactly what he said."

Stella did.

"So he wants you to confess to the murder? Or is there something else he wants you to confess to?"

"Heavens no!" Stella was outraged. "I haven't done anything wrong. I wish I'd never gone into the pool. I wish I hadn't tried to be friends with Althea. I wish we hadn't disagreed about the uniforms. Glory be, who would think I'd kill somebody over *that*."

Zeke studied her. "Victims have been killed for less."

Then out of the blue he asked, "Did you start the rumors about Claudia Moore?"

Instead of becoming more outraged, Stella looked totally defeated. Still she answered him. "I had nothing to do with the murder or the rumors. You can believe me or not. Do you think you're going to solve this anytime soon?"

"I know you're frustrated, Mrs. Cotton. We are too. We're trying to make good decisions and follow the leads that we believe will take us somewhere. But even good people with good intentions make mistakes. So this investigation might take longer than you want it to." He said to Daisy, "I can show myself out."

And he did. Daisy considered what he'd said—*even good people make mistakes*. She had made a mistake by talking to him about Jonas. But she didn't think Zeke was talking about her.

Was he talking about himself . . . or Brenda?

The following morning, the first thing Eva asked Daisy was, "Have you made any progress in the investigation?"

Since Eva knew all about the rumors, that Stella might have started them about Claudia, Daisy told her about her evening with Stella.

"Do you think the detective believed Stella?"

"I think he did, but I don't know for sure."

"We have to do more," Eva prompted. "What if we go to Floyd Hirsch and ask him what he was truly arguing about with Lucius."

"He might order us off his property for interfering."

"He might, but he also might appreciate what we're

trying to do. After all, Lucius had the best motive. He
inherited the farm. I can go with you after work."

Brielle and Jazzi weren't working at the tea garden
after school today. They'd joined a committee to help with
the May Fling float. They were submitting the float with
the peer counseling group and they wanted to win after
the parade marched down Market Street. They were building it in a garage at one of Jazzi's friend's. Stacy's mom
would be bringing the girls home around six. If Iris closed
up the tea garden, Daisy and Eva could leave and she'd be
home by six.

To Eva she said, "Let me check with Iris and Tessa. If
they'll close, we can leave about quarter to five." Eva gave
Daisy a smile that said it was the right thing to do. Daisy
hoped that was so.

Around five o'clock, they were pulling into the property
beside Althea Higgins's farm. This farm was well maintained. The barns wore red siding and the outbuildings had
a bright white glow in the end-of-the-day light. A paved
lane led to the house. It was definitely smaller than the
Higgins's homestead. It looked as if it might be a story
and a half, with white siding and black shutters. The porch
railing was freshly painted and the porch floor was concrete. So were the steps.

After Daisy and Eva exited the PT Cruiser, they looked
toward the house. They were going to head that way when
they heard noises coming from near the barn.

"That sounds like sheep," Daisy said, familiar with
barnyard noises because of the Fisher and Esh farms.

As they listened more closely, though, they heard a
radio or some other device playing music. With raised

brows Daisy pointed in that direction. "He might be feeding the animals. It's that time of day."

"I know nothing about livestock," Eva mumbled.

As they approached the barn, Daisy noticed the hangar door was open. Floyd was talking to sheep who were corralled in a large stall. They were young ones, Daisy thought. Two horses huffed on the other side of the barn, also in stalls. They were dipping their heads into buckets and Daisy believed she had surmised correctly. It *was* feeding time.

The sheep baaed and Floyd laughed. Daisy could see he was enjoying his livestock.

Eva cleared her throat and Floyd looked up, spotting them. He stepped toward the radio that was plugged into an outlet and switched it off. "Hello, ladies," he said with a smile. "I didn't think we'd meet again so soon." Then he looked at Eva. "Sorry, you certainly aren't as old as the last lady who came with Daisy." There was nothing suggestive in his voice, just amused.

Eva stretched out her hand. "I'm Eva Conner. I work with Daisy at the tea garden."

"Do you ladies always travel in pairs?" Again his tone held humor.

"Reinforcement and support," Daisy explained honestly.

Floyd's brows arched. "What can I help you with?"

Instead of diving right in, Daisy nodded to the sheep. "They're too cute."

"I'm going to be raising them for wool. Everything I do is as green as it can be."

"That concept is alive and well in this area," Daisy admitted.

"Oh, I know it is, and I've learned from the best. I'm

friends with Amish farmers who explain the old methods that work and aren't harmful to the land or the livestock. But I've got to admit, I'm not about to plow my fields with mules."

They all laughed at that, and Daisy thought the ice had been broken sufficiently to get to the point. "We were hoping you could tell us a little more about Lucius and about his feelings toward his grandmother's farm."

"Are you following up on police questioning?" Floyd asked, brows raised.

Daisy told him the truth. "Stella feels she's a subject of suspicion. She doesn't want to be a person of interest in the detectives' eyes. Yet she doesn't feel she can nose around at all. *We* can."

Floyd looked thoughtful. He took off his work gloves and laid them at the corner of the stall housing the sheep.

"You know," he said, "to raise any kind of livestock or even pets, I have to be observant." He glanced toward one of the little lambs. "That's Cricket because she makes a noise like a cricket sometimes. I think she's going to be a pet. Anyway, like I said, I have to be observant. I have to notice their behavior, watch what they do, if they're off their feed, if they aren't walking right, if anything looks amiss."

Supposing that was true, Daisy nodded. The best farmers were the vigilant ones. When Daisy glanced at Eva, she saw that Eva had no idea where this was going, but Daisy could guess. She waited.

"Lucius and I were arguing because he's thinking about selling the Higgins farm to a developer. He sees the dollar signs and that's all he can see, like many kids his age. Me, on the other hand, I see a farmer as a neighbor who could treat the land well. I see someone who can share knowledge and instincts. Do you know what I mean?"

Both Daisy and Eva nodded this time. However, knowing she had to return home soon, Daisy prompted, "Floyd, what else have you observed about Lucius?"

When Daisy could see Floyd hesitate, she guessed he might impart knowledge that he didn't know if he should. So she said, "I'll keep anything you tell me or us to myself and I'm sure Eva feels the same way . . . unless in some way it will help the police with their investigation."

"You don't seriously think they suspect Lucius." He sounded surprised.

"He had motive," Eva said, and Daisy knew she was thinking of Althea.

Daisy played devil's advocate. "We don't know if he had motive. Simply because he inherited doesn't mean he wanted the farm or the responsibility of selling it."

One of the bay geldings pawed at the straw in his stall. Attentive to the animals, Floyd looked that way and then back at Daisy. "I watched Lucius with Althea. I believe he pretended to be interested in the farm so she'd leave it to him. He knew from experience that if he made a wrong move, she'd disinherit him."

That news surprised Daisy. "How did he know that?"

Again Floyd seemed uncertain, as if he didn't want to reveal what he knew, but then he sighed. "I suppose a lot of people know about this. Any of them could tell the police."

Eva took a small step forward as if she wanted to hurry Floyd along, as if she wanted to know anything that might clear Stella and solve this murder.

Floyd looked down at the toe of his work boot and then

shrugged. "Lucius stole a car and took it for a joyride. Althea stepped in so he didn't go to juvenile hall. But she pulled the money she would have given him for college. He couldn't go. His mother didn't have the funds to pay for it, so he had plenty of motive to want his grandmother dead."

Daisy supposed the young man did, but then she asked Floyd the important question. "Do you feel he'd be capable of strangling his grandmother?"

This time Floyd didn't hesitate. He looked Daisy straight in the eye and answered, "I'm not sure."

Chapter Fourteen

In her office taking care of bookwork the next morning, Daisy looked up when Tessa rapped on the door.

"I have something to show you." Tessa's smile was conspiratorial and Daisy couldn't imagine what she had in mind.

"Good or bad? I'm only in the mood for good today."

Entering Daisy's office with a newspaper in her hand, Tessa stood in front of her desk. "I suppose that depends on your perspective."

"Did Trevor do something I'm not going to like?" Daisy asked, eyes narrowed.

"That depends. As I said, it depends on your perspective. I think it's cute."

The *Willow Creek Messenger* only printed a newspaper once a week now, though stories were posted online at their website every day. Although she was trying, Daisy couldn't read anything specific from Tessa's expression.

Tessa held out the newspaper and Daisy reached for it, intrigued now. At least, she was intrigued until she saw the article Tessa was referring to on the front page. And the surprise wasn't just the article.

"You and Gavin look cute," Tessa repeated.

The photo was typical of the *Willow Creek Messenger*'s front-page news. It often shared a human-interest story there. Today Daisy's Tea Garden was the human-interest story. That would have been fine except the picture on the front page was of her and Gavin. Gavin was playing his guitar with children gathered all around him. Daisy was standing at his shoulder, her head close to his as she sang along.

She groaned. "This is not what I want Jonas to see. It's the last thing we need right now."

"I understand. Believe me, I do," Tessa sympathized.

"Did you know about this?" Maybe Trevor had shared that the article would be going to press today.

"Trevor told me there was going to be a story on the children's tea, which would be good for our business. I texted him several photos. I had no idea the one the editor would choose would be one of you and Gavin."

"It makes sense," Daisy said, studying the photo again. "It captures the spirit of the tea. The parents are in the background eating their treats while they watch their kids having fun."

"My guess is the next children's tea is going to be sold out. That's a good thing," Tessa assured her.

"I know. It's just . . . it would have been so much better if Ned hadn't had the flu. Jonas wouldn't have taken any mind of my picture with *him*."

"He's jealous of Gavin?"

"I don't know if he still is, but this shows a level of

communication between me and Gavin that Jonas and I don't have right now."

Tessa lodged one hand on her hip. "And whose fault is that?"

Daisy dragged her hand through her hair. She had worn it down this morning since she was working in her office. "I'm not sure whose fault anything is at this point. I can blame Detective Rappaport for the whole thing but that wouldn't be fair either."

Leaning against Daisy's desk, Tessa warned, "Sometimes I think you're *too* fair."

"What's that supposed to mean?"

"You and I have never minced words. I think Jonas is acting like an idiot. He deserves a swift kick."

Tessa's words almost brought a smile to Daisy's face . . . almost. "Rappaport insists Jonas and Zeke are just stubborn males. I think we all have that stubborn streak in us when we care enough about something. Trust isn't a bond I should have messed with."

"Trevor's article is really good. You should read it. It might cheer you up. He explains how this was a teaching moment for the kids too. They learned to express themselves in a different way and had to think."

"I'll read it," Daisy assured her. "I need to know what the basis of gossip will be around town."

During the rest of the morning Daisy could have groaned at least a hundred times. It seemed everyone had seen the article. Each time she ventured into the tearoom to help serve a table, take Iris's place at the sales counter, or even peek into the kitchen, someone had something to say about it.

One of her regulars, an older woman who often bought soup and baked goods she liked to take along home for the next few days, winked at her. Fiona asked, "Are you dating the gentleman in the photo now? You look so comfortable together."

Daisy answered patiently that Gavin was a member of the family now, and they were friends. Fiona accepted that and went on her way. But Daisy saw the looks from other members of the community who came in. There were curious looks, studying looks, frowning looks. In her mind, it all added up to one big mess. Nevertheless, the article was a good one, and it would probably bring more business in. She did have to be concerned with that.

Of course, that afternoon they were supremely busy and Daisy couldn't hide in her office. She and Foster were serving a table for six when her cell phone played its tuba sound. Taking it from her pocket, she saw a number she didn't recognize. When she answered it, immediately she realized the other side had hung up. She slipped the phone back into her apron pocket, not suspecting anything wrong. The only problem was that within the next hour she received three more hang-up calls on her cell phone. Only a group of her closest family and friends had her cell number, so a strange number coming in was unusual.

Foster saw her face after the last one and asked, "What's wrong?"

"For the past hour I've been receiving hang-up calls, and I don't know the number."

"Give me your phone," Foster said. "I'll go to your office and check it out."

Did she want Foster to do that? She could tell she was beginning to bury her head in the sand and that wasn't like her. She handed over her phone. "I'll ask Tamlyn to help me finish serving the table," she said.

With a concerned look that meant he was going to figure this out, he gave her a nod and went to her office. Fifteen minutes later when their table was standing to leave and customers were telling Daisy how much they appreciated the service and the food, Foster returned to her. The afternoon tea service was over. She could breathe a sigh of relief and follow Foster to her office. She had a feeling she wasn't going to like what he had to say.

Her chest tightened. "Did you figure it out?"

"It's not that difficult. There's a website I use when I want to find out where someone lives now or when I want to check out a phone number. But you're not going to believe where the calls came from."

"Probably not," she murmured.

"Those calls came from Althea Higgins's cell phone."

Daisy felt her mouth drop open. "You can't be serious. How's that possible?"

"It's very possible. It's the same way spammers and telemarketers use your own telephone number when they call you so you'll pick up. There are websites that nefarious callers can route their calls through. Any number can be used."

"The police probably have her phone."

"No doubt . . . or they never found her cell phone. You really should let them know."

Could she bury her head in the sand or stand up to this? She didn't need Jonas to tell her she should stand up to it.

Jonas. Was he the reason she was feeling as if she wanted to duck away from the world? Maybe so, but she couldn't. And if Jonas determined that they were finished?

She'd have to deal with it somehow. She'd dealt with losses before and she'd deal with them again.

Instead of dialing Detective Rappaport's cell phone—after all, this wasn't an emergency—she dialed his office number. Voice mail picked up as she figured it would. She left a message explaining what had happened and what Foster had discovered. That was that. The rest was up to the police. She'd go back to serving blueberry coffee cake and be happy about it.

Of course, that wasn't what happened. She kept thinking about the phone calls, hoping she didn't receive another one. She didn't. Did that mean anything?

Daisy was taking inventory of the walk-in refrigerator when Cora Sue came bustling into the kitchen. "Detective Willet's here and he wants to see you. Should I send him back here?"

They were closing down the kitchen for the day and Daisy didn't want to talk to him in the midst of other people. "Send him to my office," Daisy told Cora Sue. "I'll be there in a minute."

Zeke looked put together today—black slacks, tan shirt, lightweight camel blazer. His face, however, told a different story. Lines on his brow and around his eyes, and a frown instead of a smile made him look ten years older than he was. Emotional baggage could do that as well as his job. She doubted he and Detective Rappaport were sleeping much as they tracked down leads.

He started by saying, "Detective Rappaport wasn't available so your call was switched to me."

"I hated to bother either of you. This might be nothing." Since Zeke looked as if he needed nurturing care, Daisy asked, "How about soup and blueberry coffee cake? We're at the end of the day and the tea garden's quiet. It will probably tide you over until you find more donuts."

His frown eased a bit but it didn't turn into a smile. "Why are you being nice to me?"

"Everyone needs a little kindness now and then, don't you think?"

He rubbed his hand down over his face. "Okay. If you can find me a quiet corner, we can talk over a bowl of soup. I haven't had anything since I grabbed a donut for breakfast."

Donuts and cops just seemed to go together. She hoped to change that to—coffee cake and cops . . . or snicker-doodles and cops.

In the main tearoom, Daisy motioned Zeke to a corner table in the spillover tearoom. They'd have privacy in there. Then she quickly scooped cabbage sausage soup into a bowl and set it on the tray. Cora Sue handed her a glass of iced peach tea and she added that as well as a square of blueberry coffee cake and a cinnamon scone that he could take along if he didn't eat it now.

From the large sink where she was washing teapots, Brielle, who had appeared with Jazzi after school, asked, "Is he going to arrest you?"

Daisy shook her head. "Hopefully he's going to arrest someone else . . . soon."

From where she was disinfecting the counters, Jazzi added, "Mom knows these guys. They listen to her and she listens to them."

Brielle still seemed puzzled, so Jazzi said, "I'll tell you all about the cases she helped them solve later."

Daisy wasn't sure that was a good thing. But right now she had Zeke on her mind. Carrying the tray to the spillover tearoom, she set it on the table.

He said, "The general public discounts how strong you have to be to carry those trays, don't they?"

"Everything I do around here keeps me strong," she said, meaning it.

Cora Sue had sent in another glass of iced tea on the tray and Daisy took hers too and had a sip.

Zeke started in on his soup. "This is good," he said with his brows raised.

"Of course it is. I wouldn't serve it if my customers didn't like it."

He gave a half-hearted shrug. "So hand me your phone and let me see what's going on. By the way, Detective Rappaport was checking on subpoenas. He wasn't trying to avoid you or hand you off."

"I know both of you are working hard on Althea's murder."

"I'm glad you think so. The mayor isn't too sure. I don't know why he thinks we need to solve a case in a week, and I know the trail gets cold if it takes too long. But interviews take what they take."

Zeke's frustration with the powers that be was understandable. "Does the chief work on this too?"

"Not when he has two of us on it. He sifts through everything and studies the interviews and gives his input when he can." After a pause, Zeke asked, "So Foster found out where this phone number came from?"

"He found out it belonged to Althea's cell phone. Do you have the phone?"

The policy of not sharing information still stood, but

again Zeke gave a shrug. "Yes, we have it. So this call didn't come from her cell phone. Someone who knows her number spoofed it." Zeke finished the soup and pushed the bowl away. He reached for the coffee cake and had soon devoured that. The man had been hungry.

"I don't like the fact that someone's trying to harass you. You need to be careful," he warned.

"Just what does that mean, Zeke? Stay in my house and not talk to anybody? That's not going to happen. Customers come here all the time with rumors and gossip to share about Althea and everyone else. Believe me, I haven't gone out of my way to make myself noticeable. But after this, I might have to."

"No, you don't," he said forcefully. "You're already on someone's radar. I know you don't want to think it, but it could be just as easily Stella or Claudia or Lucius who sent the call."

She knew he was right. Then he said something that really shook her.

"Whoever called you could also be tracking your movements. Maybe Jonas could run a scanner over your vehicles to make sure there isn't a tracker on one of them."

The mention of Jonas's name made her so sad. She might as well tell Zeke the truth. "Jonas and I aren't communicating right now."

"It's my fault, isn't it? This whole sorry mess is my fault." He sounded dejected as well as frustrated.

"The past is what it is, Zeke. Somehow we just have to find out how to go forward."

Zeke took the napkin at his place, wrapped the scone up in it, and stood. "I'll send a patrol officer over to scan your vehicles. Are they both here?"

"Today they are."

"All right. I'll have someone here in fifteen minutes so you can get home. Are you driving alone today?"

"No, Brielle and Jazzi are here with me."

"Just go straight home, Daisy. Don't invite trouble."

After they said their good-byes and Zeke left the tea garden, Daisy knew she wasn't going to invite trouble, but she might not be able to avoid it either.

As good as his word, Zeke sent a patrol officer who arrived within fifteen minutes. It was Bart Cosner and Daisy was glad the officer was someone she knew. She met him out back because she didn't want everyone else to know what was going on. There was no sense for the rest of them to worry, especially not Jazzi and Brielle.

It didn't take long for Bart to scan her PT Cruiser. He found a device under the rear wheel well. When he showed it to her, she knew she would have never found it. It was small, round, and magnetic.

"Where do people get these things?" she asked him.

"It's not so hard anymore. Spy shops sell them. Little chips can be embedded in key rings so you can always track your key ring. As soon as there's an innovation, somebody will figure out how to misuse it. Let me do your van."

As he wanded her van, he found another of the devices up near the front bumper. He wanded the vehicles again to make sure there weren't any others that he hadn't found. But the van and the Cruiser seemed to be clear.

"Please don't tell anybody about these," she said to Officer Cosner. "I don't want them to worry."

"I have to tell the detectives."

She nodded. "That's fine. They should know."

She could see Bart's patrol car parked out on the street in one of the slanted spots marked for buggies. With a concerned look, he said to her, "Be careful," and then he was on his way.

Daisy just stood there studying the vehicles, wondering where and when the tracking devices had been attached. Anyone could do it here, and no one would necessarily see them. It could be somebody she knew or somebody she didn't know who was involved in the murder. She must have stood there thinking about it longer than she expected because Foster emerged from the back door.

She waved him off. "Go on back in, Foster."

"I saw the patrol car though I don't think anyone else did. What happened?"

Although she didn't want any of her friends or family to worry, Foster already knew part of the story. He would keep poking until he figured it out. He knew she didn't have Jonas to confide in right now, and that might be why he was being overprotective. She certainly didn't want him bringing Gavin into it.

"Zeke had Bart Cosner check my vehicles for tracking devices. Officer Cosner found one on each."

Foster didn't say anything right away, but he looked thoughtfully over the grounds and down to the creek, away from the vehicles and away from her. After a few moments he concluded, "I can purchase a scanner and check your vehicles every day before they leave your garage. It's the only safe thing to do. Once I do that, you should forget about Althea Higgins and her killer."

Daisy could try to forget about it, but could the person who put the tracking devices on her car and her van forget about *her*?

Chapter Fifteen

Brielle had asked Daisy if they could visit her grammy again. Liking the older woman, and wanting to ease Brielle's mind, Daisy suggested she call her grandmother to find out if she wanted visitors. Glorie enthusiastically invited them to come.

On the road after she'd closed the tea garden, Daisy lowered the windows in her PT Cruiser and let the almost springlike breeze blow through. The girls liked the idea of having the wind blow through their hair.

Brielle said, "My parents believe in cold air and hot air. Nothing in between. This is nice. Smell that manure?"

Daisy had to laugh in spite of herself. "I do. It's common around here. Farmers are fertilizing their fields."

Jazzi wrinkled her nose. "I could never be a farmer."

Daisy gave her daughter a quick glance. "You like having a garden."

"That's different," Jazzi responded airily. "Our garden isn't that big and it's easy to keep. It's not like having to till fields and harvest crops. Sure, we grow a few tomatoes, zucchini, peppers. But that's not the same as farming."

Daisy couldn't disagree with that. Glancing in the rearview mirror, she saw that Brielle was avidly watching as they passed fields with horses and cows and even donkeys. She seemed interested in everything. Her curiosity was good and spoke of her intelligence.

As they drove up to Glorie Beck's cottage, Brielle said, "Grammy thinks her ankle is pretty well healed now. But she still has trouble walking sometimes. I told her to take her walker outside if she wants to go for a walk."

"With a bad ankle, carrying it out there could be a problem in itself," Daisy explained.

"I never thought of that." Brielle was quiet for a few seconds. "I wonder if she'd let Mom have a ramp built to her back door. That would make everything easier, wouldn't it? Then she could go outside more easily if she wanted to."

Daisy turned back to Brielle. "Do you think she'd agree?"

Brielle shrugged. "Maybe."

They parked. It wasn't long before Glorie had invited them inside where she had prepared iced tea. An oven buzzer sounded and Glorie asked Brielle to pull a pan of peanut butter blondies from the oven. Today she wore a hot pink T-shirt with jeans, and she looked better than the last time Daisy had seen her.

"Those are my favorite cookies," Brielle noted, as she brought the pan of cookies and a trivet to the table so her grammy didn't have to. Jazzi pulled the iced tea from the refrigerator, obviously feeling at home too. This house and Glorie Beck were like that—comfortable, heartwarming, and inviting.

After small talk, catching up on incidentals, and eating

blondies with their iced tea, Brielle found Grammy's list in the kitchen drawer and she and Jazzi went to empty wastepaper baskets.

"She likes feeling useful," Glorie said. "I don't think her parents make her feel useful."

"She's never mentioned any chores."

"Of course she hasn't," Glorie agreed. "My daughter and her husband have maids and a housekeeper. Brielle lets her dishes lie in her room when she's finished with food. The maid picks them up and takes them to the kitchen to wash them. That's a terrible way for a child to learn to live, don't you think?"

"I guess there are all different kinds of childhoods. I certainly had chores when I was growing up. My parents owned a nursery and when I went along with them to work, there were always things I could do there too. It did make me feel worthwhile."

"Exactly. Brielle tells me you have an Amish friend who has a store in town."

It seemed Brielle talked to her grammy about *everything*. "I do. When my parents started Gallagher's Garden Corner, the Eshes let them plant and start some of their trees and shrubs there. I often spent time with Rachel, feeding the chickens, grooming the horses, in general learning about farm life. Even though we live different lives, hers Amish and mine English, we were good friends. We still are."

"It's good to have different kinds of friends, especially for children. It teaches them about the world."

Glorie looked at the blondies and then shook her head. "I'd better not. My doctor doesn't want my sugar to jump up." She picked up her glass and took a long swallow, then she grinned at Daisy. "Not that sweet tea is any better, but a woman has to have some little pleasures."

"Yes, she does," Daisy agreed, and took a drink of her tea too.

Glorie glanced over her shoulder to see where the girls were. She could hear them chattering in the back of the house. Leaning close to Daisy, she asked, "Have you made any progress finding out who murdered Althea?"

"I've been warned to be careful," Daisy said truthfully, and told Glorie Beck about the tracking devices.

"Who would have thought of such a thing," Glorie said. "And they can find you by using their phone?"

"Or a computer. My son-in-law will be checking my vehicles every day now."

Glorie shook her head, a frown on her face. "I wonder if Althea had quit teaching, if she'd still be alive today."

"She was getting ready to retire from what I understand."

"She could have quit teaching last year," Glorie said certainly. "I think she could have retired after forty years of teaching and received her full pension. At sixty-two, of course, she could have received social security too."

"Why didn't she retire?"

Glorie made designs on her glass with her thumb as it sweated in the warmth of the kitchen. "Because teaching and her students gave her life meaning. We all need purpose, don't we?"

Brielle and Jazzi came into the kitchen then. Jazzi assured Glorie, "We tied up your garbage bag and put it in the can near the driveway."

"Thank you, girls. I didn't have much on my list today

because I've been feeling better. Since I am, I'd like you to do me another favor."

"Anything," Brielle said brightly.

"I'd like to go for a walk. I haven't done that for a while. I'm afraid to go too far by myself. I don't want to fall. But I have memories all over this farm and I'd like to revisit some of them now and then. Can we walk out back and down the yard? I have potatoes and onions in the springhouse. Joachim delivered a few bags of each to me. They keep well in there and I don't have to worry about running out. I need to bring some to the house."

Joachim supplied Daisy's produce at the tea garden. Daisy was glad Glorie did have people stopping in.

"Shall we take your walker?" Brielle asked her grand-mother, and then gave Daisy a look as if remembering their conversation about it.

"No, I'll take my cane. If I have one of you on either side of me, I won't need the walker."

A few minutes later, Daisy noticed the path leading down the back of the yard came from footsteps trampling ground, stones, and grasses. To her surprise, however, daffodils were beginning to bud along the side of the trail and also appeared in patches throughout the lawn.

"The daffodils are going to be pretty," Daisy said, aware of Glorie leaning on her arm.

"They spread each year," the older woman said. "I should divide them and dig up some of the bulbs, but they look so pretty when they bloom. They're usually over by the first grass cutting."

"I might have to plant bulbs in my front yard," Daisy said. "They bring spring alive, don't they?"

Brielle pointed to the hyacinths peeking up in borders

along the outside garden. "They'll soon be blooming in blue, yellow, and pink. They'll smell like perfume."

Jazzi kicked her running shoe against a loose stone on the trail and addressed Daisy. "Mrs. Beck could fall walking along here, even with her walker. Stepping-stones might really help. You know, those octagonal-shaped ones. Or even square."

"Stepping-stones would be a great idea and fairly easy to place," Daisy acknowledged. She pointed to the springhouse in the immediate distance. "They could probably be laid in a day . . . all the way to the springhouse."

At the springhouse, Daisy smiled. She'd been in springhouses before. Rachel's farm had one and the Eshes' property did too. Rachel's springhouse had been fashioned entirely of stone. Springhouses were situated over a spring and used for cool storage. Originally this was the one way to keep spring water clean, keeping it clear of leaves and other debris. But the small house had often stored milk, cheese, and other foodstuff.

Glorie's springhouse was stone at its base and wood the rest of the way to the roof. Forsythia bushes grew on either side of the door and a pussy willow bush covered the side corner. On approach from the outside, Daisy could see the heavy weathered-wood door.

Glorie turned the latch on the door and it swung open. The stones around the base of the springhouse were all different types, rough in their appearance. Daisy knew springhouses had often been built from stones that came from fields being cleared. Most of the stones around here were reddish and could be sandstone, and bluish which could be granite. The wood-framed part of the structure was still tightly paneled and didn't look as if it had been repaired or needed to be. This springhouse had been well built.

"Let's go inside," Glorie said. "It's a spot where me and my husband spent time even when we were young. We carved our names on the wall. I'll show you."

Brielle and Jazzi stepped inside too. Jazzi said, "It seems cooler in here than outside."

"When I was a little girl, we stored our fresh farm milk in here. But now I just keep my potatoes and onions here, and maybe a watermelon now and then. Those milk cans over there are left from the old days."

The girls took a cursory look around the inside, not really appreciating the history of a little house like this. Daisy moved toward the ladder that led to a small window.

"Can we go out and explore the woods a bit?" Jazzi asked.

Daisy looked to Glorie for approval. After Glorie nodded, Daisy said, "Just be careful."

With a wave and the nonchalance of youth, the girls hurried outside and around the springhouse.

"That window up there opens," Glorie said. "When I was a child I'd come in here and play, like it was my own private playhouse. I'd climb the ladder, open the window, and sit on the ledge. I could easily drop outside since it's situated on the side of a hill. I'd get tangled in the ivy but I didn't care."

Glorie moved carefully to the ladder, holding on to it for support. She pointed to the wood wall above the stone about five rungs up. A heart was etched into the wood there and two names were inscribed inside of it.

GLORIE AND PHILLIP.

"Phillip did that for us," Glorie explained. "He told me it would always be there, joining us for all eternity. He was a bit philosophical."

The burlap sacks of onions and potatoes were large ones. Daisy imagined that Glorie just took out one or two onions or potatoes as she needed them. "How many onions and potatoes would you like me to take back to the house?"

"Just two of each would be good."

After Daisy plucked two of each from sacks, she dropped them into her jacket pockets. Both of them stood quietly, listening to the babble of the spring as it passed through the springhouse.

Daisy said, "This would be a good place to come and think."

"Do you have something to think about?" Glorie asked, "Besides Althea's murder."

"Oh, I do," Daisy answered. "But it's so complicated that my thoughts are in a jumble. Hurt and too many feelings weave around my thoughts too. It's hard to sort them out."

"So it's about love, then," Glorie said, as if she were sure of it.

Daisy's gaze met Glorie's. "It is, but it could be about lost love. I did something stupid."

Leaning against the ladder, Glorie shook her head. "I doubt that. You seem like a woman who thinks out what she intends to do."

"I regret what I did."

"A mistake then," Glorie said with certainty. "Mistakes can be fixed."

Daisy still wasn't certain that this one *could* be fixed.

* * *

After her visit to Glorie's farm, Daisy and the girls drove home. She wanted to check in on Vi and she told Jazzi and Brielle that they could stay at the house if they wanted to. Instead, they came with her. Daisy noticed repeatedly that Brielle wanted to be involved in anything that had to do with family. Because she felt alone in hers? That wasn't good for any child.

The girls had run up the stairs to Vi's apartment and Daisy followed more slowly. She'd almost reached the top of the stairs when Foster came rushing down. He looked perturbed and in a hurry.

"Hi, Foster. Are you off to class?"

"I am. Vi's mad at me. I'm sure she'll tell you all about it."

Daisy didn't know whether to press Foster further, or go upstairs and talk with Vi.

Foster said, "I'll see you later. I'll be riding my new motor scooter and Vi's panicked." He threw up his arms. "I don't know what to do about it."

Daisy asked, "Do you want me gone when you get back from class?"

"I don't think it matters. I don't mind one way or the other. If Vi and I are going to fight, we're going to fight, whether you're here or not."

With that, he galloped down the remainder of the stairs and out the side door. Not two minutes later, Daisy heard the rev of an engine, a motorcycle or a motor scooter engine. Without more hesitation she went up the steps to the apartment.

Once in the open concept space, she immediately saw

that Sammy was in his playpen. What Daisy wanted to do was run over, pick him up, hug him, smell him, and cuddle him. That's what babies were for. Instead, she went to her daughter, who was sitting at the table with Brielle and Jazzi. Jazzi had gotten sodas from the fridge for them all and was pouring them into glasses.

Vi was shaking her head. "What is he thinking? Do either of you understand how men think?"

Daisy saw that Sammy was babbling to himself, kicking his arms and legs and watching the mobile that Vi had apparently started. She went into the small kitchen and leaned against the counter. "Do you want to talk about what's going on?"

Vi's face was red, and there was emotion in her eyes. "I can't believe he bought it. Sure, it's good on gas. Sure, he'll have his own wheels. But what's he going to do in winter?"

"Did you ask him?" Brielle inquired.

Vi gave her a narrow-eyed look. "Of course, I asked him. And do you know what he said? He said we might win the lottery by then. We need to keep my car in good shape, but this will be fine for him."

"I take it this was a surprise," Daisy commented.

"It was a *huge* surprise. I don't like surprises. We usually talk about everything first."

"Is there a reason you didn't talk about this?"

"Foster said he was tired of trying to come up with a solution, tired of trying to figure out how we were going to pay for everything. His car needs more than those parts they ordered. It needs a new transmission. That's way too expensive for us. Somebody at school was selling this motorcycle because he needed the money for books."

"What's going to happen to Foster's car?"

"He's going to sell it for parts. In other words, to a junkyard. His father actually thought that might be the better way to go."

"So he talked to Gavin about it," Daisy noted.

"I guess. I think Gavin looked over the scooter to make sure it was in running condition. Thank goodness for that."

"Have you ever ridden a motorcycle or a scooter?" Jazzi wanted to know.

"No, and I don't intend to."

Daisy knew this couple had to figure out solutions to their problems. However, Vi's attitude was going to cause more of a problem than a solution. Daisy said to Brielle and Jazzi, "Why don't you give Sammy a little playtime? I'm sure he'll appreciate it."

Jazzi caught her mother's meaning right away. She tapped Brielle on the arm. "Come on. He's such a cutie when he smiles. He's going to be crawling soon."

After the girls left the table and went over to the playpen, Daisy pulled out one of the chairs and sat.

Vi crossed her arms over her chest. "Are you going to lecture me?"

"Do I lecture you?"

"Sometimes you do."

Daisy took a deep breath and asked reasonably, "Do you and Foster buy lottery tickets?"

"Once in a while he buys a scratch-off, but *no*, we're saving our money, not spending it."

"Then I guess Foster was just teasing since he said you might win the lottery."

Vi uncrossed her arms. "I suppose so. He was trying to lighten things up and I wasn't in the mood for it."

"What money did he use to buy the scooter, if you don't mind telling me?"

Vi played with a strand of her hair that had swung forward. "I don't mind. He used the money he's been earning from the website business. But that's our emergency fund."

"I guess he considered this an emergency so you both can have a set of wheels."

Pushing her soda away from her, Vi frowned. "I know what you're going to say, that he could have bought a horse and buggy. That would have been worse because we would have had to feed the horse."

Daisy bit back a smile. Vi still *did* have a sense of humor. "In the short time you've been married, you've learned that marriage is all about compromise."

"That sounds good in theory." Vi sighed. "Foster has compromised on a lot. He's trying to work and go to classes and take care of me and Sammy too. I know it's not easy. And I do need my car and transportation so I can work at Pirated Treasures and earn money. It's not a lot but it helps with diapers and clothes."

"Sure, it does." Hopefully if Daisy acted as a sounding board, Vi could talk her way through the situation.

"Sometimes I see Foster looking at me as if he's afraid I'm going to slip back into a depression again. I try to be open with him about everything so he doesn't have to worry."

Often Daisy worried that Vi could slip back into the anxiety that had plagued her first weeks as a mother. "Partners worry about each other. You love, you care, you want to nurture. Worry is part of it. Sometimes I think we worry because we think we're planning while we worry.

If you worry about enough stuff, you'll be able to take care of it all."

"Sort of like having Plan A, B, and C?" Vi asked.

"Maybe. But planning is different from worrying. You know what Aunt Iris says about worry."

Violet thought a few seconds and then remembered. "Worry is like rocking in a rocking chair. It gives you something to do but you don't get any farther doing it."

"Exactly. This motor scooter is Foster's plan. Maybe so neither of you have to worry. Can you go with that?"

"And what happens in winter?" Vi asked.

"Winter's seven or eight months away. There is no knowing what could happen until then. Maybe he thinks he'll have enough website business until fall to be able to afford a car payment each month. I don't know, Vi, but I do know you have to believe in each other."

Vi glanced over her shoulder when she heard Sammy's giggle, then turned her attention to Daisy once more. "Whether you lecture me or not, you usually make me feel better."

Daisy let loose a smile. "That's good to know." She patted her daughter's hand. "I'm going to spend a little time with my grandson. When I get back to the house, I need to feed Marjoram and Pepper."

"Brielle and Jazzi are welcome to stay here. I was just going to order a pizza. You can come back and eat too."

"I think I'll let you enjoy a girls' night with Brielle and Jazzi. It will give them something different to do."

"You just want alone time," Vi teased.

"It wouldn't hurt." Although in some ways it would hurt because she'd be thinking about Jonas.

For the next hour or so, Daisy helped Vi bathe Sammy

and ready him for bed. Afterward, she returned to her house. Brielle and Jazzi decided to stay with Vi and enjoy the pizza they ordered.

After Daisy let herself into her barn home, she found two hungry felines eyeing her as if she'd been away for two weeks. She kept a light on a timer in the living room and it had switched on.

Marjoram padded toward her with a loud meow, then sat on her foot. Pepper, on the other hand, went straight toward the kitchen and her bowl as if she needed to guide Daisy that way.

"We're going to have a quiet evening together," Daisy told them.

Marjoram gave another meow.

"After I feed you," Daisy conceded. Taking off her jacket, she laid it across the back of a chair on the way to the kitchen. She'd just fed the two felines and opened the refrigerator to study what was inside for her own supper, when her cell phone played.

Could it be Jonas?

It wasn't until Pepper looked at her with an inquisitive glare that Daisy realized she had spoken out loud. Marjoram tilted her head as if waiting for the answer to the question.

Daisy picked up the phone and saw it wasn't Jonas calling but Trevor Lundquist. "Not Jonas," she said to Marjoram.

Marjoram gave a short little meow as if in sympathy, then lifted her paw to wash her face. She apparently had better things to do than worry about a phone call that wasn't arriving. Daisy should take a hint.

She answered the call. "Hi, Trevor. What's up?"

"That depends," he said. "Isn't Harry Silverman a suspect in the Higgins murder?"

"I don't know if the police consider him a suspect or not."

"Maybe he's on *your* list?"

"Possibly," she said warily. "Why?"

"He was in a fight at Bases. I think you should come on down if you want the scoop."

Did she want the scoop? Did she want a quiet evening alone thinking about Jonas? Or did she want to help solve Althea's murder?

"Are you sure he'll still be there?" Daisy asked.

"He'll be here. I'll make sure of it."

"All right. I'll see you in about ten minutes."

Daisy forgot about supper. Trying to forget about Jonas, she told Marjoram and Pepper, "I won't be long," grabbed her jacket, and headed out.

Chapter Sixteen

Daisy second-guessed herself the whole time she drove to Bases. When she turned off Market Street, she parked in the lot and saw that there were plenty of cars still there. Bases was a sports bar but served mostly burgers and fries, pickles and peanuts.

Daisy climbed from her car, thought again about what she was doing, and walked quickly to the establishment. As she opened the door, the aroma of sizzling burgers and bacon wafted out. Inside, she took a look around.

As its name purported, the restaurant was about bases—baseball bases. Photos of Fenway Park, Camden Yards, Yankee Stadium, and Wrigley Field were displayed along one wall. Enlarged to poster size, they were framed in narrow black plastic frames. Photos of players in their uniforms along with shots of avid baseball fans, most of them probably patrons of this bar, also hung nearby. She'd been here before when she was investigating another murder.

It always surprised her that this room wasn't dark. Track lighting gleamed from the ceiling along the edges of the room. There were tables along the outskirts as well as a long wooden bar with a mirror at the back. She noticed two chairs overturned, liquid on the floor along with shattered glasses that a server was cleaning up. Trevor was sitting with Harry Silverman at one of the back tables.

Strategically circling the mess and the server, Daisy didn't know if she wanted to sit with the two men. Both of them looked roughed up. Trevor bore a cut over his right eye and Harry Silverman's bruised cheek would probably be purple in the morning.

Spotting Daisy, Trevor stood and pulled out a chair for her. "I helped break up the fight," he said in explanation.

Instinctively, Daisy knew she needed to maintain her composure and not act as if their appearances bothered her. She'd project more confidence as an interviewer that way. Trying to remain unruffled, she asked calmly, "What was the fight about?"

Trevor dabbed at the cut on his forehead that appeared to have stopped bleeding. "It was just an ump's call."

Harry stared down at the table and took swigs from a glass of water . . . at least she hoped it was water and not vodka. She glanced from Trevor to Harry, not exactly sure what to do or what to ask. Trevor had asked her here for a reason, so she might as well try to pry information out of Harry.

She tapped on the table in front of the young man and asked, "So you got upset about an ump's call? Enough to break up this place?"

"It was that guy at the bar who said the ump was fair," Harry said, motioning over to the stools where no one was sitting now.

Daisy raised her brows at Trevor.

"The other guy left," Trevor said. "No one called the police. Harry said he'd cover the breakage."

Daisy again addressed Harry, feeling more like a mother than anyone else. "Were you really mad about the ump's call or something else?"

Now he directed his gaze at her. "I hate my job. I'm supposed to be playing football."

Daisy just cocked her head to listen.

"I told you that before, didn't I?" he asked.

"You did."

He scowled. "The police came around to talk to me. Was that your doing?"

Shaking her head, Daisy answered, "It wasn't my doing. I didn't mention you to the police."

Angrily, he snapped, "Well, someone did. I don't need them in my business."

Daisy pushed her chair closer to the table. "If you're not doing anything wrong, then you don't need to worry."

He shook his head vehemently, his hair falling down over his forehead. "It doesn't work that way. I have friends—" He clammed up.

"Friends who have gotten in trouble, and they don't have a fancy lawyer for a way out of it?"

He grimaced, took a moment, and then answered, "Maybe. I don't even want to think about a lawyer. You know, everybody should have a chance to go after their dream. Mrs. Higgins's daughter is trying it."

That was news to Daisy. "Phebe?"

"Yeah."

"What dream does Phebe have?"

"You know, don't you, that Phebe resented her mother? And now *especially* does."

"Because—" Daisy prompted.

"Althea should have left Phebe the money, the farmhouse, anything she could get out of it. But she didn't. So Phebe is trying to convince Lucius to lend her enough money to flip a house. He's not sure he wants to do it. He's not sure about anything he wants to do."

This was news about Phebe. "Do you think she'll go after her dream, even if Lucius doesn't lend her the money?"

"I think she might. Lucius and I hang together now and then. His mom's pretty cool. I mean, she's not giving him a hard time every two minutes. Mrs. Higgins did. Just like she did to her students. If it weren't for her—"

If it weren't for her, Harry might be playing in the NFL. *Could* Harry have killed Althea? He was big enough, and strong enough, and maybe angry enough. She exchanged a look with Trevor, who had been letting her take the lead. She didn't want to dwell on the murder. "What do you really want to do besides playing football?"

Excitement shone in Harry's eyes. "I'd like to own my own business, maybe open a sports equipment store. I'd be good at that, telling kids what they need. I don't want to have to work three jobs like my dad. I want something solid that will last. I know football wouldn't have lasted forever, but I could have made enough money for life."

"Maybe. If you didn't have an injury that took you out," Trevor noted.

Harry leaned back in his chair and stretched his legs out under the table. "Nothing's ever going to get any better."

Daisy realized that was the shortsightedness of youth

talking. "It could, but you'll need to work at it for a while first."

"You mean work at the storm door place and save enough for collateral so the bank will give me a loan?"

"That's possible, isn't it?" Daisy asked.

"If I want to devote my life the next five years to storm doors." He sounded dejected and put out.

"What's the alternative?" Trevor wanted to know.

"Spending whatever I make now, buying a new car, coming in here, and—"

Daisy cut in. "Getting arrested for a brawl?"

He looked contrite. "Yeah, not such a great idea, huh?"

"Mrs. Higgins might have put a temporary stop to what you wanted to do with your life," Daisy said, "but now the future's ahead of you and it's up to *you*."

"Yeah, I guess it is." Harry slid his chair back and stood. "I'm going to leave before the manager changes his mind and *does* call the police. All we did was spill two drinks and break glasses."

"You might want to pay the bartender for that before you leave," Trevor advised. "You know, a sign of good will? Then the manager might not cringe the next time you walk in."

Harry nodded as if he thought that was a good idea too. He turned to Trevor. "Thanks for helping me . . . for pulling me off before we really got into it."

"My good deed for the day," Trevor said lightly with a smile.

After Harry walked away, Daisy asked Trevor, "Do you think he could have murdered Althea?"

With a shrug, Trevor shook his head. "I know firsthand he's strong enough. It's not out of the realm of possibility."

Had she really learned anything here tonight?

Just that Phebe wanted to flip a house. But who knew how that might fit into other information Daisy might pick up? Sometimes clues built one on the other. In time, those clues would create a picture, a picture she might not want to see.

On Friday evening, Portia arrived and Daisy welcomed her with a smile. Jazzi had told Portia that Brielle was still staying here. Portia's hair was black like Jazzi's and her eyes dark brown. Her layered cut fell along her cheeks. She was a few years younger than Daisy.

Jazzi introduced Brielle to her and then, looking a bit uncertain, Portia settled in. Daisy had planned supper with bowls of beef and lentil soup that she had started in the Crock-Pot, an antipasto plate with salami, mozzarella, carrots, celery, pickles and olives, and the cookies from the tea garden that they could enjoy now and later.

Conversation flowed at dinner, though Portia and Jazzi chatted to catch up since they'd last visited with each other. After dinner, Daisy suggested that the four of them sit around the table to play Cat-Opoly.

About fifteen minutes into the game, Brielle took a card and asked Jazzi, "Do you play games often?"

"We have a closet full of games," Jazzi assured her. "We've always played board games since we were little. Card games too—hearts . . . gin rummy."

"We never played games," Brielle said, looking at Portia and then at Daisy. "On weekends Mom and Dad went out Saturdays and Sundays, or else had work to do in their offices."

Portia addressed Brielle. "My husband and I play board games with our two girls too. It's a chance for all of us to relax."

"Did you play games with the housekeeper?" Jazzi asked, never shy about asking a friend something important.

"Mostly the housekeeper took me to the park or a supervised playground. Housekeepers always had their own stuff to do too."

For Daisy, the picture Brielle set up was of a lonely child who didn't get the attention she deserved.

Brielle kept her cell phone with her at all times. Now it dinged with a text message. She said to everyone sitting there, "It might be Mom. I'd better look. Is that okay?"

"It's fine," Daisy told her. "I'll refresh our drinks. How about hot cocoa?"

"Sounds good," Brielle agreed, already looking at her phone screen. Daisy glanced over her shoulder and saw Brielle read the message. The teenager then typed something in quickly.

There was another ding and Daisy suspected Brielle's mother had answered her. She didn't know whether to pry or not, to ask questions or not. But when she reached the table, she saw the disappointed look in Brielle's eyes.

Conversation had stopped and even Jazzi looked a little awkward.

"How many marshmallows do you want in your hot chocolate?" Daisy inquired, hoping all was well even though she sensed it wasn't.

Brielle looked up at her, her eyes wet. "None for me."

"Whipped cream?" Daisy asked.

They all nodded except for Brielle.

Daisy put her hand on Brielle's shoulder. "Why don't you come with me into the kitchen and help me with the cocoa. I'm going to make it from scratch."

At first, she thought Brielle was going to refuse, but then the teenager stood and followed Daisy.

Daisy retrieved the pan from the cupboard and set it on the burner. She asked Brielle, "Can you get me the milk from the fridge?"

Brielle opened the fridge and grabbed the half-gallon container. She set it on the counter next to Daisy.

If Brielle wanted to shut her down, she could, but Daisy felt she had to ask. "Are your parents having a good time?"

"I guess so. They met one of their international clients over there. They made a couple more appointments too, so they're probably going to be gone another week. She wanted me to ask you if it was okay if I stay. If not, she said I could go home and stay with the housekeeper."

As a mom, Daisy couldn't imagine being out of the country and sending her daughter to an almost empty house with a housekeeper! "Of course it's okay if you stay. I imagine you miss your parents."

"I do, but . . . Mom didn't even ask me if I was having fun. She said they'd gotten back from a late party and they'd be traveling tomorrow and she didn't know if she'd have service to call me."

Daisy wondered why in the heck Brielle's mom hadn't called her instead of texting. Didn't she want to talk with her daughter? After all, Brielle had never stayed with Daisy before. Wouldn't she want to know that Brielle was happy?

Brielle asked, in almost a little girl tone, "Are you sure you don't mind?"

"I don't mind. You're company for Jazzi, aren't you? She misses her sister."

"But she has you. . . ." After hesitation Brielle added, "And she has Portia."

"I know. But it's important that Jazzi has bonds with someone her own age too. To tell you the truth, I don't think I've ever seen her connect with someone the way she's connected with you."

"Really?"

"Really. It reminds me of me and Tessa when we went to school together. I wasn't always happy at home because of arguments with my sister and my mom. Tessa didn't have a great home life. We just seemed to understand each other from day one, and it's still that way now. She can tell when I'm upset or when I'm mad. She doesn't let me get away with anything either." Daisy gave Brielle a smile.

"I guess that's the way friends are supposed to be."

"I think they are."

"We've moved often so I haven't had time to make real friends," Brielle confided.

"And here in Willow Creek, you have your grammy too."

"Yes, I do. I really think I want to go live with her."

"You'll have to discuss it with your parents when they come home."

Somehow Daisy didn't think Brielle's parents were going to be very understanding or open to listening to their daughter.

By bedtime Friday night, Daisy had seen that Brielle felt left out, her bond with Jazzi more tenuous with Portia in the house. Daisy had given Portia her bedroom and she slept on the sofa. She could hear Jazzi and Brielle talking late into the night. Not wanting Brielle to feel like a fifth wheel, Daisy made a decision.

In the morning, Daisy suggested to Brielle that she come with her to the tea garden for the day. Jazzi and Portia would have their time together and Daisy would spend time with Brielle.

Brielle asked, "Do you mean it? Without Jazzi? I'll mess up with her not telling me what to do."

"You've been busing tables with her. You'll be fine. Besides, if we go in early, you and I can brew special teas before anybody arrives. I'll show you how to do it, then maybe you can do it during the day. Would you like that?"

Brielle broke into a wide smile. "Yes!"

When they arrived at the tea garden, Daisy took Brielle to the kitchen, where Tessa was mixing up scone batter and Iris scooped cookies from the dough that had been in the freezer.

After Daisy showed Brielle exactly how they brewed their teas, Brielle was eager for their first customers to arrive. She bused tables, doing well, until midmorning. Daisy had gone to the kitchen for a table of four women who had asked for cinnamon scones and snickerdoodles. One wanted to taste the blueberry coffee cake. She sent Brielle ahead with a dish of cookies and scones and the one dish of blueberry coffee cake.

Soon after, when she followed her with pots of oolong tea as they'd ordered, she heard the woman say to Brielle, "You're awfully young to be working here, aren't you?"

Brielle stood her ground, put the cookies on the table

followed by coffee cake, and answered brightly, "I'm sort of interning, shadowing Daisy for the day."

The woman's eyebrows rose and she frowned. "You're not quite what I'd expect to see in a tea garden, with your hair and nose ring and all those holes in your ears."

Daisy set the pot of tea on the trivet on the table. Instead of pouring it into the teacups, she put her arm around Brielle's shoulders. "Brielle is exactly the type of server I like to hire here. She's responsible, efficient, and can take direction well." Her glare challenged the other woman to say more against the young woman.

"I see," the woman said with a disapproving frown again. "I just think maybe an Amish girl would make a better presentation."

Daisy felt Brielle's body sag. She started to return to the kitchen.

Daisy said quickly, "Yes, Willow Creek is in Amish country, but here at the tea garden we welcome diversity, inventiveness, and unique personalities. That's what spices up life."

Brielle looked up at Daisy with her eyes glistening. She said quickly, "Excuse me," and headed for the restroom.

The other three women at the table seemed embarrassed. They jumped into conversation, eager to change the subject. One of them said, "I can't wait to sample that oolong tea and your wildflower honey."

Daisy quickly poured the tea and didn't linger as she usually did to chat with her guests. Instead she just gave them all a nod and then headed for the powder room.

It wasn't a surprise to Daisy to see Brielle crying. The powder room was small and Daisy stood at the sink with

Brielle, putting her arm around her shoulders again. "You can't take what she said seriously."

"My parents don't like the earrings or the nose ring or the hair either."

Daisy couldn't say anything against Brielle's parents. However, she leaned against the vanity and turned to face the teenager. "You're going to have to make a choice, honey. Either you live by everybody else's rules or you make some of your own. You can try and gain the whole world's approval and you're never going to. Doing something just to rebel doesn't get you very far. But if you actually do what you think makes your personality shine, then that will serve you well as you get older. Does that make any sense?"

Brielle took a Kleenex from the box on the vanity and blew her nose. Sniffing, she nodded. "I guess it does."

"I know you can't forget what that woman said, but remember it was all about appearance. She wasn't saying anything about you as a person or what's in your heart, right?"

Brielle nodded again.

"Are you going to be okay?"

Brielle stared into the mirror. "I just need to wipe the mascara off my face." She had raccoon eyes from crying.

Daisy smiled at her. "Take as much time as you need. I'll either be in the kitchen or in my office if you need me." Then she left Brielle in private to pull herself together and to think about everything that had happened.

Ten minutes later when Brielle stuck her head inside Daisy's office, she said, "Tessa wants to show me how to make scones. Is that okay?"

"That's fine. And before we leave today, be thinking

about what cookies you'd like to take along for tonight. We might play more board games."

"I know Jazzi likes peanut butter. I'll include some of those."

It seemed Brielle had recovered from her experience with the customer. Daisy just hoped that was so.

After having black coffee and a cinnamon scone, Portia left early Sunday morning.

Since Jazzi and Brielle would be working on the parade float at Stacy's for most of the day, Daisy made a big breakfast with waffles, eggs, and country ham. Brielle enjoyed the blueberry syrup on her waffles as she and Jazzi discussed what progress they could make on the float today.

The girls had gone upstairs to get ready to leave when Daisy's cell phone played. Taking it from the counter, she was surprised by the caller's ID. It was Glorie Beck. Had something happened to Glorie again . . . or to Brielle's parents?

Perplexed, Daisy simply said, "Hello?"

"Is that you, Daisy?" Glorie asked, as if she wasn't used to using a cell phone.

"It's me. Is everything all right?"

"I'm not sure. Can you stop over here today . . . alone?"

After only a moment's thought, she answered, "I'm soon leaving to drop off Jazzi and Brielle at a friend's. They're working on the parade float for most of the day."

"I don't want to interrupt your day, but I think this is important."

"I'll be at your place in a half hour. Okay?"

"That sounds just fine. I'll have the teapot ready."

After Daisy ended the call, she knew she shouldn't wonder what this was about. She'd find out soon enough.

When she pulled into Glorie Beck's driveway, Glorie was standing at the door as if she'd been waiting. She was holding on to the doorframe instead of using a cane or walker.

As soon as Daisy went up the steps to the porch and stood before the door, Glorie said to her, "Don't scold me for not using my cane. I'm feeling better today. I have enough furniture around that I can hold on to things."

As if that was safe, Daisy thought, but she didn't say it aloud. She followed Glorie into the kitchen as the woman held on to the back of the chair and then the table.

Daisy suggested, "Why don't you sit. I'll pour the tea."

After a sideways glance, Glorie agreed. "Have it your way."

Once they were seated at the table, honey in their tea, Glorie took an envelope from under the placemat and slid it over to Daisy.

"What's this?" Daisy asked.

"Althea gave me this for safekeeping last year. I forgot all about it. I found it in my safe box this morning when I was looking for my homeowner's insurance to check when I have to renew it. I wanted to make sure I have enough of a balance in my checking account to pay it. Anyway, I spotted the envelope and since Althea is gone now, I opened it. But in a way, it was Althea's personal business. I thought about giving it to the police, but I'm not sure it means anything and they'll just laugh at me."

Daisy didn't think they'd laugh at Glorie, but even

Detective Rappaport could be condescending at times. "Are you sure you want me to see it?"

"I hate to say this," Glorie murmured, "but we don't know if Phebe or Lucius had anything to do with Althea's murder, do we?"

"I don't know anything for sure. I don't think the police do either."

"Exactly."

Studying the envelope, Daisy suggested, "You could give it to Althea's lawyer."

"And what would *he* do with it? Stick it in her folder? Or give it to Lucius or Phebe? Not a good idea."

Daisy picked up her mug and took a sip of the hot tea, buying herself a little time. Did she really want to open this envelope? She could be opening a Pandora's box.

Maybe Pandora's box needed to be opened.

Picking up the envelope from the table, she flipped up the flap. Then she emptied the contents onto her placemat, keeping it away from her mug of tea.

She was surprised at what fell out. Maybe she'd expected something formal. Maybe she'd expected a letter to Althea's lawyer. What she found was a teacher's ID. The thing was, it had Althea's photo on it, but another name— Thea Hathaway!

"What do you think of this?" she asked Glorie, holding up the ID.

"Keep looking," Glorie directed her.

Next Daisy picked up a conference brochure. It was in color and glossy. On the front, she read "Shakespeare in the Classroom." As Daisy opened the trifold brochure, she noticed speakers' photos and the schedule for a conference for English teachers. The date was 2005.

Again, she glanced at Glorie but Glorie just arched her brows. Daisy picked up the last item that had been in the envelope. It was a piece of paper torn from a hotel notepad. On it was written—

Thea. This time with you means so much to me.
I wish everything was different.

Will

"I have no idea what any of this means," Daisy said. "Can you put it all together?"

Glorie put a lined finger to her bottom lip. Then she tipped her head to the side. "I thought about that date— 2005. Fifteen years ago. Fifteen years ago, Althea was a different person. Around that time, she seemed to have a new outlook. She smiled more. Her comments weren't as biting. It was quite a change. That's why I remember."

Daisy could imagine going down this road and where it was headed. But she waited in case Glorie had more to say. The older woman did.

"You know, when Althea was younger, I'd say twenty-five or thirty years ago, she was kindlier. She'd always been around animals and liked them."

Twenty-five to thirty years ago would have been when Eva had experienced Althea as a teacher. She remembered Eva's comments about how kind Althea had been, how she'd brought their family food, and made clothes for Eva.

"Life hardened her? Teaching took its toll?" Daisy offered.

Glorie's lined face became even more lined. "Possibly. But I also think her marriage wasn't what she wanted it to be. Around that 2005 date, kindness that I'd seen in her as a young woman came back again. I remember because it was fall, harvest time, and the town was getting ready for an Amish auction that would benefit a family with medical bills. Althea and I were going around to neighbors and collecting items for the auction. She was so happy and told me she'd been at a conference that had been worthwhile. I wondered what had happened at that conference because after it, Althea took trips some weekends to Harrisburg and York. She told me she was working on a book and needed to do Shakespeare research. Her husband even grumbled to me about her interest in Shakespeare and her time away from the farm. Did you know Phebe's and Lucius's names are from Shakespearean plays? Phebe's name is from *As You Like It* and Lucius's from *Julius Caesar*."

"And you think . . . ?"

Glorie looked sad as she sighed. "I believe Althea was sorry she'd married a man with less education than herself. But she'd wanted to have a family and no one else had seemed to be interested in her. So she'd settled."

"And that's what made her bitter, sharp, and cutting?"

"I think so." Glorie tapped the envelope on the table. "But I also think that maybe at that conference she met someone she cared about. And maybe, just maybe, that man had something to do with her murder."

Daisy leaned back in her chair and caught her breath as her heart raced. This possibility opened a new avenue for investigation. Did she want to investigate? Or should she just turn the envelope over to Detective Rappaport?

Chapter Seventeen

One thing Daisy's parents had told her as she was growing up was, "Don't waste time." Often Daisy scheduled as much in a day as she could . . . especially since Ryan had died. Every moment of life was precious. If she could make a difference, she wanted to. Therefore, instead of becoming caught up in what she should or shouldn't do regarding the envelope Althea had left with Glorie, she decided to do something about it—visit Phebe.

She'd heard from Stella that Althea and her daughter weren't close. If that was the case, Phebe might not know anything about Althea's life, outside of what Althea *wanted* her to know. On the other hand, children picked up things. Little kids *and* big kids. Fifteen years ago, Phebe would have been around twenty-five. The only way Daisy was going to secure any information was to ask for it. She was deeply into this case now, and she really had nothing to lose.

When Daisy arrived at the row house on Juniper Avenue where Phebe Higgins lived, she saw that it was two stories . . . but a very narrow two stories. Steps and a railing led up to the red front door. The siding was beige and the shutters on the second-floor window were red. She didn't know if Phebe would be home or not, but it wouldn't hurt to find out.

After a minute or so, Phebe opened the door. She wore a navy headband to keep her hair away from her face. Her yoga pants and top were loose-fitting. Her appearance was similar to Althea's and yet it wasn't. Her nose was long and sharp but the rest of the features of her face balanced it out.

"Hi, Phebe. Do you have time to talk for a few minutes?"

"Is this about Lucius? Are the police going to question him again?"

"Not that I know of," Daisy responded with empathy in her voice. She knew how anxiety-filled worrying about a child could be.

Phebe looked uncertain about inviting Daisy inside, but she didn't seem to have the blatant rudeness of her mom. "I'm leading a yoga class in half an hour but we could talk for about fifteen minutes."

A short visit was fine with her. If she learned anything that helped, their discussion would be worthwhile.

As Daisy followed Phebe inside, she saw that the house was indeed narrow but the wood plank flooring gleamed. A small foyer led straight into a living room while stairs on the right led to the second floor.

Phebe motioned Daisy into the living room. "Go ahead in there. I do like tea. I'll brew us some. Is cinnamon rooibos all right?"

"Perfect," Daisy agreed.

The living room had French doors that led into a dining room. The kitchen was beyond. Phebe had decorated all in a minimalist but comfortable fashion.

Glancing around the living room, Daisy noticed the sofa had loose cushions that a guest could arrange any way they wanted. That and the double-wide armchair took up the entire room while pole lamps added light. Daisy liked the French doors. They were an old-fashioned touch with their glass doorknobs and multipaned windows. The dining area beyond was only large enough for a small table for four and no other furniture. Daisy wondered how long Phebe had lived here. Since her divorce?

Phebe returned to the living room with two cups of tea, one balanced in each hand. She set them on the small round chrome-and-glass coffee table. "Do you need sugar or lemon or anything?"

"No, this is great. Do you enjoy yoga?"

"I teach the class," Phebe said. "I earn enough to pay the rent and put food on the table. That's what matters. Lucius was paying me rent for his bedroom but now that's changed."

"I spoke with Lucius recently. He doesn't know what he wants to do with the farm." It was a prompt that Daisy hoped Phebe would follow.

"I know he's indecisive. I gave him ideas but he'll do what he wants, no matter what I say. Are *you* interested in the farm?"

"Oh, no," Daisy protested. "I have enough on my hands with my home and the tea garden. No, I came to ask you about your mom. Do you know anything about a man in your mother's life?"

Phebe's eyes widened. "You mean after Dad died?"

Daisy wasn't exactly sure what to tell Phebe when nothing was definite. But Glorie had given her the envelope to take along, and now she showed it to Phebe. "What do you think about this?"

After Phebe examined everything in the envelope, she returned it to Daisy. "I don't know what to think. I don't know anything for sure."

"But you know *something*?"

Phebe adjusted the pillow behind her. "I lived at home after my divorce until I could get back on my feet. I probably stayed longer than I should have. I remember my mom got a phone call on her cell. She was standing near me and I could hear a man's voice. At first, she seemed happy to receive the call. She went to another room, but when she came back, she was sad. I asked her if something was wrong. She insisted nothing was."

"But you believed there *was* something wrong?"

Phebe didn't meet Daisy's gaze until she answered her. "My mother didn't expect much from me. She underestimated me. She thought I didn't notice things that I did. But I noticed more than she ever thought I did."

Keeping her voice as casual as she could, Daisy asked, "What exactly did you notice?"

Closing her eyes as if she needed to do that to remember, Phebe related, "My mother had Shakespearean sayings laminated and framed for her bedroom. After the day that she received that phone call, she hung a new one. 'Star-crossed lovers are doomed until eternity.'"

That was heavy, Daisy thought. Apparently it had been meaningful to Althea. Was she comparing herself and whoever the man was to Romeo and Juliet?

Phebe picked up her cup of tea. "Something else she told me after my divorce was that timing was everything. I wasn't sure what she meant. She might have meant that my husband and I married too young, that we didn't know what we wanted until it was too late. She believed Lucius suffered because of that, and she was probably right. No matter what was going on between me and Clark, I tried to make Lucius the focus of my life. It wasn't always easy. Mom didn't like Clark and Clark didn't like her, so she didn't see him much for most of our marriage. It wasn't until after our divorce that I felt Mom got to know Lucius better."

"Was that when he started helping her with chores on the farm?"

"He had been staying over now and then. But when we lived there, he and my mom grew closer. I think my mom thought she could keep him on the straight and narrow. But he still got into trouble again by joyriding in someone else's car."

"I'm sorry to hear that. Teenagers have it hard enough these days."

"Yes, they do, don't they? I keep telling Lucius what my mother told me that timing is everything. Not only timing in relationships, but timing for taking the right jobs . . . timing for taking a risk with a career."

Daisy knew well that her timing and Jonas's had been skewed more than once. Just when they thought they were getting really close, something else happened. Were they supposed to be together?

As she sipped her tea, thoughts of Althea kept running through her mind. Had Althea loved someone else while she was married? Was this *Will* married too? Just who was Will, and how could Daisy find him?

* * *

The following evening Daisy had asked Stella and
Claudia to have supper with her and the girls. Just for an
occasion such as this, she kept deli tortellini in the freezer
as well as her own meatballs. It wasn't long before she
had a tall jar of tomato sauce that her aunt Iris had canned
simmering on the stove with the meatballs steaming in it.
She'd just put water on to boil and dumped the tortellini
in when the doorbell rang.

Jazzi called from the living room, "I'll get it."

Soon Daisy heard chatter in the living room and it
sounded as if Claudia and Stella had come together.
Moseying into the kitchen, Brielle asked, "Do you want
me to set the table?"

"That would be great, Brielle. You know where the silverware and the plates are. The placemats are in the top
drawer of the hutch. We'll use those tonight."

Over the past few weeks, Daisy had noticed that Brielle
seemed happy to have dinner around the table just as
she was when she was sharing tea with Glorie. However,
Daisy didn't want to bring the girls into her plans for
tonight. She knew after dinner they'd probably return to
Jazzi's room upstairs, do homework, then find something
to entertain themselves. Hopefully, something worthwhile.
The last time she'd gone into Jazzi's bedroom when they
were there, they had been streaming runway shows with
the latest fashions, commenting on outfits they liked and
those they didn't.

Marjoram and Pepper, who usually made themselves
scarce when company came, seemed to like Claudia and
Stella. They hung around, hoping for treats, but just enjoyed a pet here or there from anybody who would give
it. While Daisy served dinner, Marjoram sat under Jazzi's

chair and Pepper under Brielle's. The women talked with Brielle and Jazzi about the floats and the parade. They listened to the tensions and interactions that had happened between the girls and their classmates. Not everyone agreed on projects like that, but Stella assured both Brielle and Jazzi that that was quite normal.

"Projects come together," Stella said, "when everyone can compromise."

Brielle shook her head. "Some of the kids want to use cheap materials. If we use cheap stuff, it will look cheap."

"Tissue paper will disintegrate in the rain too," Jazzi added. "There are new types of cloth that Rachel's store sells that would make beautiful flowers. They would hold up a lot better."

"But the cost is the problem?" Claudia asked.

Brielle nodded.

"This is just a thought," Daisy suggested. "But what if you made some kind of trade?"

"I don't understand, Mom." Jazzi looked pensive.

"You know Rachel well enough to bargain with her. What if you offered to advertise her store on the back of your float if she donates some of that material? You'd have to check it out and make sure it's appropriate first, but I don't see anything wrong with materials donated by Quilts and Notions, do you?"

Brielle and Jazzi exchanged a look. Brielle nudged Daisy's arm. "You know how to market, Mrs. Swanson."

"I think it's time you start calling me *Daisy*."

Brielle's smile told Daisy that she'd just handed her some sort of present that made her happy.

After tortellini, meatballs, and salad Daisy brought out a dish of snickerdoodles. "Why don't you girls grab a few of them and take them up to the room. I'll make hot chocolate later. Claudia, Stella, and I would like to talk for a bit."

"About the murder?" Jazzi asked, always seeking the truth, not wanting to be kept in the dark.

"It might have something to do with the murder. We're not sure yet. We just need to explore a bit."

Offhandedly Brielle said, "If you need us to help explore, just yell."

They all laughed because they knew she meant it.

Marjoram and Pepper trotted up the steps after the girls.

Daisy quickly cleared the table and left the plate of cookies in the center. "We might need these," she said.

"What are you planning?" Claudia asked. "You told us to bring our laptops."

"I thought working on a laptop would be easier than working on our phones. This is what I think we need to do."

As they sipped tea and ate cookies, Daisy explained what Glorie Beck had told her about Althea, the conference she'd attended, the ID, the change in her personality, and the trips to Harrisburg and York. Afterward Daisy explained about going to Althea's daughter's home and how Phebe told her that something had happened with a phone call, the new quote she'd put up on her wall . . . how "lovers are doomed until eternity" meant something important to Althea.

"So what can we do?" Stella asked, looking more relaxed than the last time Daisy had seen her. She looked over at Claudia and said, "By the way, I did *not* start any rumors about you."

Claudia nodded. "I believe you. The person who started them is probably the killer. But rings of rumors just intertwine in a small town and you can never untangle them. Let's see what Daisy has in mind."

Daisy pulled out the conference brochure that had been in the envelope Althea had left with Glorie Beck. She showed the other two women the fake ID with *Thea Hathaway* printed on it.

"She had a secret life?" Claudia asked. "That doesn't seem like her at all."

"We all have more than one side," Stella said. "After I divorced, I was a different person. I did things I never thought I would do, thought things I never thought I'd think. I was filled with resentment, bitterness, and anger. It took a long while to find an even keel again. So Althea possibly having an affair— We'll just have to try to think of her as an ordinary woman who wanted a love of her own. If she was in a stale marriage, if she'd felt trapped into the life she'd settled for, a man who could bring her to life again might be all she'd ever wanted. She could have pushed her own marriage into the back of her head."

"If we use computer skills and track down the organizers of the conference, we might find things out. We might even be able to find this Will," Daisy decided. "If we do, then I think we'll be getting somewhere. Maybe we should each take one of the conference organizers. There are three names here—Calinda Dietz coordinated the total conference and the schedule. If we could get a list of her committee members, we'd be making headway. The second person to contact—I thought you could do that, Claudia—is Sue Henry. She's the one who put together all of the workshops. I'll take Ted Mann. He kept track of the conference attendees. I thought we could start by calling them. If that doesn't work, we can e-mail them. If we're lucky, they'll still have their files."

"From fifteen years ago?" Claudia asked.

"When I was a classroom teacher," Stella said, "I never threw anything away. You never know when you can use it. My guess is, each of these organizers has all their materials in envelopes or a drawer in their office or their desk. Let's get to work and see what we can find out. All the tea and cookies we can possibly drink and eat will help."

Stella went to the living room to make her phone call while Claudia stayed in the kitchen. Daisy migrated to her bedroom but left the door open.

Fifteen minutes later, they met back in the living room. They had all made contact with their targets. Daisy, Claudia, and Stella were expecting e-mails within a short amount of time. They came together at the table again and waited for dings or beeps.

"Do you really think we'll find him?" Stella asked.

"If his name's Will, we will," Daisy said, selecting another snickerdoodle from the plate because she was stress eating.

Stella's phone pinged first. She scrolled to the e-mail and scanned a list. "I don't see any Wills or Williams on here. Calinda even included periphery staff. Maybe this Will was a fake name like Thea."

Next Claudia's tablet dinged. She checked her e-mail and opened her list, which included the names of the presenters of each workshop. "No Wills or Williams here either," she said.

Daisy was beginning to lose hope. This *was* like looking for a needle in a haystack and it was a long shot.

When her phone played a tuba sound, she saw that

Ted had sent the list as a text message. With it appeared a PDF file.

"I have a printer in my bedroom," Daisy said. "I'll print this out and then we can look at it."

A few minutes later she was back in the living room with three sheets of paper. The conference had about one hundred and fifty attendees. Each of the women took one of the sheets. With steady intensity, they each went down their list of names. Daisy's finger stopped. She found what she was looking for.

"I have one. His name's Will Mooney." She looked over her list to make sure there weren't any other Wills or Williams. "It's the only one. It has to be him. Althea Higgins's name is on my list too," Daisy pointed out. "They both must have been attending the conference. Maybe they met there and, afterward for their liaisons, Althea used the name Thea Hathaway."

"Where does Will live?" asked Stella.

Daisy's gaze met hers. "He lives in Lancaster. Tomorrow after work, I'm going to pay him a visit."

The address for Will Mooney felt like a burr that was rubbing against Daisy's skin while she was making scones, cinnamon buns, and blueberry coffee cake in the tea garden the following day. She was planning what she'd say to the man. On the other hand, he might not even open the door to her. Should she just be forthright and pursue information that way?

Brielle and Jazzi had a peer counseling meeting after school. As soon as she counted receipts and money with Iris, she could be on her way to Lancaster and Will Mooney.

Finally, maybe there would be answers. She thought of calling Detective Rappaport or Zeke. She thought of calling Jonas. But she didn't really know anything. Once she had information in her pocket, so to speak, she'd talk to the authorities. If she didn't get any information, so be it.

Iris would be making the bank deposit tonight. Daisy was just grabbing her jacket and her purse when her cell phone played. She didn't recognize the number but she did recognize the caller ID. It came from The Style Corner. She recognized the name as a dress shop where Jazzi and Vi had often bought clothes. The styles there were for young adults so Daisy didn't often look there for her own fashions. Without knowing what to expect, whether or not she was going to receive a solicitation, she answered with a simple "Hello."

A male voice asked, "Can I speak with Daisy Swanson, please?"

"This is Daisy. What can I do for you? I was just on my way out."

"I have a situation here," the male said. "My name is Rudy Weber. I'm the owner of The Style Corner."

"I see," Daisy offered, though she really didn't see.

"There are two young women in my office. One says she's your daughter, Jasmine Swanson?"

Daisy's mother alert bell started ringing. "Yes, Jazzi's my daughter."

"There's another young woman here too. She says she's staying with you while her parents are out of the country."

"Yes, if you're talking about Brielle Horn. She is staying with me. But I don't understand. What's the situation? Did they come into your store to shop?" They were supposed to be at the high school!

"Yes, well, one of the young women, Brielle, tried to shoplift a scarf—a Hermès scarf."

There was no need for Brielle to shoplift *anything*. She'd told Daisy she was an authorized user on her mom's credit card. Before Daisy could ask any more questions, the man went on. "My security guard caught her in the act. We have it on video. I was going to call the police but your daughter begged me to call you instead. This is highly out of the ordinary, but she seemed quite well-spoken and she was very upset and she said that you could make things right."

Oh, if only Jazzi was right about that, Daisy thought. If only mothers could solve all the problems their children encountered.

"*Are* you going to call the police?" Daisy wanted to know.

"If I do that, this girl will be arrested and charged with retail theft. There are varying degrees of that. They would range from a simple citation all the way to a felony. This scarf, which was on sale, would require a simple citation. But if I call the police, she would be arrested, taken to the police station, photographed, and fingerprinted. After that, she would be released into her guardian's custody. A court date would be set and a judge would determine what happened next."

"I'm leaving the tea garden now. I can be there in fifteen minutes, twenty at the most depending on traffic. Can you please wait until I get there to make any decision?"

"Your daughter said you're the owner of Daisy's Tea Garden. My wife and I have been in and enjoyed tea several times."

"I own the tea garden with my aunt, Iris Albright. We

run it together. Jazzi works here. In fact, while Brielle has been staying with us, she's been working here with Jazzi some days busing tables. I can't express how much this situation upsets and terrifies me. My daughter's not a troublemaker. And from what I understand, Brielle isn't either. I spoke to the counselor at school about her before I decided to let her stay with us."

"You sound like a very responsible mother. I won't call the police or make a decision about it until you talk with me in person."

As Daisy flew out the door of the tea garden, she wondered just how responsible a mother she was if her daughter had become involved in a situation like *this*.

Chapter Eighteen

Jazzi hadn't said a word on the way home, and Brielle . . . Brielle had a look in her eyes that Daisy could only call defiant. But she wasn't saying anything either.

What did an adult do with one child who looked as if she was about to break into tears any minute, and another who looked as if she wanted to fight a mixed martial arts match? Could life get more complicated?

She shouldn't even ask.

Once inside the house, they all took off their jackets and hung them in the closet and Daisy pointed to the living room. "Go sit. We're going to talk."

"Oh, Mom," came out of Jazzi's mouth.

A tight "Mrs. Swanson" came out of Brielle's.

But Daisy didn't pay any attention. She didn't care if the girls liked her at this moment. They had to get something straight. She pointed to the sofa again.

Marjoram and Pepper came hopping down the steps from upstairs. Marjoram went to Daisy and sat on her foot. Pepper, however, took one look at her and turned in the other direction toward the kitchen. Pepper didn't like direct confrontation and Daisy's cats always picked up on the moods in the home.

To calm herself down, Daisy picked up Marjoram and snuggled her around the neck. The cat didn't squiggle as she usually did when someone picked her up. Daisy thought, not for the first time, that the cats had more emotional intelligence than many humans.

The two girls were sitting on the sofa. Daisy chose the armchair with the hassock and carefully settled Marjoram on that. The feline sat there in a bread loaf position as if she wanted to be part of this discussion. Maybe she'd have more wise words to share than Daisy did.

Daisy began with, "Brielle, you should have thanked the store manager for his kindness. If he had called the police, you would have had a mark on your record, one way or another. They could have given you a citation, finger-printed and booked you, and brought you before a judge. Do you understand that?"

Brielle said nothing.

Daisy turned her attention to her daughter. "You could have been arrested as an accomplice."

"But I didn't *do* anything," came out of Jazzi's mouth.

"You were with Brielle and she shoplifted. How would anyone know that you weren't going to shoplift too?"

"But I *wouldn't* have. I didn't know what Brielle was going to do."

Daisy eyed Brielle. "Did you plan to go into that store and take something?"

Brielle wouldn't look at Daisy, but she shook her head.

Trying another direction to move this discussion, Daisy said, "Brielle, Jazzi and I have an agreement. It has to do with phone privileges and curfews and chores and merely our daily life. Since she's a minor, I want to know at all times where she is. I don't have that phone app that tracks her phone, but after today maybe I'll put it on my phone and use it. Mostly, she and I have respect for each other. She knows where I am, and I know where she is. If plans change, we text each other or call each other. Do you understand that?"

Again Brielle wouldn't look at Daisy . . . but she nodded.

"The two of you were supposed to be at a peer counseling meeting. I want to know how you got from school to The Style Corner. Let's start with that."

When Brielle didn't say anything, Jazzi leaned forward, stroked Marjoram's head, and looked at her mom. "Brielle thought it would be fun if we went shopping. Peer counseling broke up early. So she called her housekeeper and she came and picked us up and took us into town."

"You mean into Lancaster, not to downtown Willow Creek."

"Yes, into Lancaster, Mom. I don't get much chance to go to those shops."

Even though Jazzi was driving, she didn't have her own car yet, and she didn't often ask for Daisy's. So it was true she had to go where Daisy took her. But she hadn't expressed an interest in going to downtown Lancaster. Maybe Daisy had missed that wish of her daughter's or just hadn't listened.

"Was there anything in particular you were going to shop for?" Daisy asked, trying to get to the bottom of this.

"Brielle wanted to buy a new outfit, and I thought if I could find a top or something on sale, I could use my money for that."

"Did you buy a new outfit, Brielle?"

"No, I didn't," Brielle said tightly.

Jazzi nudged Brielle's arm. "Why did you shoplift when you have your mom's credit card and you're authorized to use it? I don't get it. Why would you get me in trouble with you?"

Hunching her shoulders, Brielle admitted, "I wasn't trying to get anybody in trouble. I thought I could get away with it."

"Brielle! Do you realize what you just said?" Daisy asked, astonished. "You wanted to get away with stealing."

"It was only a scarf," she mumbled. But this time her voice caught. She wasn't as unaffected as she was making herself out to be. That was a good thing.

Daisy gentled her voice. "Brielle, I said you could stay here with Jazzi because I thought the two of you would become good friends and it would be good for both of you. But I never expected you to get her into trouble."

Brielle put her elbows on her knees and dropped her head into her hands.

Softer now, Daisy asked, "Tell me why you did it, honey."

It must have been the "honey" that broke Brielle's defenses. When she looked up, her eyes were filled with tears. "Mom texted me earlier today and sent photos. Only she's in the photos, so I don't know where Dad was. She looked like she was having a great time with the ski instructor. If she was with him, Dad was probably off on his own. That's what they're like at home. Separate. They don't care about me. Jazzi has *two* moms and they both love her. You adopted her and you treat her as if she's the same as Vi."

Daisy's heart ached for Brielle. She knew the teenager wanted her parents to grow closer on this trip, not further apart. "Jazzi is the child of my heart, just like Vi is. It doesn't matter that she didn't come out of my body."

"See what I mean?" Brielle said to Jazzi as she turned toward her. "You have so much love you don't know what to do with it all. And then there's Portia. I can see in her eyes that she thinks the sun rises and sets with you. I get that you don't have a dad, but you had one and he loved you. You don't need one, with two moms and a sister and brother-in-law who love you. Jazzi, do you know how lucky you are?"

Jazzi's eyes filled with tears too. "I didn't know you felt that way. I guess I take it all for granted most of the time. You have your grammy. *She* loves you."

At the bottom of all this, Daisy knew what the problem was. Brielle didn't feel lovable. That was because of her parents' attitude.

Rising from her chair, Daisy crossed to the sofa and sat on the other side of Brielle. Without hesitating, she hung her arm around the girl's shoulders. Brielle turned into her and cried. Daisy let her sob for a while as Jazzi handed Brielle tissues.

Finally Brielle blew her nose and wiped her tears away.

Daisy lifted the girl's chin. "I want you to know something, and it isn't like anything you learn in school."

Brielle's wide eyes stayed on Daisy's.

Daisy went on, "You deserve to be loved. Everyone does. Sometimes maybe we don't do things that we think anyone will love us for." She pointed to Brielle's chest. "But you have a good heart. Jazzi recognized that right away and so did I. I want you to know you're part of our family now too. We have a crazy family sometimes. My mom and I didn't always get along. My sister and I don't always get along. Vi and Jazzi don't always get along. But we all love each other and we're family. You are now included in that craziness."

Brielle sniffed. "You mean, you don't want me to leave?"

"Do you *want* to leave?"

"No, I don't want to leave. I want to stay here with you as long as I can. But I know you're going to get tired of me."

"Maybe we will," Daisy said with a bit of a smile. "But that doesn't mean we'll stop caring, and that doesn't mean you won't have a place here."

Brielle gave her a very small smile. "Thank you."

Daisy could tell that "thank you" came from the bottom of Brielle's heart.

"But there are repercussions from today. Brielle, there's something I want you to do for me."

"Anything," Brielle said.

"I want you to e-mail Mr. Weber. Thank him for not calling the police, and assure him again that you will perform the fifty hours of community service he and I agreed on by working at A Penny Saved. It will help convince him that you're responsible. Can you do that?"

Brielle looked at Jazzi. "Will you look over it after I write it to make sure I did it right?"

"Sure, I will," Jazzi said.

"Jazzi, for your part in this situation, I want you to work at least ten hours at A Penny Saved. I'll set it up with Amelia."

"I'll fit it in somehow, Mom. And I promise I'll let you know where I am. If you want to put that tracking app on our phones, you can."

"Let's just table that for now."

Daisy glanced into the kitchen. "I didn't have anything planned for supper tonight because I was going to run errands before picking you up."

Jazzi asked, "Do you want to run those errands now?"

Daisy thought about visiting Will Mooney and the questions she wanted to ask him. But maybe that deserved more thought and input from Tessa. "No errands tonight," she said. "How about we make omelets and put in anything we can find in the refrigerator that we think would be good?"

"Peppers too?" Brielle asked. "My dad hates peppers."

"I think I have a pepper or two in there. I know I have cheese, ham, maybe even some asparagus." Both girls turned up their noses.

"Don't knock it until you try it. I have salsa to put over the whole thing after it's done."

Daisy stood and Jazzi came over to give her a hug. "Thank you, Mom. Thank you for getting us out of the mess. I promise that you won't have to clean up any more of my messes."

Daisy wasn't sure that day would ever come. After all, she was a mom, and moms helped right their children's lives no matter how old they were.

Last evening, after Jazzi and Brielle had gone to their rooms, Daisy had called her mother. In the past, it wasn't something she would have done. But after everything that had happened, the talks they'd had, the secret that her mother had divulged, Daisy felt the need for advice. There were times when a woman just needed her mom.

She'd asked her mom to meet her in the back booth of Sarah Jane's for lunch.

Daisy was a little nervous about this talk with her mother. In the past, she would have been afraid to confide in her, thinking her mom would blame her for whatever the problem was. And maybe she still would. Maybe this situation with Brielle and Jazzi *was* all Daisy's fault.

Her mother came rushing into Sarah Jane's, saw Daisy in the back booth, and headed her way. She sat across from Daisy, curiosity in her expression. "You said this was an emergency."

"Thanks for coming at the last minute. I know you're really busy at the nursery right now. Spring is your busiest season."

"It is," Rose agreed, shrugging out of her jacket and laying it on the seat next to her. "But I deserve an hour to myself now and then too. I just told your dad I was having lunch with you so he wouldn't worry. But I've been worrying. What's going on?"

"As I told you, nobody was hurt or anything like that. I just need some advice."

A waitress, one who Daisy knew, came to their table with a smile and two menus. "What can I get you to drink?" Joanie asked.

"Just water," both Daisy and her mother said at the same time.

"Do you want to order?" Rose asked. "Then we won't be interrupted much."

Daisy nodded. "I saw the special today is shepherd's pie. I'll take that with coleslaw."

"Same for me," Rose said, handing Joanie her menu.

Daisy did the same. Minutes later Joanie had brought their waters and said the food would soon be out.

Rose took a sip of water, then reached across the table and patted Daisy's hand. "Come on, tell me what's going on. Isn't Jazzi's time with Brielle working out?"

"How did you guess?" Daisy asked.

"It's not easy to take in a stranger. You didn't know that much about her. Is she causing a disruption with Jazzi? Didn't Portia's visit go well?"

"Portia's visit went fine. I thought for a while that Brielle felt left out."

"Iris told me you took her into the tea garden so Jazzi and Portia could spend time together."

"I did, but something happened there that upset Brielle." Daisy told her mother what the customer had said and Brielle's reaction to it.

"It sounds as if you handled that well."

"I thought I had. I thought I was beginning to know Brielle and how she was feeling. But I got a call yesterday from the owner of The Style Corner in Lancaster. Brielle had shoplifted a scarf and Jazzi was with her. They were supposed to be at an after-school meeting. Jazzi never lies to me. It's hard for me to believe she would have had anything to do with the shoplifting."

Instead of jumping on Jazzi's actions as she once might have, Rose asked, "What did you do?"

"This incident could have gone on Brielle's permanent record . . . and Jazzi's too. The store owner thought Jazzi was an accomplice. Fortunately, after we talked, he was understanding. He's been in at the tea garden. We worked it out. Brielle's going to do fifty hours of community service at A Penny Saved. Jazzi's going to do ten. Apparently

Jazzi didn't know what Brielle wanted to do. Brielle's housekeeper picked them up and took them shopping. I think Jazzi was afraid of my disapproval so she didn't tell me. When the excursion turned into shoplifting instead, Jazzi was mortified."

"Can you ground someone else's teenager?" her mother asked. "Because that's what I would have done."

"As soon as we got home, I confronted both of them. At first Brielle was defiant but then the truth came out." Daisy leaned in toward her mother. "I feel so bad for her, Mom. She sees Jazzi and who she has around her who love her—me and Portia, you and Dad, Iris and Tessa. She's said Jazzi has two moms who love her and Brielle feels she doesn't even have one."

"What kind of parents are they?" her mother asked. "I mean, I know I made mistakes. We've certainly talked about those. But if they're lawyers, they have to be intelligent."

"That doesn't mean they understand a child," Daisy offered. "I'm not sure Brielle has ever gotten the love she needs or deserves. She's had material possessions, but even she knows that's not what matters. She wants to go live with her grammy, Glorie Beck. Glorie could use somebody around, and I think Brielle needs her. But that's a conversation for after her parents return home. In the meantime, I have to decide the best way to deal with her."

"And that's why you want my advice?"

"Yes, it is. Raising Vi and Jazzi was not the same as this. What if Brielle had actually been arrested? What would I have done?"

"You would have gotten her parents on the phone and

told one of them to come right home. You know, this isn't your responsibility, Daisy. Brielle is *their* responsibility."

"I know, and I need to talk to her mother or father or both of them as soon as they have time to listen. But they're traveling right now, skiing in the Alps or something."

"You don't show your disdain for them around Brielle, do you?" Her mother's question didn't have criticism in it.

"I try not to. I try to be positive. But that's hard, especially when I know how Brielle feels. I can't turn her over to Glorie without her parents' permission. Actually, in the state Brielle's in right now, with a real lack of self-worth, she's probably better off with me and Jazzi."

"Create boundaries, Daisy. That's what you have to do. Give her structure. Apparently Brielle hasn't had rules or chores."

"She has chores while she stays with me. There hasn't been a need for rules before now."

"Make them and make sure she sticks to them. Jazzi will understand. I'm surprised she's still speaking to Brielle."

"Last night when we were alone, she asked me if Brielle stole the scarf to get attention. I told her that was one reason, so I think she understands."

"One time, she'll probably forgive. More than one, she probably won't. Maybe you should tell Brielle that."

"Maybe. Or maybe Jazzi should."

Rose nodded. "You're right there. You're handling this, Daisy." Her mother finally smiled. "I'm not sure you need my advice. I want to ask you something and I don't want you to get upset," her mother said.

Daisy had a suspicion what was coming. "Go ahead."

"Have you and Jonas talked? Your father ran into him when he was making a delivery. He said Jonas didn't look happy, and Jonas said he hadn't seen you for a while. Did something happen?"

This was a dilemma. Her mother had never been enthusiastic about her dating Jonas. Now she wasn't sure what to say.

"Jonas seems to be working through his past—the fact that his partner got pregnant, that she died on what he considered his watch, and that Zeke told him that the child might be his, not Jonas's."

"I thought the two of you were working on that together."

"We were, but I wanted him and Zeke to be friends again. I went to Zeke to talk to him about it and I shouldn't have. Jonas considered that a breach of trust, and then he saw me and Gavin together at the children's tea."

Daisy felt tears burning in her eyes. "I don't know what to do. He doesn't want to talk to me."

Her mother leaned across and took both of her hands in hers and squeezed. "If he loves you, and I think he does, he'll forgive you. Are you going to be able to forgive the heartache he's putting you through?"

"Of course I can. But Brenda broke his trust too, and so did Zeke. What if mine is the last straw?"

Frowning, her mother moved her silverware around and said what she was thinking. "I know this isn't what you want to hear," her mom warned. "But if Jonas doesn't come around, you *will* find love again. You are the kind of woman who men are lucky to have in their lives. I think it's harder for men to swallow their pride than women, and Jonas has to do that on a couple of fronts. Keep yourself busy, hold Sammy tight, and give Jonas more time. I don't think you'll be sorry if you do that."

Opening up real conversations with her mother had meant the world to Daisy. Today was a day she'd looked forward to all of her life. She could confide in her mother and feel accepted.

Their waitress arrived with a tray with two steaming dishes of shepherd's pie and two smaller dishes of cole-slaw. After she set it all down, she asked if they needed anything else. When they said they didn't, she left the table.

Before they went on to other subjects, before the timbre of their conversation changed, Daisy said, "Thank you for coming today, Mom. It means a lot."

"Thanks for asking me. That means a lot too."

Daisy picked up her fork, knowing having lunch with her mother wouldn't be the ordeal it used to be. Sure, she knew they'd have disagreements again. Sure, her mother might even disapprove of her methods of raising kids or something else she did. But now they seemed to have an understanding. That understanding would be the basis for them going forward.

They were enjoying their meal together when the tuba sound erupted from Daisy's purse. She quickly dove for it and saw that the caller was Stella.

Her mother waved at her phone. "Go ahead and take it. I don't mind."

Since they were in the back booth and the booth in front of them was empty, Daisy knew she could keep her voice low and not bother anyone else in the restaurant. "Hi, Stella."

"Have you given any more thought to the job training

program for the homeless shelter? I really think you'd be an asset." Stella had asked if she wanted to be involved and she hadn't given an answer.

"How soon do you need an answer?" Daisy asked. The situation with Brielle might take up more time than she thought it would. She didn't want to commit to something and not be able to do it.

"Within the next few weeks."

"Are *you* going to help?" Daisy asked.

"I might volunteer to counsel in the evenings. I like to keep busy. Sometimes the evenings and the nights are long. So the homeless shelter might benefit me as much as anyone I help."

"Are you still worrying about the police thinking you're a suspect?" Daisy glanced at her mom. She usually didn't tell her much about the investigations that she was involved in, but maybe the time for that secrecy was over too. Maybe it was time for everything to be out in the open.

"I haven't heard from them lately. I haven't heard any more rumors either. Though I do think Claudia is considering resigning."

"Why?"

"Althea's death has really spooked her, and I've got to admit, I think about Claudia's major question to me too."

"What was the question?"

"She asked what if the killer is one of the teachers?"

"I can't say I blame her, I guess. But if all of you felt that way, everybody would resign."

"She somehow feels she's a target, but I'm not sure why."

"Maybe because of the rumors," Daisy offered.

"That could be it. There was tension between Althea

and so many people, not just the teachers. I can see that the police are going to have trouble solving this. Are you still going to question Will Mooney?"

"As soon as I get the chance."

After another minute or so, she ended the call. Looking up, she saw Trevor waving at her from the front of the restaurant. He came her way. After hellos all around, he sat in the empty booth in front of where Daisy and her mom were sitting.

Her mother asked, "I heard Tessa and Trevor have been dating since Thanksgiving. Are they serious now?" She'd kept her voice low.

"They seem to be getting along well. It would be nice if they decided to commit to each other."

"If they're right for each other," her mother said. After a pause, Rose gingerly noted, "I heard you talking on the phone. So you're involved in the investigation?"

"Not really. I've asked a few questions." She studied her mother, and then she said in the same low voice her mother had used, "Althea seemed to have a second life. I think she was dating a married man. I'm thinking about talking to him."

"Do you know who the man is? I mean, have you met him before, or has anyone you know met him before?"

"No."

"Daisy," her mother said with that exasperation in her tone that Daisy knew well. She suspected what was coming.

"You think I'm going to tell you not to do it."

"Aren't you?"

"No. But what I'm going to tell you is—if you have to do it, don't do it alone. Make sure you have some kind of backup. If it can't be Jonas, make sure it's someone else."

Daisy looked over at Trevor, who was studying his menu.

Glancing over her shoulder, her mother said with resignation, "It wouldn't hurt to have a man backing you up. Trevor's tall and muscled."

"Mom."

Her mother smiled. "I'm serious, honey. Talking to a stranger about an affair he might have had could be more dangerous than you think."

Daisy didn't rush through lunch with her mom. She wanted to give her mother as much time as she wanted to chat. Eventually, however, Rose said, "I'd better get back to the nursery. I don't want to leave your dad in the lurch. He counts on me to keep things organized behind the desk."

Her father did count on her mother, and her mother counted on him. That had been her example growing up, and her example now.

After her mom left, Trevor was still eating. Daisy hopped out of her booth and went over to Trevor's.

Trevor pointed to his coffee. "I was just about to order dessert. Do you want to join me?"

"No dessert, but I do want to join you."

Trevor was wearing a beige polo shirt with khakis and a brown denim vest. He looked unwrinkled and spiffy.

Daisy said, "I'd like to go over the suspect pool for Althea."

Trevor rubbed his hands together. "Nothing I'd like better. This surprises me. You weren't getting involved the last time we talked."

"Someone was tracking me," Daisy revealed.

"Tracking you?" He looked genuinely surprised.

"There was a tracker on both my PT Cruiser and the van. Foster goes over both vehicles every morning with a scanner to make sure nothing's hidden on there now." Daisy stared at Trevor. "Who do you think the suspects are?"

He held up one finger at a time. "Harry Silverman, of course. Lucius Higgins and Phebe Higgins. Then there are the two teachers that the police have their eye on— Stella Cotton and Claudia Moore."

Trevor went over his reasons to believe those suspects had motive. "Harry Silverman might still have revenge on his mind. Lucius gained from his grandmother's death. Phebe might have known about the will and been resentful for the will leaving her son Althea's estate. I think the teachers' motives are a little less potent. Of course, we could be missing something. But straight out not liking someone and arguing with them doesn't seem rage-filled enough or passion-filled enough for either teacher to commit murder."

"Speaking of passion," Daisy said, keeping her voice low.

"Are we going to talk about you and Jonas?" Trevor asked eagerly.

Daisy had no doubts that Tessa had spoken to Trevor about her and Jonas. "We're not," Daisy objected firmly. "Jonas doesn't want to talk to me."

Trevor gave Daisy an odd questioning look. "You do know this is the twenty-first century. We're not living in the nineteen fifties or the nineteen sixties or even the nineteen seventies when women had to stand down. Now you can go right up to a man and say what you want."

"I tried that and it didn't work," Daisy protested. "I

don't want to talk about me and Jonas. I do want to talk
about Althea and maybe her lover."

That got Trevor's attention.

Daisy explained about Althea and Will.

"Hathaway," Trevor repeated. "Wasn't that the name of
William Shakespeare's wife?"

"It was—Anne Hathaway. There's definitely symbolism
there."

"So what do you want to do?" Trevor asked.

"I want to go to Will Mooney's home. I want to talk
to him."

Trevor said, "You can't go alone."

Daisy rolled her eyes. "You sound just like my mother.
She said the same thing."

After studying her for a long moment, he concluded,
"I think it's simple. I should go with you."

Daisy's response was immediate. "Do you want to
go now?"

He grinned. "I'm free."

Daisy decided, "I'll give Tessa a call. If the tea garden
is calm, we can make a quick trip to Will Mooney's house.
I'll tell her I'm going with you to keep her in the loop.
For all we know, no one will be home. For all we know,
the man won't talk to us."

Daisy took out her phone and called Tessa.

Chapter Nineteen

Daisy sat in the back seat of Trevor's sporty red sedan. He himself admitted that he'd bought the car because he'd wanted to be noticed. He wasn't a reporter who wanted to fly under the radar or stand behind the crime scene tape. Sometimes his in-your-face style alienated officials. But when Trevor was out to get a story, he did that. That's why Daisy appreciated the respect they had between them. If she didn't want to reveal details in an investigation, he waited until she did. It was a deal they'd made several times, including today as he drove to the address Daisy had given him for his GPS.

Daisy was nervous but tried not to show it.

She hadn't known what to expect at the address in Lancaster. What they found were two cement tracks with mown grass running down the center that led to a single-car garage. Trevor turned into the so-called driveway.

Eying the house, Daisy saw that it was a Dutch Colonial. The windows all looked like replacement windows. The lot itself might be a third of an acre and was dotted with mature trees—maples and elms—and a variety of bushes along the front from arborvitae to boxwood. An interlocking cement-block retaining wall lined both sides of the path to the front door from the driveway. A side entrance farther up the lane toward the garage was covered with an awning roof. The home looked well-kept and maintained as did the grounds.

"Let's do this," Daisy said to Trevor. They both unlatched their seat belts and opened their doors.

Trevor and Daisy didn't speak as they walked up the path to the front door. Once there, Daisy hesitated, then pushed the doorbell.

A moment or so later, a man who looked to be much older than Daisy's dad opened the door. She guessed he was around seventy. He had a long oval face and white to gray hair that he had slicked back over his forehead. His heavy mustache was also gray and white and dipped over his lips on either side. Large tortoiseshell glasses balanced on the bridge of his nose. He was wearing a blue plaid shirt and jeans along with black high-top sneakers.

Daisy took the lead as she and Trevor had discussed. "I'm Daisy Swanson," she said. "I own Daisy's Tea Garden in Willow Creek."

"I've never heard of it," the man responded gruffly.

"Are you Will Mooney?" Daisy asked.

He frowned. "I am. Did something happen at your tea garden that concerns me?"

Stepping forward, Trevor introduced himself. "I'm Trevor Lundquist, a friend of Mrs. Swanson. My girlfriend and Daisy were both acquainted with Althea Higgins."

At Althea's name, Will Mooney's face went white.

Suddenly a woman stood behind Will. "What do they want?" she asked him. "Are they selling something?"

The woman who had appeared behind Will was dressed

in an orange knit top and gray sweatpants. She looked to be his age, maybe a couple of years younger. Her hair was curly and steel gray, like a bubble over her head. Gold hoop earrings dangled from both ears and she wore orange lipstick. She had a wide mouth and brown eyes behind rimless glasses. She was staring at Daisy and Trevor with open curiosity. Overweight, her round bosom and belly were about double the size of Will's.

Will stepped aside so the woman behind him could come forward. He said to her, "They want to talk about Althea."

The woman gave Will a sideways glare and her lips pressed together. After a moment, she asked sharply, "Why are you asking?"

Daisy said, "Althea Higgins was my teacher when I went to school. I'm searching through her background to see who might have hurt her."

The woman scoffed, "Teacher, my foot. That woman was a home wrecker. I told her to stay away from my husband, and she did. I don't have anything else to say on the subject, and neither does he."

Will patted his wife's shoulder. "Go on inside. I'll just talk to them a minute or two, then I'll be in, I promise."

Will's wife narrowed her eyes at him, turned, and went inside.

Lowering his voice, Will asked, "What do you know about me? What led you here?"

"We put a few pieces together that Althea left behind," Daisy answered. "I know you met Althea at a conference on how to teach Shakespeare to children. I think there was a lot more to your meeting than that. Althea saved the brochure and there was a note in it from you. I believe afterward she used the name Thea Hathaway. Her fake ID was with your note."

With his voice lowered, Will looked over his shoulder. Then he said, "When my wife found out about the affair, Kay physically confronted Althea. She pushed her and knocked her down. I . . ." His face reddened. "I didn't want anything to happen to Thea. Look, I have to get back inside."

Daisy had been ready for something like this. She pulled a card from her pocket and handed it to him. "This is my contact information. You can get hold of me at the tea garden. My cell phone number is on the back. I'd like to talk to you more about this." She hesitated, then added, "Before I give any information to the police."

Will's face went even paler, if that was possible. He nodded. "I'll be in touch." Then he stepped back inside and closed the door.

Daisy and Trevor swiveled from the door at the same time. "Do you think he will be?" Trevor asked.

Daisy started down the front path. "I don't know. I'll give him twenty-four hours. But if I don't hear from him by then, I'll have to tell the police what I know. It might not have anything to do with Althea's murder, but it might too. His wife looks capable of murderous rage, don't you think?"

Trevor sighed. "A woman scorned and all that. I'd say it's a good possibility."

The next day, Tessa had the day off. Iris, Tessa, Cora Sue, and Daisy were all full-time and each took off one day a week. On days like this, Cora Sue worked in the kitchen to cover for Tessa, and Foster served along with Jada and Tamlyn. The tourist season had been picking up week by week. The long tourist buggy with its six horses had traveled up and down the street at least once every two hours with sightseers who wanted to enjoy an actual buggy ride.

Daisy was peering out the window in the spillover tearoom, watching the happy faces on the tourists, when her cell phone played. She took it out of her pocket, and she didn't recognize the number. A scam call? She'd been getting more of those even though she blocked them when they came in. Or . . . hoping beyond hope, she answered, "Hello?"

"Mrs. Swanson, it's Will Mooney."

"Hello, Mr. Mooney. I was hoping you'd call."

"I have to be quick. My wife went outside to tend to the garden. Can you meet me in the parking lot at the American Music Theater in a half hour? I'll tell Kay I have errands to run and she won't think anything of it."

The American Music Theater, a Lancaster County events facility that hosted live concerts with renowned entertainers, was about twenty minutes away. Daisy knew the meeting itself probably wouldn't take long if Will wanted to get home to his wife before she became suspicious. That meant she'd be gone an hour, maybe an hour and a half at most. The tearoom had slowed down this afternoon as the buses that had stopped in the public lot went on to Kitchen Kettle Village at Intercourse or even to the outlet mall in Lancaster.

She motioned to Foster.

Crossing to her quickly, he asked her, "What's up?"

"Can you cover for me for an hour and a half?"

"Sure. No class tonight so I intended to work a full shift and then go home to Vi and Sammy."

"That sounds good."

"Does this have something to do with the investigation?" he asked with interest.

"It might. I'm going to meet Will Mooney at the American Music Theater's parking lot."

She got back to Will on her cell phone. "No problem. I'll be there in half an hour."

After she ended the call, Foster asked, "Isn't anybody going with you?"

"I'm going to call Tessa and see if she can meet me there. And if she can't, maybe Trevor can. You know where I'm going, and certainly there will be people around."

"I know I can't come with you because I'm needed here. What about Jonas?"

Daisy stared down at her yellow clogs, thinking about what to say. She hadn't talked about Jonas with Violet and Foster.

"Are you still not speaking to him?" Foster asked, almost like a father would.

"Foster, Jonas and I will take care of our relationship. Right now, we're giving each other time."

"What you mean is—that he's ghosting you."

"He's *what*?"

"You should be up on the latest slang since Jazzi's a teen. Ghosting is when a guy won't answer your texts or disappears."

"Jonas hasn't disappeared."

"Well, he might as well have."

Exasperated, she explained, "I just saw him the day of the children's tea. As I said, we need time."

Foster gave her a sideways glance, then lifted his hands in surrender. "Fine. I'll give you two hours, and if you aren't back, then I call Jonas or Zeke or Detective Rappaport. Got it?"

Daisy shook her head. "You've matured too much since you've gotten married and had a child."

He grinned at her. "That's the best compliment you've ever given me."

Daisy smiled a bit as she snatched her jacket and her purse and went out the back door, heading for her car. She tried calling Tessa and reached voice mail. So she texted Tessa where she'd be. When she called Trevor, she also only reached voice mail. She texted him too. I'll be at the American Music Theater in half an hour to meet Will Mooney. Just wanted you and Tessa to know.

They were probably together. She wouldn't think about when, where, or what they were doing.

Twenty minutes later she was pulling into the parking lot at the theater. She suddenly realized she had no idea what Will's car looked like or he hers. As she had his number, she texted him. I'm here in the purple PT Cruiser.

The parking lot was practically empty. But she soon saw Will emerge from a white pickup truck and head her way. She kept her cell phone in her hand just in case. Just in case of what, she didn't know.

"I don't have much time," he said.

"That's fine. As quickly as you can, tell me the truth about you and Althea."

Will's face fell and he really looked grief-stricken. She

tried not to feel sorry for him because she didn't know if he could be the murderer.

The breeze lifted his thinning hair and he brushed it back into place. "Althea and I did meet at that conference in 2005. We kept up an affair for two years. I claimed I was coaching the debate team during that time, but I wasn't. There are often meets in nearby towns so Althea and I would meet wherever those meets were taking place."

"You were both married." Daisy attempted to keep judgment from her voice. "I guess neither of you were happy in your marriage."

Will shifted from one hip to the other. "Thea's husband didn't pay much attention to her. It was no problem for her to get away. When she met me at a hotel or motel, she used the name Thea Hathaway. My wife and I had lost our connection. Kay thought it was just part of me earning a living as a teacher to go away to debate meets until she stumbled upon the fact that a debate was cancelled for one of the weekends Thea and I went anyway. It was stupid for us not to check the last-minute schedule. Maybe I wanted to get caught because I knew it was wrong. I don't know. I just knew Thea gave me understanding and . . ." He suddenly cut off his words. "Anyway, that was that. At least for then."

"You said your wife accosted Althea. After that, did you and Kay patch things up?"

Looking pained, he admitted, "We went to counseling—about six sessions. Kay said if I never mentioned Thea's name after the counseling sessions, she wouldn't divorce me. So that's the way it stood."

"Until it didn't?" Daisy guessed.

Will leaned against Daisy's car and looked about as sad

as she'd ever seen a man look. "I knew Thea's husband had died. I saw the obituary. But I didn't contact her because my marriage vows *did* mean something to me. Even though my marriage was rocky, I had made a commitment a second time."

"But something else happened?"

"A week before Thea was killed, she called me. We had dinner together. That dinner convinced me I was stupid for staying in a marriage I didn't want to be in. Thea . . ." His voice caught. He cleared his throat and continued. "She said she was going to retire and maybe we could spend more time together, even if we simply did it as friends. But I wanted to be more than a friend. Now I want out of a marriage that isn't working."

Daisy stared him straight in the eyes. "Are you telling me that you loved Althea and you had nothing to do with her murder?"

Looking horrified at the thought that he could have, he raised his hand as if he was swearing on a Bible in a court of law. "I promise you, I never would have done anything to hurt Thea. Never. I had nothing to do with what happened to her."

"Do you have an alibi?" Daisy probed.

"I do. I was substituting, teaching *Much Ado About Nothing* to a class of eleventh graders that day."

Daisy figured she might as well keep pushing. "Let me ask you—does your wife work?"

"She works part-time at Walmart. Why?"

"Do you know if she was working the day of Althea's murder?"

Will rubbed his hand down his face, then closed his eyes as if he didn't want to think about it. "I don't always know her schedule. I'm not sure what time she was working that day."

"Do you think Kay has enough anger and resentment that she'd want to kill Althea? That she'd be *able* to kill Althea?"

Will's jaw went slack and his eyes grew wide. "I can't believe she would do that."

"Does your wife have access to your phone records?"

"We're on the same plan, so I suppose she could if she looked."

It wasn't difficult to calculate the fact that Will's wife might have never forgiven him, that she had radar where he was concerned, that she could see that Althea had phoned him or he'd phoned Althea.

Daisy spotted Trevor's car spin into the parking lot at a speed higher than it should have. She could see that Tessa was with him. They spotted her and drove over to a parking spot nearby where she and Will were talking.

Will looked shaken to his very core as he stared at Trevor and Tessa. "I have to go. I don't know anything else. Are you going to tell the police what I told you?"

"I have to."

"It doesn't matter," he said, shaking his head. "I'm leaving Kay anyway."

Then Will hurried to his truck, climbed inside, backed out of the parking space, and drove away.

Tessa and Trevor came over to her. Before they could say anything, she said, "I have to text Foster so he knows I'm okay. I told him where I'd be." It only took her a few seconds to send him a text. Then she told Tessa and Trevor what Will had revealed to her.

"Are you going to call Jonas?" Tessa inquired.

Daisy shook her head. "He doesn't need to be involved in this."

After Tessa exchanged a look with Trevor, he said matter-of-factly, "Then you need to call either Detective Willet or Detective Rappaport right now."

Daisy knew he was right.

As she made the call, Tessa and Trevor watched over her as if they were afraid she was in danger right then. However, she couldn't reach either Detective Rappaport or Detective Willet. She didn't want to blurt it all out in a voice mail message, but neither man was picking up. She did the only thing she could. She left a message with the office voice mail—"I need to talk to Detective Rappaport or Detective Willet because of information I have about the Althea Higgins case." She also left messages on each of their cell phones. Hopefully one of them would get back to her soon.

That evening, Daisy was in the kitchen emptying the dishwasher when the doorbell rang.

Checking her phone and the monitoring app there, she saw Zeke Willet was standing outside her door.

Jazzi and Brielle were upstairs. Jazzi had an app on her phone too, so Daisy knew her daughter wouldn't bother running down the stairs. Closing the dishwasher, Daisy wiped her hands on a dish towel and went to the door. She hadn't expected Zeke to come to the house. Maybe he sensed this was serious.

She opened the door to Zeke as he was shoving his hand through his hair, as if he was thinking about his appearance now that he stood at her door. "I got your message. So did Detective Rappaport. So did our office machine. Considering you left a message at all three places, Detective Rappaport and I decided I should pay you a visit."

"Come on in," she said, gesturing inside.

Zeke's sport jacket was rumpled and his tie a bit askew. He looked as if he'd had a long day . . . or maybe a long week.

She asked, "Are you finished for the day?"

"Do you mean, am I going to go back to the office and maybe sleep there tonight?"

"I wondered if you could take a break, have a cup of tea or coffee, and maybe a slice of blueberry coffee cake. I brought a pan home for the girls for supper. There are a few pieces left."

He studied her and sighed. "You *are* the nurturing type, aren't you?"

She wrinkled her nose at him. "That doesn't sound like a compliment. I do like to cook. And if there's someone around who likes to eat it . . ." She trailed off, then added, "Isn't that what the tea garden's all about?"

Studying her again as if his dark brown eyes were trying to figure something out, he nodded. "All right. I'll have a cup of your famous tea and a piece of blueberry coffee cake. This *is* my supper break. I was going to grab something at the fast food restaurant on the way back."

"Fast food," she scoffed. "How about a meatloaf sandwich?"

"Are you trying to bribe me?" This time there was humor in his voice.

"Not a chance, Detective. I could be arrested for that."

He finally chuckled and followed her to the kitchen.

Daisy was hoping he wouldn't ask about Jonas. And he didn't. By the time he'd finished his sandwich, drained half of his tea, and started in on the blueberry coffee cake, Zeke looked more relaxed.

She had busied herself around the kitchen, not wanting to make small talk. She was putting the last clean dish away from the dishwasher when Zeke leaned back in his chair.

She said conversationally, "You really should take better care of yourself—regular meals, a few more hours of sleep."

He drained the rest of his mug. "Do you think that would make me more productive?"

"I don't know, but you might feel more alert and maybe more energetic."

He gave a sound that might have been approval or disapproval. He sat up straighter, pushed his plate to the side of the island's counter, and said, "Tell me what you've got."

"There are two parts to this," she explained, taking the envelope Glorie Beck had given her from one of the drawers. When she laid it in front of him, she told him, "Althea Higgins had an alter ego named Thea Hathaway. She apparently used the name after she went to this conference in Harrisburg. I'm not sure why. Maybe it was just a play on the Shakespeare thing that she loved so much. Maybe she just wanted to escape the life she was living."

Zeke opened the envelope and looked inside.

Daisy hurried on with, "From what I understand, her marriage might have not been that successful. Her husband didn't pay much attention to her and just expected life to go on. He took care of the farm and she taught school, and that was that. She wasn't close to her daughter, though it seemed she wanted to be close to her grandson. He helped her husband with chores before her husband died."

Zeke studied the conference brochure.

"Back to the conference," she said, pointing to the flyer in his hand. "Apparently she met a man there named Will Mooney. I guess it was just a coincidence his name was Will."

Zeke looked up at her, perplexed.

She explained, "You know. Like Will Shakespeare?"

The detective shot her an odd look. Zeke apparently didn't understand.

"Will and Althea thought they were kindred spirits. They were both teachers. They both loved Shakespeare. They were both in marriages that might have been loveless."

"Might?"

She didn't want to lose Zeke's interest in her info. "Let me finish explaining, then you can ask all the questions you want, though I might not have the answers. Althea left that envelope with Glorie Beck, who is Althea's neighbor. It just so happens that Glorie is Brielle's grandmother so I've been getting to know her. After Althea died, Glorie remembered Althea had given her that envelope when she went to her fireproof box for her insurance papers. Her home insurance yearly payment was due. She opened the envelope and because she didn't know what to do with it, she asked my advice. Maybe when Althea gave it to Glorie, she'd wanted to keep it away from her grandson's eyes. Maybe she forgot she had given it to Glorie. I don't know. But you can see the fake ID and the note was from someone named Will."

Zeke ran his hand up and down the back of his neck.

"I can tell this is heading somewhere that I'm not going to like any more than Detective Rappaport will like it, right?"

"I can't help what you like and what you don't like. I do have more information for you."

He arched his brows at her.

With haste, she continued, "One night, Stella Cotton and Claudia Moore came over for supper and we decided to try and figure out who Will was."

Zeke made a disapproving noise.

She went on. "It was obvious he'd been at the conference. So we each contacted one of the conference organizers—one for workshops, one for registration, one for general organization. They each sent us a list either of volunteers on their committee, or in the case of registration, the conference attendees. That's where we found Will Mooney's name. He was the only Will in the whole situation."

Zeke tapped his fingers on the conference brochure on the table. "Now you're going to tell me something I'm *really* not going to like."

"I'm careful, Zeke. I've had too many close run-ins not to be. I don't know if you knew it but Trevor Lundquist and my best friend, Tessa Miller, are dating now."

"I've seen Tessa around," Zeke said with a quirk of his lip. "I didn't know she was dating Lundquist."

"They've been dating about four months. It might or might not work out, it's hard to say. But, anyway, Trevor didn't want me to go alone to see Will Mooney."

Zeke sucked in a breath. "You didn't."

She plunged right in because Zeke wasn't going to like however she framed her words. "Trevor drove and went up to the house with me. Will's wife wasn't at all glad to see us, especially when Will told her why we were there—to talk about Althea. I told him Tessa and I had her as a high school English teacher. It was a good excuse."

"It was an excuse that put you in danger! Why didn't you just bring this information to us?" He looked outraged and angry.

"Because I didn't even know if he was the man Althea had had an affair with. Not until we asked him. He admitted he was. When he talked about Althea, he looked grief-stricken. I gave him my card. His wife seemed domineering like she wanted to rule the roost, so he couldn't talk to us that day."

"So Mrs. Mooney knew about Mrs. Higgins?"

"His wife, Kay, is the reason he broke off the affair. She knew Althea was Thea Hathaway."

Zeke blinked. "Okay, you lost me."

"Will called me. We met in the American Music Theater's parking lot."

Zeke narrowed his eyes at her. "Alone?"

"I tried to call Tessa and Trevor and I texted them. They were together and they came to the parking lot as soon as they could. Will was just leaving."

Zeke seemed to be holding his dismay in check to listen to the rest of her story.

"Will told me when his wife discovered his affair and confronted Althea, he was concerned Kay would hurt her. He decided to save his marriage. Kay's condition was that he never talked to or about Althea again. He told me that after years of no contact, he had dinner with Althea a week before she was killed. I asked him if they were reconnecting, but he didn't know for sure. However, he was hoping.

He told me he was going to leave his wife whether he and Althea connected again or not. He knew Althea was going to retire, and they were going to spend time together, as friends if nothing else. The thing is, his wife had access to his phone records because they were on the same plan. So his wife could have seen that he'd had recent conversations with Althea before she died."

Running his hand across his forehead, Zeke looked down at the conference brochure and the note again. When he looked up at her, his gaze was as serious as she'd ever seen it. "Do you think Will's wife could have killed Althea Higgins?"

Daisy had considered the possibility long and hard. "I think she had enough anger, resentment, and bitterness to have a good motive, especially if she knew her husband might be picking up the affair again . . . or even leaving her. What do *you* think?"

"I think you just handed me my next four to six hours' worth of work—background checks mostly of Mr. Mooney and his wife." Zeke motioned to the table. "Thanks again for supper. I'm not going to give a lecture on how you should not have gone after this information."

"You just did."

He rolled his eyes in a way Detective Rappaport often did. Maybe he'd learned it from him.

At Daisy's front door, he told her, "I don't want to think that you're going to have repercussions from everything you've told me. But . . . if there's even a hint of something amiss, you call me."

"I will."

After Zeke was gone, Daisy turned around to see Brielle

halfway down the stairs. She looked scared to death. "What's wrong?"

"I thought he came to arrest me."

Daisy hurried to the bottom of the stairs, and Brielle came down to meet her.

Daisy didn't hesitate to put her arms around her. "No, he came to ask me some questions. It had nothing to do with you, I promise. I told you, as long as you do your community service, we're good with The Style Corner's owner. Do you believe me?" She leaned away from Brielle and studied the girl's eyes. They'd filled with tears.

Still, Brielle nodded, then hugged Daisy again.

Chapter Twenty

On the way home from the tea garden the following evening, Daisy glanced in her rearview mirror once and then twice. Was that green sedan following her?

She was just getting paranoid. Maybe it was because she didn't have Jonas to rely on. Maybe it was because she'd found out too much about Althea. Maybe it was because someone had seen her speaking with the police. No, they couldn't have. Zeke had come to her house.

Still . . .

She told herself to calm down.

Yet when Daisy made another turn and the sedan still followed her, her heart raced and her hands became sweaty on the steering wheel.

Yes, she *was* paranoid. Yes, she *had* been spending too much time around Detective Rappaport and Zeke Willet. She stepped on the gas and went over the speed limit in a hurry to get home.

In no time at all, she was driving on the more rural roads that led to her house. She checked in the rearview mirror and the green sedan was still there. She would *not* lead trouble to her home where Jazzi, Brielle, Vi, and

Sammy were probably spending time together right now. Jazzi and Brielle had strict orders to disembark from the school bus and go straight to Vi's.

All of a sudden, Daisy made the decision to pull into a lane that led to a neighboring farm. She knew it was a long lane. She hoped the other car would pass it by.

The car kept on her tail and followed her down the lane.

Her pulse racing, scared beyond her limit, she quickly said into her car's Bluetooth— "Call Zeke." When his voice mail picked up, she could have screamed. But that wouldn't do any good.

She left a message: "I'm being followed. I turned into Abraham Lapp's driveway and the car followed. I don't want to drive up to the house, but if I have to, I will. He has three sons who work on the farm and hopefully they can all help me if necessary."

She stopped the car. Her doors were locked and her windows were up.

The green sedan stopped behind her. The person who climbed out was . . . Kay Mooney. She stalked to the driver's side of Daisy's car and peered in Daisy's window.

Daisy shouted, "I called the police."

Kay lifted her hands in a surrender gesture and shouted back, "I just want to talk."

Though she knew she might be a fool, Daisy decided the best course was to lower her window an inch. They could easily hear each other through that space.

Daisy kept silent and waited but delved her hand into the purse on the seat beside her for the pepper spray vial she kept there. It was not only pepper spray, but a glittery heart with an alarm on it also dangled from the attached ring. She'd bought it on a whim because it was cute. She didn't feel so glittery or heart-filled right now.

Lowering one hand, Kay shook her finger at Daisy. "I don't want you talking to my husband about Althea."

"No problem," Daisy said, willing to placate this woman any way she could.

Kay seemed surprised at her response, and her eyes filled with tears. "I can't keep him close in our marriage when he keeps thinking about a woman who wanted to tear us apart."

Her voice had risen, but she didn't look angry anymore . . . just torn apart.

Daisy told herself she should keep her mouth shut. Maybe Jazzi was rubbing off on her because she couldn't. She said simply, "If a dead Althea can tear you apart, what do you have?"

A red glow spread over Kay's face. She slammed her hand so hard on the hood of Daisy's car that Daisy thought Kay might have put a dent in it. Will's wife's hand fisted as if it hurt. As well it might, Daisy thought.

All at once, Kay rounded on her heel, ran to her car, climbed in, and backed down the lane like a banshee. It wasn't five seconds after she had zoomed up the road when Daisy recognized Zeke's car pulling in behind her. He got out and hurried to the driver's window. She opened her door, put her feet on the ground, her elbows on her knees, and breathed in several quick breaths.

"Are you hyperventilating?" he asked. "Did she hurt you?"

Daisy waved her hand at him, trying to indicate that he was wrong . . . that she hadn't been hurt . . . that she was fine.

He crouched down to the ground and looked up at her. She could see the worry on his face and the possibility that he'd been too late.

Her chest felt tight and she realized she probably had been about to have a panic attack. After another few breaths, she pulled herself together, lodged her feet on the ground, and stood. "I'm fine. Really, I am. She scared every thought out of my head. I had my pepper spray." She brought up her hand to show him the dangling glitter heart and the tube hanging with it.

"Just what good is that thing?" he asked with disbelief.

"You don't want me to try it on you, believe me. The sound this thing can make rivals your patrol car's siren."

After a deep, frustrated, blown-out breath, he ordered, "Tell me what happened."

"Kay doesn't want me to talk to Will—her husband—about Althea. I told her that wasn't a problem and I wouldn't." Daisy looked up at the sky—a beautiful pinkish purple with the sun setting.

"Anything else?" Zeke prompted.

"She said if her husband was thinking about a dead woman, he wouldn't be invested in their marriage. I said something like if a dead woman could tear them apart, what good was their marriage?"

"You didn't!"

Daisy turned around and stared at the hood of her car. If there was a dent, it was a very small one. She turned back to Zeke. "I did. And she pounded her fist on the hood of my car. Then she roared off."

"Did she touch you?"

"No. And I can't really say she damaged my car either."

His stance relaxed a bit. "Do you want me to warn her off?"

"That just might make things worse."

"You could get a restraining order."

"I could, but again that might just make the situation worse. I don't think she'll bother me again if she knows I'm staying away from her husband. Have you questioned Kay?"

"She and her husband are on my list. I had some other things I needed to take care of today. But believe me, I'm on it. You stirred the pot, and I think it's going to soon boil over."

She gave him her entire attention. "What do you mean?"

"I can't talk about it, Daisy."

"If you're still interviewing, then you're not ready to charge someone."

"We're closing in. That's all I can say."

If they were closing in, soon everyone would be safe. If they were closing in, maybe she'd be able to sleep at night. Or maybe not. Either the murder investigation was keeping her awake . . . or Jonas was.

At the tea garden on Saturday, Daisy could only think about what Zeke had said. "We're closing in." Who did the police have in their crosshairs? Distracting herself, she wondered how Brielle and Jazzi were faring at A Penny Saved. They'd begun their service hours today.

Last night, Brielle had asked Daisy to do something for her. "Can you ask my grammy if I can stay there after my mom and dad come home? I can help her, I know I can. And she can watch over me. I'd even sign a contract if I had to . . . to make my parents believe me. I promise I'll go to school, study, and just hang out with Jazzi. I can swear on Grammy's Bible that I won't get into trouble."

Daisy had been aware that Brielle knew exactly what Glorie's Bible meant to her. It was a serious thing for her to offer that. She'd told Brielle she'd visit Glorie today after the tea garden closed. Iris was going to pick up Brielle and Jazzi and drive them home. When Daisy got there, they'd make something easy for supper like BLTs.

On another front, Daisy considered what might be going on with Tessa. She'd been fine in the morning when Daisy had told her all about last evening and what had happened with Will Mooney's wife. Tessa had warned her not to go too far afield and Daisy had assured her she wouldn't. However, after Tessa's lunch break when her friend had left the tea garden, Tessa had avoided Daisy.

Whatever was bothering Tessa, eventually she'd confide in Daisy. After all, they were best friends.

On her drive to Glorie Beck's, Daisy found herself looking forward to dinner with the girls and Iris. Hopefully, she'd have good news for Brielle.

Daisy was surprised when her Bluetooth signaled a call was coming in from an unknown caller. She answered automatically, "Hello?"

"Mrs. Swanson? It's Lucius Higgins."

This was a shock. She wondered why Lucius was calling. Had his mom put him up to it? To check with her again if he was on the police's suspect list? She really didn't know. All of them could be.

"Hi, Lucius. What can I do for you?"

"I found something, and I'm not sure what to do with it."

Something could be anything. "What did you find?"

"I've been going through the desk in the farmhouse. The police were through here after my grandmother was killed, but they didn't take much . . . just her laptop."

"Okay."

"I found records . . . a ledger of my grandfather's and grandmother's that I want you to look at. Is that possible? Because if you think it's important, then I'll call the police. But I don't want to call them and put myself on their radar for nothing."

Daisy thought about it.

"Where are you?" she asked.

"I'm at my grandmother's house."

Sometimes serendipity was serendipity. "I'm on my way to Glorie Beck's. Can you meet me there? Or I can come over to the farmhouse after I finish my discussion with Glorie."

"Wait a minute," he said sharply.

She kept her eyes on the road, staying silent for a while.

She heard the click of Lucius's boots on the floor, then she heard the door to the outside porch open and close. "Is something wrong?" she asked Lucius.

"I thought I heard something, but I guess I was mistaken. I think I'd feel better if I met you at Glorie's. But I really don't want her to know about this. Can you meet me at her springhouse?"

"You want me to meet you there before I go in to Glorie's or in about a half hour?"

"I'd rather do this now. Ever since I found it, it's been

making me antsy. I need to either put it away or call the cops."

"I'm pulling into Glorie's driveway now. I'm going to tell her that I'm here, then I'll meet you at the spring-house. Do you have a problem with that?"

If Lucius did have a problem with that, Daisy would know she shouldn't meet him out there alone.

His reply came immediately. "No. I don't have a problem with that. I'll meet you there."

After Daisy stopped to see Glorie, just to tell her she was meeting Lucius at the springhouse and why, she went through Glorie's house and out the back. Spring was definitely on its way, but even at the beginning of April, there was a chill as dusk settled in. She was glad she'd worn her jacket and kept it on during this little jaunt. Whatever could Lucius want to show her?

He certainly couldn't mean her any harm because she'd told him she was stopping at Glorie's first, so Glorie would know where Daisy was.

Suddenly filled with trepidation, Daisy stopped and turned around. She saw the older lady at the back door, watching her. Keeping her mind on something other than Lucius while she walked to the springhouse, she consid-ered Brielle staying with Glorie. She had the feeling that Glorie would like the idea of Brielle staying with her, but would Brielle's parents accept the arrangement as feasible?

Whether she was right or wrong, Daisy hadn't told Brielle's parents about the scarf incident. She would, of course, once they returned home. It simply wasn't a situation she wanted to discuss in text messages. And that seemed to be the way Brielle's mom intended to communicate.

Maybe if they discussed what had happened and then the idea of Brielle staying with Glorie, it would all work out.

Jonas once said Daisy had a Pollyanna outlook. On the other hand, she hoped she was just a good judge of character.

A squirrel ran across the path in front of her as the scents of grass, damp earth, and something sweet like hyacinth teased her nose. Inhaling that breath of spring, she reached the springhouse door. As she reached out to open it, she heard a loud *crack*. She froze with her heart banging against her chest.

She'd gone with Jonas to the firing range once. She knew what that sound was—a gun. Someone shooting groundhogs? Someone practicing shooting targets?

Self-preservation kicked in, and she quickly opened the springhouse door. About to duck inside, she heard a shout. With a quick glance to the side of the springhouse, she spotted Lucius hobbling toward her. Was that blood on his shirt near his waist?

Without thinking twice, she took out her phone, found Zeke's number in her contacts, and tapped it.

He answered with a sharp "What?"

She wasn't letting his tone deter her. "Zeke, I'm at Glorie Beck's. At her springhouse. Lucius is running toward me and I think he's been shot."

Zeke's voice changed to one of horrified concern. "Are you safe?" he asked.

"I will be . . . as soon as Lucius gets to me. We'll duck into the springhouse."

"Is there a lock?"

"No, but I'll figure out something. Hurry."

Lucius was almost at the springhouse now. She ran a

few yards through the long grass to meet him, took his arm, and helped him toward the little building. "Inside," she directed him.

They both moved inside, and she slammed the door.

Lucius leaned against the wall, then slid down to the ground. She had to look at his wound, but she had to keep him safe too. Loose burlap sacks were stacked in the corner along with sacks of potatoes and raw dairy milk cans that once sat in the spring to keep them cold.

She took one of the sacks and tossed it at Lucius. "Can you put pressure on your wound?"

"I think so," he answered in a gravelly voice.

"Press hard," she commanded him, hoping he wouldn't pass out.

There were four large sacks of potatoes against the wall. She hefted one and set it against the door. "Who shot you?"

"It was Floyd. And I know why."

She hefted another sack into place. "Tell me what you know."

As if adrenaline took over instead of the pain, with one hand pressing the burlap onto the wound at his side, his other hand revealed papers that he'd stuffed into his shirt pocket.

"He overheard us. He must have. When I came outside to come over here, he was coming around the side of the house. He acted like he'd just arrived, but something in his face was different."

Daisy hefted a third sack in front of the door.

"Before I could take another breath, he raised his gun and pointed it at me. He said he wished I'd never found my granddad's ledger. My grandfather kept records of loaning Floyd money. There were payments from Floyd for a while, but then I found the page my grandmother had entered and an IOU. The payments stopped without the bulk of the money being paid back. My grandmother had written notes in the ledger that outlined talks she must have had with a lawyer for a civil suit against Floyd. I think he was hanging around me and the farm so much to see if I found the ledger and her notes. Or maybe he thought he could eventually find the ledger and destroy it."

Daisy piled sacks of onions on top of the potatoes. Seeing that Lucius seemed to be putting firm pressure on his wound, she realized she had to see what was going on outside. She climbed the ladder up to the high window. Floyd was coming toward the springhouse, but he was limping.

Easing down the ladder quickly, she asked, "Did you hurt Floyd?"

"I threw a shovel at him that was along the porch. It hit him."

Daisy knew she and Lucius couldn't run because of his wound. They wouldn't get very far from the springhouse. She also didn't want to bring trouble into Glorie's house. The only other option was to hide in the woods.

About to press herself against the door if she had to protect Lucius, she heard a siren. When she glanced at Lucius, she saw he looked exceedingly pale. How much blood had he lost? She reached for one of the milk cans and handed it to Lucius. "Use this to defend yourself any way you have to."

Daisy felt panic pressing against her chest as Floyd banged on the springhouse door and heaved against it.

He yelled, "I want that ledger."

Although Lucius was bent over now, pressing his side, he shook his head vehemently. "Never. It shows his motive, right, Daisy?"

Oh, Lucius was right. Did he want to lose his life over the evidence?

Glancing up at her, Lucius admitted in a low, gravelly voice, "My grandmother wasn't the best person, but she was good to me. I was the one who screwed up by stealing that car. She left this place to me. If I want to go to college, now I can. I'm not going to give up the proof of who killed her."

That settled that, Daisy thought. Not that Floyd would accept the papers and go away. She'd dealt with enough killers to know that.

Floyd was big. His weight against the door was making a difference. Sacks of potatoes couldn't prevent the two-hundred-fifty-pound man from breaking in.

Suddenly the door popped open halfway. Daisy screamed. She was so tempted to back up and cower with Lucius.

Instead, she hefted a sack of potatoes to her shoulder. When she did, she not only saw Floyd, who was still pushing at the door, intent on getting inside, but she spotted Zeke, running toward the springhouse. To her astonishment, Jonas was running toward her too. How had he known she was here?

Apparently hearing the two men, Floyd swung around and took aim to shoot to Zeke. However, he was spoiled by Jonas, who ran interference. To her horror, Floyd shot Jonas!

She screamed again, whether to distract herself or to distract Floyd, she didn't know. While he was aiming to shoot Zeke for sure this time, she managed to lift the sack of potatoes over her head. She brought down the full weight of it onto Floyd's shoulders. Potatoes flew everywhere. Turning, she grabbed a sack of onions and swung that at Floyd's head, stunning him.

By then, Zeke was on Floyd, flipping him over to his stomach, cuffing his hands behind him.

Patrol officers rushed toward them.

Daisy called to one she knew. "Help Lucius. He's in here."

Without thinking of anything or anybody else, she ran to Jonas. He was so pale, and his eyes fluttered as Daisy knelt down beside him. Blood was spurting from his thigh. She pressed her hand to it, not knowing what else to do.

"I'm so sorry," he gasped. "Zeke was reading me the riot act about you . . . about us. Just like Tessa had earlier. I realized I'd lose you if I didn't get my head on straight."

Bart Cosner knelt beside Daisy. He didn't push her away but rather wrapped a strip of burlap around Jonas's thigh. The blood stopped spurting.

Zeke came over to Jonas too. He said to Daisy, "Tommy is seeing to Lucius." Then he knelt on the other side of Jonas. "Why did you run in front of that bullet?"

Jonas's lips thinned, the scar on his face dark against his white cheek. Then he murmured, "Because that's what cops . . . and friends . . . do."

Daisy took Jonas's hand and squeezed tight. She wasn't going to let go . . . not ever.

* * *

The hospital in Lancaster was noisy as hospitals always were—trays rattling on service carts, machines beeping, nurses talking. Daisy had waited with Zeke, other patrol officers, and Detective Rappaport for reports on Jonas and Lucius. Both of them had been taken into surgery. Lucius's mom, Phebe, had arrived too. Daisy was grateful that Zeke explained to her what had happened to her son.

Lucius had passed the pages from the ledger to Zeke before the paramedics had taken him away. Lucius had made sure everyone understood the situation between Floyd and Althea. He'd made certain that everyone understood that his grandmother was about to bring a civil suit against Floyd and that would have ruined him.

Daisy had called her mother so she wouldn't see the news and freak out. She explained everything that had happened, told her that she was fine, and she was waiting to see Jonas. She heard tears in her mother's voice when her mother asked, "Do you want me to come to the hospital?"

Daisy had nixed that idea. She wanted to give all of her attention to Jonas. She'd reassured her mom, "Just tell everyone that I'm fine." Before they'd ended the call, her mom had said to her, "Thank you for calling me."

Daisy understood what that meant. At one time she might have called her aunt Iris first. Although she and her aunt were still close, Daisy and her mother were establishing a bond too.

Finally word came through a blue-scrubbed tech that Jonas was settled in a room. Daisy went in, anxious and hopeful. She pulled a chair up by his bedside, and his eyes fluttered open.

"Hey," he said.

"Hey back," she said, and brushed his black hair from his brow. "You scared the living daylights out of me," she chastised him.

"As if you didn't scare them out of me? A sack of potatoes? Really? When did you get that strong?"

There was amusement in his voice, and he was trying to make light of what had happened . . . for both of them. "It's lifting those trays at the tea garden. I have muscles."

He gave her a wan smile. "I know I have painkillers in me, but I want you to believe everything I'm saying." Reaching his hand out, he took hers.

All she could manage was a wobbly "All right."

"I've been such a fool, letting something you did out of love become a barricade between us. Tessa showed me that . . . and Zeke too. He was yelling at me when he got your call. There was no way I was staying behind and he knew it."

"You took a bullet for him," she reminded Jonas.

"Yeah, I did, but that's not what I want to talk about. I want to talk about *us*."

There was a noise at the doorway, and Zeke peeked into the room. "I don't want to interrupt." He came over to stand beside Jonas's bed. Clasping Jonas's shoulder, he said, "Thank you."

Daisy could hear the emotion in Zeke's voice and see it on both men's faces. They had been friends once, and they would be again. She was sure of that now.

Zeke wagged a finger at Daisy. "And you—"

"Don't say it," she murmured.

"I won't. We were about to close in on Floyd, but we can talk about that another time. Lucius is going to be okay. He's out of surgery. He's one brave young man."

Zeke patted the rail that was raised on Jonas's bed. "You stay in here as long as they tell you. No leaving early."

Jonas narrowed his eyes, but then he smiled. "Whatever you say."

As Zeke left the room, Daisy felt the tears she'd been holding in check begin to fall. But that was okay . . . because the world had righted itself again.

Epilogue

Two weeks later, Jonas helped Daisy carry casseroles from the kitchen island to the dining room table. She'd invited friends and family for a gathering to simply celebrate life.

Jonas spotted her glancing at his leg as he limped to the dining room table. "It's better each day," he told her. "I hardly notice it's there. Physical therapy this week was tough but I know it's making it stronger. I got through it with my shoulder and I'll get through it with this."

She and Jonas had talked a lot since his stay in the hospital. He'd even let her drive him to his town house and stay overnight to make sure he was okay that first day home. Then as usual, he'd wanted to do the rest on his own. She'd taken him to a physical therapy appointment or two, and so had Zeke.

Zeke had joined them today. He was in the living room, talking to her dad about the new video equipment the police department had added. Her mother had brought a casserole of homemade pot pie. Iris had contributed ham and cabbage. Tessa and Trevor had brought coleslaw and fruit salad, respectively. Daisy had baked two trays of blueberry coffee cake and made sure she had plenty of whipped cream to top it. Even Brielle had insisted on helping when she was invited. She and her grandmother had brought pasta salad and a tray of deli meats. Vi and Foster had asked if they could buy something instead of making something, and Daisy had suggested rolls and condiments. Looking over the table, she knew they had a real feast.

"Okay, everyone," she called. "Let's dig in. We're going to do this buffet-style, so sit wherever you're the most comfortable. Drinks are on the kitchen counter."

As Daisy returned to the kitchen to make sure she emptied the refrigerator of anything necessary for their dinner, Glorie sidled up beside her. She was using her cane today, but seemed to be doing well. "I still want to know how you worked magic with my daughter. She's agreed to let Brielle stay with me."

"Once I explained what had happened with the scarf, and how Brielle needed a sense of self-worth, I suggested that taking care of you would help her with that. Since the school bus will pick her up right down at the end of your lane, that wasn't a problem either. Brielle knows she's on probation of sorts, but she loves you. I think she'll do well with you."

"It *is* nice having someone there every night, and knowing if I need her, all I have to do is text her."

Daisy laughed. "So is the way of the world now."

Jonas came up beside Daisy and circled her waist with his arms. "I don't want to interrupt, but Trevor has Zeke cornered over by the deacon's bench. Zeke said he can explain everything to us if you want to come join us."

Glorie patted Jonas's arm. "I'm so glad to see that you two have each other to love." Then even more agile than Daisy could believe Glorie could be with her cane, she went toward the dining room table and some of that luscious food.

Jonas squeezed Daisy's waist. "I do have somebody to love. I'm never going to forget that again."

"Ditto," Daisy said, gazing into his eyes and believing it.

There was a buzz around the deacon's bench. Anyone who wanted to hear what had happened with the investigation was gathered there.

Zeke looked out over them and said, "I feel like I should have a podium."

Then he continued, "It's pretty simple, really. Althea's husband lent Floyd money to buy additional land. The thing was, Floyd was deeply into debt from buying new expensive farm machinery."

"I guess he was telling the truth when he said he didn't want to farm with mules," Daisy commented.

Zeke continued, "He just wanted to run a green farm but in an expensive way. After Althea's husband died, he paid her a little at a time, but then he stopped. She was looking toward retirement and needed that money to keep her farm going. When we questioned her lawyer, he told us she decided she was going to file a civil suit against Floyd to recoup the funds. After her husband died, she learned exactly how much he had lent Floyd during their marriage. She hadn't known or she probably would have put a stop to it. If she had brought that suit against Floyd to retrieve the funds her husband had loaned him,

Floyd would have lost his farm and everything he was trying to build."

Tessa chimed in, "I suppose he never expected Lucius to care who had killed his grandmother."

"That and the fact that he thought Lucius was clueless," Zeke said.

"So it's true that Floyd has confessed?" Jonas asked.

"It is. What else was he going to do when we have the proof? This plea agreement will buy him the rest of his life in prison."

"What about Lucius?" Tessa asked.

"Lucius has decided to sell the farm to an Amish family instead of a developer. That way he can use the money to go to college as he always intended to do. He sees that as a gift from his grandmother."

When everyone had dispersed from the little group and surrounded the table to fill their plates, Jonas whispered in Daisy's ear, "Come with me to the sliding glass doors, would you? I have a surprise for you."

"What kind of surprise?"

"You'll see."

Jonas had apologized to her more than once about his stubbornness concerning her visit to Zeke. She'd told him she'd forgiven him and asked if he'd forgiven her. He said he had and she could see in his eyes that he'd meant it. She had no idea what this surprise would be.

He opened the sliding glass door and pulled her outside onto the patio. There she saw a wooden glider with heart-shaped seatbacks. Instead of running toward it, she turned to Jonas. "It's beautiful."

"You didn't even look at it up close."

"I don't have to. You made it, didn't you?"

Wrapping his arms around her, he nodded. "I did. I know you said you didn't want any more apologies, and this isn't an apology. This is a symbol of what I know we share, and the days and nights going forward that we can share together."

In her mind Daisy could see the two of them sitting on the glider looking up at the stars. She could see the two of them as the weather warmed, watching Sammy run around with his mom and dad. She could see the two of them speaking with Jazzi about her plans for the future. She could see so much . . . because of Jonas.

Taking his hand, she led him over to the glider. They sat, gently swaying forward and back . . . forward and back. It had taken her a long while to overcome her grief about Ryan. It had taken her a while to learn to trust Jonas and for him to trust her. But now, here they were, together on the glider, looking forward to days and nights together, looking together toward whatever life brought them next.

ORIGINAL RECIPES